FRIENDLY FIRE

BOOK 7

ALASKAN SECURITY-TEAM ROGUE

Jemma WESTBROOK

CHAPTER 1

"YOU'RE SURE YOU don't want to come?" Lennie clearly didn't believe what she was hearing.

"Positive." Elise forced on a smile. "I think I'm just tired."

It was a lie.

One she'd been telling everyone for the past few months.

And that included herself.

Lennie frowned, the space between her brows narrowing more with each passing second. "Maybe you should go see Eli. Have him make sure you're okay."

Her friend's concern made the twist of guilt in Elise's gut pull tighter. "I'm sure it's nothing. Probably just the time change."

"You've lived here for months. You should be used to it by now." Lennie clearly wasn't going to let this drop easily.

Probably because this was the fourth time Elise had passed on an evening of fun with everyone at Alaskan Security.

Which was the exact problem.

The night would include *everyone*.

"I'm sure it will pass soon." It wasn't a complete fib. She hoped like hell it would. Things needed to get back to normal.

She needed to get back to normal.

But the chances of that happening got slimmer with each day that passed.

One of Lennie's dark brows slowly lifted. "And if it doesn't?"

"If it doesn't, then I will go see Eli." Another lie.

The on-site physician at Alaskan Security wouldn't be able to do anything to help the problem she had.

The only solution she'd been able to come up with was extreme.

And depressing.

But she couldn't keep living like this.

Tiptoeing around corners.

Ducking into empty rooms.

Hiding out in her office.

Her room.

It was a slippery slope, and eventually she would fall. Stumble back into old ways.

And she'd worked too hard to get where she was.

Lennie finally sighed. "Fine." She bumped the door to Elise's room open a little wider, grabbing her in a hug. "I just want to make sure you're okay."

Her throat went tight. "I'm okay. I promise."

Lennie gave her one last look before heading down the hall to join the gathering Elise spent the last week planning.

And now, instead of spending the night with the first women she'd ever felt safe around, she was alone.

Cut off from the world she'd been so excited to step into.

This was supposed to be her fresh start.

Her do-over.

And she'd fucked it all up already.

Elise closed the door and fell to the mattress, dropping onto the pile of blankets she planned to wrap up in during an evening spent eating her feelings and binge-reading.

Just like she had so many nights before.

But tonight it wasn't coming as easily.

Instead of the safe haven it had been, her room seemed more like a cage.

A prison of her own making, where she was both inmate and warden.

Her foot tapped the floor as she watched the clock, counting the minutes as they passed. Waiting until everyone would be at movie night, lined down the plush leather sofas in the theater room. Eating snacks and drinking beers.

At least they were watching a movie she hated. One that was almost as much of a deterrent as the main issue she was facing.

The second the clock passed seven Elise grabbed a sweatshirt, pulling it on over the t-shirt and flannel pants she already wore. It was still technically summer, but Alaska was always flipping cold.

Even when everywhere else in the US was sweltering.

On the plus side, the sun was still up, and since Pierce recently spent an ungodly amount of money reinforcing the perimeter of the property, her sneaky evening strolls were about as safe as it got.

Until the snow was as tall as she was, but that was a bridge she'd have to cross when she came to it.

If she came to it.

Because right now it seemed like her best option might be walking away from all of this.

Mostly one very specific part.

The part that brought back all sorts of feelings she'd been determined to leave behind her.

The insecurity.

The doubt.

The loathing.

That was why she had to walk.

Because it was better than the alternative.

Elise peeked out into the hall, looking both ways, listening for anyone who might still be hanging around.

The silence was as comforting as it was sad.

She'd spent so much of her life isolated.

Outcast.

And here she was again.

At least this time she was the one initiating it. Not that it eased the sting any.

The building was quiet as Elise hurried down the hall toward the door leading outside. She quickly swiped her badge and stepped out, sucking in a deep breath of fresh air, closing her eyes as she looked toward the sun that sometimes seemed to linger forever.

It smelled so different here.

Looked different.

Felt different.

The thought of leaving made her chest ache. Her eyes burn.

And it had little to do with the weather.

Heidi and Lennie and Mona and Eva were the first people to ever support her.

See what she had to offer instead of her shortcomings.

And there were plenty. But with her friends around they seemed less significant.

Less consuming.

A familiar need crawled across her skin like electricity.

It was time to walk.

Elise started toward the back of the compound, making her way across the paved area where she'd watched the teams load into vans countless times, ready to do whatever it took to protect them all, usually under the cover of darkness.

She shoved one hand into the sting in her stomach, trying to force it away.

Dull the pain of a loss that might be coming. A loss that reminded her of another from so long ago. One she thought was finally in her past.

Everything had been so good here. So much easier.

Happier.

But it made the weight feel so much heavier when it came back.

Elise walked a little faster, forcing the rate of her heart to pick up as she hit the incline leading to the back of the property. The burn in her chest and thighs took over as she pushed harder, needing to feel something besides the ache.

The sadness.

The defeat.

She was close to the back corner when a twig snapped.

But she was not the one who broke it.

Her feet skidded to a stop as she listened, breath like fire in her chest as she held it captive.

It had to be an animal. They were everywhere here. Bears. Moose. They even had coyotes now.

Elise forced an exhale, making sure it was slow and steady and silent as she scanned the space around her. As much as she hated the snow, it at least made things a little easier to see. All the leafy green blocked any line of sight she tried to have through the trees inside and outside of the fencing keeping her safe from any of the bigger animals Alaska had to offer.

As well as the more human variety.

But that knowledge did nothing to slow the rate of her racing pulse.

To quell the dose of adrenaline telling her to run.

A prickle of awareness climbed up her spine, sending the hairs on her neck standing on end.

Whatever it was had to be on the other side of the fence. Far enough away she should be safe.

As long as they didn't plan to just shoot her.

A year ago she would have laughed at the possibility.

But not now.

Now she was pretty sure she might be an idiot for coming out here.

Especially alone.

While everyone else was distracted by the terrible humor of Adam Sandler as they watched a movie not even Kathy Bates and Henry Winkler could save.

Elise held perfectly still as she scanned the area around her, trying to come up with her best plan of escape. She was at the top of the incline leading to the backmost corner. It was a route she took on purpose, using the strenuousness of the grade to help refocus her mind.

But right now it might serve as more.

As long as she could get far enough down the hill, anyone on the other side of the fence would lose sight of her.

And out of sight, out of shooting range.

A softly-concentrated rustle of leaves sent her running, racing down the wooded hill as fast as her feet could carry her.

Then faster.

Too fast.

When the toe of her sneaker hooked on a root she was a goner, momentum carrying her body forward even though her feet could no longer keep up. She hit the ground hard but didn't stop. Instead she started to tumble, rolling headfirst before a drop twisted her to the side. Branches caught her clothes and dug into her skin, scraping her arms, her face.

Her thighs.

The thick base of a tree stopped her descent in a sudden, painful jolt.

The trees and scrappy overgrowth around her blacked out as pinpricks of light swallowed her vision.

That was definitely going to leave a bruise.

But she didn't get shot, so it was still a win.

Except the sound of her fall didn't stop when she did.

Someone else was coming down the hill, but they were doing it purposefully, each of their steps sharp as they hit the aging vegetation crumbled across the dirt.

And now there was nowhere to go. Nowhere to hide.

No one to save her from another mess she'd created herself.

"Elise."

The deep voice was sharp and loud.

And unmistakable.

He didn't know where she was.

She'd stopped rolling just beside a cluster of brush that sat between her and the gravelly voice that haunted her every waking minute.

All she had to do was be very quiet.

Then go pack up her room and take the next flight out of Alaska.

Because there was no coming back from this.

"*Elise.*" His voice was closer. Tighter.

He almost sounded.

Scared.

Before she could blink he was there. Beside her. Dropping to his knees. "What in the hell were you doing?"

"I'm fine." She tried to sit up.

Stupid. This was so stupid.

She was so stupid.

"You're not fine." Abe's hand pressed to her belly, pinning her in place as his eyes moved over her body. "You're fucking bleeding."

That was the least of her concerns right now. "It's fine." She braced one hand against the ground, using it as leverage to push against where Abe held her. She managed to get halfway up.

That was when she saw the thing that could make this even worse than it already was.

Elise grabbed at the tear across the leg of her flannel pants, pulling the shredded fabric together to hide the cut across her upper thigh.

It was a move Abe didn't miss.

"Why are you so fucking stubborn?" The frustration he felt was evident.

"*I'm* stubborn?" She tried to scoot away from him.

From the closeness she craved but could never have.

Again.

"I keep telling you I'm fine. You're the one who's not listening." She attempted to push to her feet, but her butt was barely off the ground when a stabbing pain stole her breath and any momentum she'd worked up, sending both hands out as she tried to catch herself as she dropped back down.

"Fine?" Abe gripped the fabric she'd dropped, pulling the tear open to reveal what she'd tried to hide from him.

From everyone.

His eyes landed on the cut. The perfect line of it.

The scab already holding it back together again.

She tried to yank her leg away but he grabbed it, moving faster than she could. His fingers held tight to her knee as he stared at the evidence of just how little she'd really managed to overcome.

His other hand snagged the hole, tearing it wider to reveal the full scope of her struggles.

Her pain.

Abe's eyes slowly lifted to hers.

She couldn't breathe.

Couldn't speak.

Couldn't think.

His gaze dropped, going back to where his hand still held her pants. One finger came out to trace the white lines stacked down her skin. "Elise."

This time when he said her name it was different. Any hint of frustration was gone.

It was soft. Quiet.

And that was almost worse.

No. Not almost. It was worse.

"Let me go." She needed to get away from him. She'd already made a fool of herself in front of him once.

Thinking Abe might have an interest in her was one of the biggest mistakes of her life.

And this moment was coming in a close second.

Abe's cool blue eyes lifted to hers. "I don't think so, Babe."

"I just want to go back to my room." *And pack it up.*

Then run away from one more fuckup.

One more failed chance to be someone better.

14

Someone she could be proud of.

Abe shook his head at her. "No."

"Please." The desperation in her voice was humiliating.

All of this was.

But she'd humiliated herself in front of Abe before. What was one more time?

His eyes slowly moved over her face. "Have you eaten?"

The abrupt shift made her blink.

Once.

Twice.

Three times.

"What?"

"Have you eaten?" This time he said it slower. Like that might help her understand the question better.

It didn't.

"I'm fine."

"That's not what I asked." Abe reached out to snag a bit of leafy twig caught in her hair. "I asked if you'd eaten."

"I don't know why it matters." She strained to watch from the corner of her eye as he gently worked the snaggle of roughage loose, carefully freeing it from the tangled mess of her hair.

"I'm gonna give you two choices, Babe." Abe went to work on another bit of dried ick, sliding it from where it stuck to the side of her head. "We can either go eat, or we can talk about that leg."

She didn't want to do either of those things. "I pick the third option."

"There is no third option." Abe's eyes came back to hers, his gaze steady and unwavering. "You can eat or you can talk."

She liked eating. Usually liked talking too.

The subject here was the issue.

"My body is none of your business."

"Dinner it is then." Abe stood. "Can you walk?"

"I didn't say I was going to have dinner with you."

"You only had two choices." He held one hand her way. "Come on."

Elise lifted her chin, fighting for the strength she worked so hard to fake. "I can say no to both of them."

Abe's hand came closer. "I wouldn't advise that."

"Why?" She ignored where he reached for her. "Are you going to run and tell Pierce what you saw?"

His head bobbed back like she'd slapped him.

Abe stared at her, his eyes narrowing a little more with each second that passed. He slowly lowered back toward the ground, coming eye to eye with her.

"Now we're sure as hell talking, because you clearly have some ideas about what kind of man you think I am," he paused, his eyes holding hers, "*Babe*."

"I don't want to talk to you." The words didn't come out as harsh as she'd hoped they would.

She'd offended him. On purpose.

But it hadn't had the desired effect she was expecting.

Most men would have called her a bitch. Left her to fend for herself.

It would figure this would be the one time Abe didn't act like most men.

"Too fucking bad." Abe grabbed her without warning, hauling her up from the ground.

"What are you doing?" It was a stupid question. It was pretty obvious what his plan was.

"I'm taking your ass inside." He scooped her up. "We're gonna eat some fucking food and talk about why you're such a pain in the ass."

"I can clear that up for you right now." She laughed, letting the bitterness inside escape. "I'm a bitch."

She'd heard it more times than she could count from any array of men.

And more than a few women.

"You're fucking full of shit is what you are." Abe shifted his hold on her, bouncing her body in a way that almost felt like he might drop her.

And it made her latch on. Grab the only thing available.

Unfortunately that was him.

"I'm not going to drop you." Abe huffed a little as he carried her down the rest of the hill. "And I sure as hell won't tell anyone your business."

He sounded mad.

Pissed at the jab that was supposed to make him leave her alone.

One more thing she'd failed at.

"Why are you even out here?" Elise tried to force her emotions to focus on him. It was the only thing that could help her now.

17

Because hating him was better than hating herself.

"You shouldn't be out here alone."

"It's safe. Pierce said it himself."

"At least I'm not the only one you don't listen to." Abe's strides were long as he crossed the courtyard leading to the medical wing of the compound. "Pierce said it was as safe as it would ever be."

That was exactly what he'd said. "I can't live my life in fear, *Babe*."

Abe's eyes slowly came her way, one brow lifting. "Why haven't you gone to any of the weekly events?"

Why had she even tried to get him to have sex with her? The man was aggravating.

Infuriating.

"Because I don't want to." She snapped it out. "Why aren't *you* there?"

"Because I hate that fucking movie you picked." Abe managed to swipe his badge, whipping the door open with one of the hands holding her hostage. "And because I knew you'd be out all by yourself again." He went straight into the building, headed right for the line of rooms Eli used to treat any random assortment of injuries.

"Again?" Elise barely noticed the room around them as Abe slid her ass onto the examination table.

He didn't answer her question. Instead Abe went to the line of drawers, pulling one open and fishing out a few items before lining them down the counter. He turned back to her, going to a scratch she hadn't noticed on one arm and swiping down the jagged line of it with a wet piece of gauze.

18

"Abe." She stared at his face, waiting for him to look back, but his eyes stayed on her skin as he carefully cleaned each scuff and scrape she'd collected on her tumble down the hill. "What do you mean, *again*?"

He finally looked at her. "I couldn't let you go out alone."

She swallowed. "You followed me?"

The extent of what Abe actually knew about her was so much worse than she'd realized.

"Someone has to make sure you're safe, Elise." He grabbed another gauze and wet it with the wound cleaner. "Make sure no one tries to hurt you."

"No one's trying to hurt me."

Abe's eyes went to her thigh, hand hovering over the healing cut there before gently wiping across the irritated skin. His gaze slowly lifted to hold hers. "Aren't they?"

CHAPTER 2

HE KNEW THERE was something off with Elise since they got back from Cincinnati.

He just never would have guessed this was what it was.

Elise was barely breathing at this point, eyes wide as they watched his every move.

Which meant he had to choose each one carefully. She was suddenly skittish as hell around him, and the last thing he needed was for her to try to run again.

Wrestling her back on this table would be...

Not as unwelcome as it should be.

"What do you want to eat?" Abe gently wiped across her inflamed skin with the wound-cleansing wipe, trying to find the calm he needed to deal with this situation.

With this woman.

Because Elise tested the hell out of his calm.

Among other things.

"I'm not hungry."

"I don't care." He ignored the urge to clean the scars he couldn't help.

Not with anything he'd find in Eli's supplies anyway.

Abe tossed the spent wipe in the trash can, pulling in a deep breath as he turned back to the drawer, taking his time as he dug through the items there. "If you don't decide what we eat then I'm going to, and I don't think your picky ass will like it."

"I'm not picky." A little of the sharpness was back in her voice and it soothed the edginess he'd been fighting.

"You are the most fucking picky woman I've ever met." He snagged a tube of medicated ointment and a few bandages before going back to her side.

"I'm not picky." She watched closely as he carefully smeared each of her cuts with the ointment. "I just know what I like."

"Then pick." He gently laid one of the Band-Aids in place, peeling back the paper to press it against her skin. The process shouldn't be taking as long as it was, but she seemed to relax a little more as he smoothed each one into place, so he took his time, letting his fingers slide over the smooth warmth of her body more than necessary.

Touching her was a dangerous thing. Even more so than he initially realized.

Because while Elise acted unbreakable, it was clear she was fragile as hell.

"Why are you doing this?" Her voice was low and lacking the fire it had seconds ago.

21

"Because you're not the only one around here who's a pain in the ass." He forced his hands from her body. "It's your damn fault I'm not at the movie, so now you have to deal with me."

"How is it my fault?" She perked up a little, the way she always did when he jabbed at her.

"You're the one who picked that fucking awful movie." Abe collected the scraps of paper left from the bandages, fisting them into a tight ball before shooting it at the trash can in the corner. "I can't believe anyone went."

"I gave them options." Elise sat a little straighter. "Your friends are the ones who made the final decision."

"My friends clearly have no taste then." He put the ointment back in place. "What's for dinner, Babe?"

Elise huffed out a breath as she slid off the table. "I said I'm not hungry."

Abe turned, crowding close, sending her feet back a few steps until her butt bumped the table he'd put her on minutes ago. "And I said I don't care."

Elise gripped the padded edge with both hands, holding tight as he eased in a little more.

"I'm going to give you one more chance to decide." The lean length of her frame was so close. Close enough he could imagine how it would feel pressed into him. "What do you want to eat?" He said the words slowly, dragging each one out to buy just a little more time of being close to her.

Because it had to end soon.

22

Elise's eyes dipped, barely moving down his face in a slow sweep that hovered on his mouth. "I'm not hungry."

She was most definitely hungry.

Just not for anything he was willing to offer her right now.

"Be that way then." Abe took a step back and the clench of her fists immediately relaxed. "Come on."

Elise stared at him. "No, thank you."

"Too late to try to be nice to me, Babe." He snagged her hand and pulled her toward the door. Her fingers were cold where they linked between his.

But she held tight, coming more easily than he expected.

He took her down the main hall and through the walkway leading to the rooming building where she stayed, stopping just outside her door. "Go in and get changed."

Elise's chin barely lifted as she swiped her badge and pushed open the door.

He shot one hand across the frame, blocking her from going in. "And don't think I won't come in after you."

She scoffed, eyes widening. "You can't just break down the door."

He smiled. She'd definitely been planning to hide inside, thinking she could wait him out. "I can, and I will."

Her eyes held his, gleaming with the defiance he appreciated even more now that he knew what she hid behind it. "What if I don't want to have dinner with you?"

Abe moved close to her, offering Elise a reminder he didn't need. "You're a lot of things, Elise." He eased in as much as he dared, stopping when the front of his company-issued shirt touched the bulk of the sweatshirt swallowing her narrow body. "But a liar isn't one of them." He jerked his chin toward the door. "You've got three minutes. Then I'm coming in after you."

Her hazel eyes barely widened. "That's not enough—"

Abe pressed the button on the side of his watch, setting a timer he hoped to need. "Two minutes and fifty-five seconds."

Elise's jaw clenched tight as she stared him down for a full ten seconds.

That was fine. She could waste all the time she wanted.

Finally she bumped past him, one of her shoulders hitting his as she shoved her way into the small room she called home and slammed the door.

Abe leaned against the wall, making two quick calls as he waited, checking his watch as he placed his orders. The seconds ticked by too slowly, each one dragging out until he was pacing outside the closed door.

He counted down the final ten seconds, his hand hitting the knob as the last one came and went.

He knew she would force him to come after her.

But the door whipped open before he could make good on his threat.

Elise stood just inside the room, her slim body swallowed up by a pair of baggy sweatpants and an equally baggy hooded sweatshirt. Her long hair was twisted into a tousled wad at the top of her head, and her face was scrubbed clean of any trace of the make-up she wore every day.

It was impossible not to take it all in. The stark difference between what he saw now and the woman who showed up for work every morning, ready to take on anything in her path.

Which usually included him.

"Ready?"

Elise lifted one shoulder and let it drop.

Close enough.

He reached for her, taking one of her hands in his for the second time tonight. Her fingers were still just as cold as last time, and it almost made him reconsider his plans.

Almost.

"Where are we going?" Elise's legs were long enough that she was able to keep up with him as he moved through the halls, working them along the path that would be least likely to be in use by anyone else.

Elise worked hard to avoid the rest of the company tonight and he wanted to make sure it still happened.

"If you wanted to know where we were going then you should have picked." Abe led her into the main garage where all the vehicles owned by Alaskan Security were stored. He snagged a set of keys from the large rack and went to where the SUV

25

he usually drove was parked, clicking the automatic locks as they approached.

"Fine." Elise tipped her chin as they walked up the passenger's side of the Land Rover. "Be that way."

Abe blocked her in, taking advantage of the forced closeness caused by the enclosed space. "What way am I being?"

He'd fought the desire to be close to her since they came back from Ohio.

Ignored the need to stop the spiral he watched spin faster every day, knowing soon it would spin out of control.

And it had.

"A pain in the ass." Elise stood tall, her spine straight, shoulders set. "But that shouldn't surprise me. You're always a pain in the ass."

He moved in a little more. "Is that right?"

She didn't shrink back. Not even a little. "That's absolutely right."

This was why he couldn't stay away from her.

Not a single bit of her was weak.

Even if she didn't realize it.

He took a deep breath, savoring the moment. The nearness.

Because soon it would be gone.

"Is that why you asked me to fuck you?"

Elise's nostrils flared at the reminder of their last night in Ohio. "I was drunk."

"No, you weren't." At least not when she propositioned him.

"I puked in the bushes, remember?" She said it like it would matter to him.

26

"Of course I remember." He leaned in. "I'm the one who held your hair back, Babe."

Then he'd scooped her up and carried her to his room, force-feeding her a couple Advil and some Pedialyte before she passed out in his bed.

"But I watched every drink that night, Elise." He held her gaze. "You were stone-cold sober when you—"

"Stop it." She squeezed her eyes shut. "It was a mistake."

"Was it?" He tipped one finger under her chin, dragging the angle of her face his way and waiting until she opened her eyes. "Because I don't remember you taking it back."

"And I don't remember you being interested, so why does it matter?" Her words snapped out, sharp and short.

"Is that what you remember, Elise?" He pressed her chin higher, bringing her mouth closer to his as he continued to speak. "Because I don't remember turning you down."

Her skin flushed and she jerked her face away. "You said no." She huffed out a breath. "And you laughed while you said it."

"That's what you got out of that conversation?" It explained a lot.

Why she'd been avoiding him like the fucking plague.

Why she ignored him when their paths did cross.

"You know what?" Elise tried to push past him. "Fuck you. I'm going back to my room."

He caught her arm, using her own momentum to swing them around until her back was against the side of the SUV. "Not happening, Babe." He pressed into her, finally allowing himself a little of what he'd been craving. "Because it turns out we have a lot to talk about."

"I don't want to talk to you." She pressed tighter to the SUV at her back.

"So you just wanted to fuck me? No talking involved?" Abe let the tip of his nose run down the side of hers. "Because that's not an option."

It was the point he intended to make to her that night, but before he could finish she stormed off, leaving him trying to figure out what in the hell happened.

"Whatever." Elise used her body to shove at his. "It doesn't matter anymore anyway."

He held his ground, bracing one hand against the side of the Rover to keep her in place. "It does matter, and you're not fucking leaving until we've cleared this up." Abe shoved one leg between hers, intending to use it as added insurance he would finally be able to finish a conversation with the woman who managed to only ever hear half of what he said to her.

But Elise immediately froze, her whole body going rigid.

He stopped everything, the odd reaction setting off every alarm bell he had.

Something was off.

Elise's eyes dipped, going straight to where his thigh pressed against her body. Her gaze held, staring at the only part of him that touched her.

She was holding her breath.

She didn't blink.

Didn't move.

Her reaction forced him back a step.

Made him rethink everything.

Again.

Elise was a walking contradiction. She was strong and opinionated. Dominant and forceful.

But she was clearly breakable. He'd seen the evidence firsthand.

She'd straight up asked him to fuck her.

But her reaction just now was not that of a woman out to get fucked.

None of it made any sense.

"Come on." He grabbed the handle to the passenger's door and pulled it open. "Let's go get some food."

Elise stared him down a second longer. Luckily she didn't pick the fight he was anticipating. She shot him a glare as she sat in the seat, crossing her arms over her chest.

Abe leaned in, grabbing the belt and pulling it out and across her body before buckling her in. "Safety first, Babe."

She stared straight ahead, ignoring him as he adjusted the slack into place.

He closed the door on her and walked to the driver's side, irritation crawling across his skin as he got in.

He started the engine and pulled out of the spot, waiting until he'd picked up enough speed to engage the automatic locks before saying anything else.

"I meant what I said, Elise." Abe glanced her way as the motion-activated door opened in front of them. "We're talking this shit out tonight."

She didn't respond.

The woman knew exactly how to get under his skin. Whether she was talking to him or not, Elise could get his blood pumping in under ten seconds.

One more reason they needed to work this out.

She was a distraction he didn't need right now.

There was too much going on and too much at risk.

The door opened and he pulled out of the garage, going straight toward the newly-installed gates at the front of the property, gripping the wheel tighter with each silent second that passed.

By the time they reached the front gate he was ready to lose what little shit he had left.

Abe rolled down his window and punched in his passcode, waiting as the heavy gate slid open. "So you're just going to keep ignoring me?"

Elise's lips stayed tight together.

He drove through the commercial area just outside the compound, headed to the first of their stops.

"You can't ignore me forever, Elise." The main road was a little busier than normal, congested with the cars and trucks of people taking advantage of what might be one of the last warm nights of the season.

Elise tipped her head to stare out the side window, making it clear she had every intention of ignoring him for as long as possible.

Fine.

30

If that's what she wanted, he'd sit and stare at her all fucking night long, because there was no way he was going to let her go back to her room and sit alone.

Especially now that he knew what she did while she was there.

The first of their stops was surprisingly quiet. He took the front parking spot, cracked the windows, and shut off the engine before opening his door. "I'll be right back."

She didn't answer, which was fine. He didn't expect her to.

There was no one at the counter when he went in to pick up the order he'd placed while Elise changed. It was a full five minutes before one of the owners of the small Cuban restaurant came out, carrying the bag of empanadas and ropa vieja he chose.

When he got back in the Rover, Elise peeked his way as he passed over the bag of food. "I wouldn't have driven away and left you here."

"I'm not willing to take that risk." Abe pulled out of the lot and headed to their next destination.

Elise held the bag in her lap, fingers crinkling the brown paper as she tried to work the opening wide enough she could see inside.

"No peeking." He pulled up in front of the next hole-in-the-wall he'd ordered food from. This time he left the engine running. "I'm taking you at your word, Babe." Abe met her gaze. "Don't make me come after my dinner."

Elise pulled the bag of food closer.

He chuckled. "I will fight you for what's in there."

31

The scent of meat and fried dough was already filling the interior of the SUV, and his stomach was growling.

But the food was still the least appealing thing in the Rover.

The Chinese take-out place was much faster than the Cuban spot, and in under two minutes he was out the door with an order of stir-fried cabbage, garlic pork, and firecracker shrimp.

Enough food to give Elise plenty of options.

He passed the second bag over before pulling away.

Elise's eyes moved around as they drove through town, but to her credit, she didn't ask where they were going.

Not that he would have told her anyway.

Abe followed the path he'd taken every morning and every night for the past three weeks, but this time he didn't check his rearview mirror every five seconds.

Thinking of all he left behind.

Because this time what mattered was sitting right beside him.

CHAPTER 3

ABE WAS ABOUT to make her look like a liar.

She wasn't hungry.

At least she didn't think she was.

Not until he had to drop two bags of something amazing smelling on her lap.

Now she was stuck with him.

But only because she was dying to find out exactly what was inside the two bags.

Otherwise she might still be considering shoving open the door and jumping out. Someone would come looking for her eventually. Probably Heidi. Maybe Lennie.

Or Mona.

"Trying to figure out a way to ditch me but still keep the food?" Abe didn't glance her way as he continued driving through town.

"It's like you're a mind reader." She managed to sound at least a little snarky with the response.

"I don't think I need to tell you that you can try to run, but you won't make it far." Abe's clear blue eyes finally came her way. "You're holding one of my favorite foods."

"So the main reason you would try to find me if I was wandering around Alaska would be because I had your dinner." She tipped her head in a little nod. "Good to know."

"I think you know that's not true." Abe eased the SUV up to a heavy gate and stopped. "Or do I need to remind you about your little tumble?"

She did not need or want a reminder about what led her to the spot she was in currently.

So she turned and stared out the side window as he punched a few numbers into the keypad.

Silence was better than revealing anything else, because Abe already knew too much. Enough that this would definitely be her last night in Alaska.

Her last night at Alaskan Security.

Her last night living in a world where she was accepted.

Of course that was only because no one here really knew what she was.

The gate in front of them opened and Abe pulled through. He took an immediate right along the freshly paved blacktop.

He'd brought her to the new townhomes Pierce built to house members of Alaskan Security. So far Lennie and Rico bought one, Bess and Wade bought one, and Heidi and Shawn bought one.

But apparently there was one more sold than she realized.

Abe pulled the Rover into the garage of the third unit in.

She'd helped Pierce with the building process, but up until this point Elise hadn't seen a single unit in person.

Looked like that was about to change.

Might as well see one before she left.

Abe cut the engine and climbed out of his seat. Elise fumbled with the two bags he left her holding, trying to work both under one arm so she could open the door with her free hand. Before she could wrangle everything, Abe pulled open her door.

"Having problems, Babe?"

"Nope." Elise climbed out, holding tight to the bags. "Just making sure nothing happens to my dinner."

"Thought you weren't hungry." Abe shut the door before punching the button to close the garage.

"I changed my mind." She marched past him and through the door leading into the bottom level of the three-story condo. "I'm changing my mind about a lot of things tonight."

Like living in Alaska.

"I wouldn't get ahead of yourself." Abe followed her into his home, not seeming bothered at all that she was barging straight in.

The place smelled brand new, which made sense considering it was. This particular unit was the first and only one currently finished. Abe must have wasted no time moving in.

She couldn't really blame him. Staying in the rooming house was nice in some ways, especially when you were new to the area, but not having a kitchen got real old, real quick.

It was almost as irritating as not having any privacy.

Elise tried to sneak a peek in the open door to her right, but the room was dark enough it was impossible to see what was in the space.

She climbed the set of stairs leading to the main living area. Each of the units in the building had the same basic floor plan. Garage, bathroom, and a bonus room on the bottom floor, living area and master bedroom on the main floor, and two additional bedrooms on the third floor.

The perfect place for people who wanted to raise families.

People like Bess and Wade and Heidi and Shawn.

Elise stopped in her tracks when she reached the top of the stairs.

"Something wrong, Babe?" Abe moved in close behind her, his gravelly voice low in her ear.

He was so close.

Close enough she could almost trick herself into thinking things that weren't true.

And wouldn't really matter if they were.

All the skeletons she tried to leave in Ohio followed her here.

Tainted the new life she tried to create.

She did a mental shake, knocking loose the past creeping in. "You have a lot of furniture."

Abe's eyes moved, but his body did not. He scanned the large sofas sitting perpendicular to the large window she'd insisted on putting in each unit's family room space. "I need somewhere to sit."

"I guess." She made herself step away from him.

From the closeness reminding her of what she would probably never have.

Because no matter how hard she tried, the truth always seemed to find her.

A large, heavy-legged table sat in the dining room space, perfectly centered under the classic lines of the pendant light she chose for the spaces that didn't already have buyers.

Elise sat the bags on the table as Abe went into the kitchen and pulled open a drawer. He came back with two forks and picked up the bags she'd just set down, taking them and going straight for the brand-new sofas.

He dropped to one, kicking off his shoes before propping his feet up on the coffee table situated in the center of the space. He tipped his head her direction, lifting one brow. "Coming?"

Of course she was coming. He'd managed to trap her into whatever this night was.

Wedged her right between good and bad, locking her into a spot she couldn't easily get out of.

Elise huffed out a breath before going toward the sofa across from him and plopping down.

His eyes followed her, holding steady as she sat. He slowly leaned forward, dropping his feet to the floor, eyes locked on hers as he started unloading the bags.

It took everything she had not to look away.

Not to buckle under the weight of his gaze.

But while she might still be a few of the things she'd always been, there was one she definitely was not.

Weak.

If nothing else, she could be proud of that. Proud that she earned the nickname slung her way so often.

Bitch.

Abe held out one of the forks.

She took it without breaking her stare. "Thank you."

"You're welcome." Abe looked cool and calm. Like uncomfortable eye-contact was one of the many superpowers he possessed.

She should never have asked him to fuck her. Not someone like Abe.

She should have gone for lower-hanging fruit. Someone more likely to be flattered by her request.

Which Abe definitely wasn't.

If anything, he'd been amused. She'd seen the way he almost smiled. The slight crinkle of his eyes when she propositioned him. It only took a second for her to realize how awful of a mistake she'd made.

Elise slapped her hand around the table, looking for one of the foam containers lined across the top. Her fingers brushed one and she grabbed it, flipping the top open before stabbing her fork in and shoving whatever it caught into her mouth.

Abe watched her with that same amused look he'd given her the night she wished she could forget. "Good?"

"Shut up." She stabbed another batter-coated shrimp from the container. "At least let me eat in peace."

"Is that what you're looking for, Elise? Peace?"

"I'm looking for silence." She jammed the giant crustacean in, almost closing her eyes as the sweet and sour sauce coated her tongue.

"Fine." Abe leaned back, stretching his arms out across the back of the sofa. "Silence it is."

If he thought staring at her while she ate would bother her, then he was about to be very surprised.

It took more than a judgmental stare or two to get under her skin.

Only Abe's stare didn't seem to be judgmental.

It was more…

Satisfied.

As soon as she reached for the second of the four containers he stood, finally breaking the staring contest she was unwilling to lose. "Thirsty?"

"I'm fine."

"Water it is." He went to the kitchen, leaving her to peek through the rest of the containers as she tasted what seemed to be stir fried cabbage.

The other containers had empanadas and an order of shredded beef with vegetables. She was halfway through one of the beef empanadas when a stemmed glass clinked onto the table in front of her—

And Abe settled onto the couch beside her, leaning close as he reached for an empanada of his own. "Good?"

She swallowed what was in her mouth, managing to hold her position as Abe's body teased hers with each move. "It's fine."

"If this is what you call fine, then I'm going to need to see your ranking scale." He took a bite of the cabbage.

"I thought you didn't care about food." She'd seen him chug down chalky protein shakes and eat unsalted eggs and pale chicken.

The man ate the most boring meals ever created.

"So did I." Abe snagged the container of beef and dug into it. "Until someone suggested I might be wrong." His eyes slowly eased her way as he chewed.

"I'm sure you're wrong a lot."

"I'll keep that in mind." Abe snagged a remote from the coffee table and relaxed back against the couch. "What do you want to watch?"

"I don't watch much television." It was a waste of time. There was so much else to explore. To learn about.

To understand.

"Looks like I'm not the only one who's wrong sometimes." Abe switched on the large flat screen that sat opposite the windows.

"Are you actually arguing that watching television is a good way to spend your time?" Now she was definitely happy he turned her down.

She thought Abe was an all-around good choice. He was physically fit. Attractive. Older. More mature.

And that voice.

"How else are you going to learn what happens to people who find love on Date an Inmate?" Abe flipped through the On-Demand section and started a show called *Love After Lockup*.

Elise looked from the television to him and then back again. "You're kidding, right?"

"Nope." Abe draped one arm across the couch behind her back. "You're not the only one around here with a guilty pleasure."

Pleasure.

That was something she didn't have any of. Guilty or not.

And at this point it was starting to become clear the fault for that might not lie where she wanted to believe it did.

Elise snagged another empanada, looking for something else to focus on besides the reality of how she really ended up where she did.

Unfortunately, the most distracting thing in the room was the television and the ensemble of messy individuals screaming across it.

She accidentally watched long enough to find out it was hard to look away. "These people are dating convicts?"

"Yup." Abe took a drink from his water glass, eyes glued to the screen as a man waved around a pocket pussy named after the woman he was picking up from prison the next morning.

"Oh my God." Elise dropped the rest of the empanada to the table. "Did he just put that—" She covered her mouth, watching in horror as the man loaded the torso-shaped sexual aid into his dishwasher.

Filled with dishes.

"That seems like a bad idea." Abe tilted his head to one side, squinting at the television. "Aren't those things handwash only?"

"Why are you asking me?" She leaned back. "What would I do with something like that?"

41

"Hopefully not put it in the dishwasher." Abe stood as a commercial break came on. He snagged a couple of the food containers. "Finished?"

She was now that she had the mental image of that man's jean juice all over his forks and knives. "Yes."

"Good." He stacked everything into a single pile, before picking it up and carrying it into the kitchen. "You'll have plenty of leftovers then."

"They're your leftovers." Elise drained her water. "I don't have a fridge."

"You can have them for dinner when you come over tomorrow." He didn't miss a beat with the explanation.

"I'm not coming over here tomorrow." Tomorrow she would be long gone. Nothing more than a blip on Alaskan Security's radar.

"Why not?" Abe brought over a pitcher of water and re-filled her glass. "Do you have other plans?"

"As a matter of fact, I do." She drank down some of the icy cold water, tempering the thirst brought on by their salty meal.

"Are they the same plans you had tonight?" He set the pitcher down on the table.

"No." Her plans for tomorrow were firm and final.

"That's good." Abe slowly sat next to her. "Because I'd be pissed as hell if I found you outside alone again." He reached out to slide one hand along her hair, pushing it behind one shoulder. "It's time to stop taking chances you don't need to take."

Was he trying to tell her what to do?

42

It seemed a lot like he was.

"It's awfully bold of you to think that I care what pisses you off."

"You should." His hand didn't move away. Instead his finger traced a line up the side of her neck before following the crease of her jaw toward the front of her chin, keeping her eyes on his.

Another staring contest.

Fine.

Elise met his gaze once again. "I don't."

"That's your choice to make." Abe's stare came closer, forcing her eyes to refocus as he leaned in. "But you're the one who will have to deal with the fallout, Babe."

She wouldn't though. Tomorrow she would be on her way back to Ohio.

Never to see Abe again.

And it would be a relief.

"I doubt it."

Abe's penetrating blue eyes skimmed her face, narrowing as his head slowly tipped to one side. "What are you up to?"

"Nothing." It came out too fast to be the truth, and Abe didn't miss it.

"You can't run from your problems, Elise." The hand at her chin shifted, slowly moving along the side of her face. "They will always find you."

He was wrong.

She could have had a fresh start here. Could have put everything behind her.

All the mistakes.

All the loathing.

All the pain.

She'd gotten it all right. She'd made friends. Proved herself to Pierce. Everything was going perfectly.

Until Abe came along and screwed it all up.

"Maybe you're right." She glared at him. "Because you're my problem and you always seem to find me."

It's why he was the man she propositioned that night. He was there. Never far enough away for her to get close to anyone else.

And again tonight, he was right there to see another of her failings.

"You should remember that then." Abe's palm curved against the side of her face, fingers stretching across her cheek and jaw, thumb pressed up the opposite side.

"Why? Because if I leave you'll come hunt me down?" The threat was ridiculous. If she left he wouldn't bat an eye.

Abe probably wouldn't even notice she was gone until someone else pointed it out.

"Is that your plan?" His thumb stroked her skin, sliding across her lower lip. "To leave?"

Shit. She'd said too much.

Not that it mattered. "My plan isn't to stay."

"And you're going where? Back to the life you left?" Abe's thumb teased across her lips again. "You left it for a reason, Babe."

"I'm leaving this one for a reason too." She smirked, ready to send the jab that would end this pointless conversation. "You."

But instead of being insulted Abe smiled. "That's good to hear."

That threw her off a little. "Why is it good?"

He was supposed to be offended. Maybe a little pissed.

But Abe was neither of those, based on the smile he wore and the slow way he continued to touch her.

He was touching her.

A fact that sort of slipped past her distracted brain.

But now that she'd noticed it, the heat of his hand was all she could focus on.

The way it covered so much of her skin. The barely rough drag as it moved.

He was touching her.

"If I'm the problem, then I can be the solution."

It was so tempting.

Thinking that someone else could clean up the mess she made.

But that simply wasn't the way life worked.

"I don't need you to fix things for me."

"I didn't say you needed me to fix it." Abe's lips were so close they almost touched hers as he spoke. "But it is my responsibility to fix the problem I created."

His breath was warm where it brushed her skin.

Another teasing touch she shouldn't allow herself to notice, much less enjoy.

"I'll be fine." One way or another she would make sure it was true.

Even if it felt like a lie right now.

"Is that all you want out of life?" This time Abe's lips did touch hers as they moved. "To be fine?"

Fine was something she'd struggled to be most of her life. Imagining being able to be fine sometimes still felt impossible. Expecting more than that?

Then she would just be being greedy.

"Sometimes fine is as good as it gets."

Abe leaned back, just enough that she could see his whole face.

The crinkle around his eyes.

The smirk on his lips.

"Fine might be as good as it gets for average people," one finger curved up the center of her chin, "but you're not average, Babe."

CHAPTER 4

"RIGHT." ELISE WASN'T as flattered as he expected by the honest compliment.

She stood up, leaving him alone on the couch to go stare out the large window overlooking the property that would eventually be filled with buildings just like the one they were in. "Can you take me back now?"

"No." Abe relaxed back on the sofa, ready for the fight he was hoping would come.

But Elise didn't fight him. Instead she turned from the window. "Fine." She went straight toward the stairs.

He barely made it off the couch and across the room in time, managing to block her at the last possible second. "What are you doing?"

"I'm leaving." She tried to step around him. "I'm done talking to you."

"And you're gonna do what? Walk back?"

"Seems like." She made another attempt to get around him.

"You can't walk back to headquarters. It's three miles away."

"You don't know what I can do." Elise shoved at him, palms spread wide across his chest as she pushed hard enough that he might have gone down the stairs if he hadn't seen it coming. "I just want to go back to my room."

"What you want is to run away." He grabbed her as she came at him with more force, barely managing to keep them both from tumbling down the stairs. "And you're going to get yourself fucking hurt doing it."

"I don't care." She struggled in his grip, elbows digging into his stomach as she twisted in her fight to get free.

"I do." He scrambled to contain her as she got more and more angry.

"No you don't." Elise broke loose, spinning to face him. "And you can stop pretending like you do. It won't hurt my feelings."

"Is that what you think this is? Me trying to spare your fucking feelings?" He chuckled a little. "You're giving me too much credit if you think I go around worrying about everyone else's feelings." He shook his head. "Because I don't."

Her glare was strong and unwavering as it leveled on him. "Unsurprising."

He didn't make a habit of being particularly concerned about how other people felt. Their feelings were just that.

Their own.

But it wasn't turning out to be so easy with Elise.

48

Especially now that he knew the full extent of what her feelings caused.

"Why am I here then?" She crossed her arms, looking him up and down with a suspicious gaze. "Were you hoping I'd ask you to fuck me again so you could turn me down again?" Her chin lifted. "Because that ship's sailed, Babe. I wouldn't fuck you if you were the last man on earth."

He put one hand on the center of his chest. "That would hurt my feelings if I thought it was true."

"Why should I worry about your feelings if you aren't worried about mine?" She straightened. "And it is true." Elise shook her head. "I'm not interested in anything you have to offer."

Abe moved toward her. "You don't have a clue what I could offer you, Babe."

Elise stood taller. "I'm sure it's unimpressive."

She was trying to push his buttons. Trying to force a reaction that would prove whatever point she was attempting to make.

It wasn't going to happen.

"What makes you so sure?" He closed in on her.

Her eyes slipped, moving down to the dwindling space separating them. "Lots of things."

"Like what?" Abe almost smiled when she started to back away.

This was how it worked between them.

A push and pull that carried a potential he'd never experienced.

"You're uptight." Elise continued backing away.

"I'm a perfectionist." Abe followed her across the room. "Trust me, that works out in your favor."

"You're bossy."

"Again," Abe slowed his pace as she backed toward the wall, "something that works in your favor."

Elise snorted. "Haven't you heard?" She stopped her retreat, a wry smile lifting her lips. "I'm the bossy one." Her humorless smile flattened. "And I can tell you, bossy isn't a compliment."

"Depends on who's giving it." Abe took advantage of her temporary pause, closing the gap between them. "I like bossy."

Elise's laugh was bitter. "Right."

He pressed against her, forcing her feet to move again, backing her against the wall. "That's why you're here." He pinned her in place. "Why I followed you when you were outside alone." He ran his nose along the side of hers. "Why I spent the past three months trying every fucking restaurant around here." He tipped his head, dragging his lips along the jut of her jaw. "Because I like your bossy ass."

"It's too bad I don't like you then." She sucked in a breath as his mouth moved to her neck.

He nosed along her skin, catching the lobe of her ear between his teeth. "Not even a little?"

Her hands gripped his arms, fingers digging into his biceps. For a second he thought she might push him away, but the shove never came. "Not even a little."

"I'm going to call bullshit." Three months he'd been kicking himself. Regretting not immediately taking her up on the offer she'd made.

Now it suddenly seemed worth it.

And it made him willing to wait a little longer.

Abe stepped away from her. "Come on." He grabbed her hand in his and pulled her toward the stairs she'd been so intent on racing down just a few minutes ago. "Let's get you back to headquarters."

"Fine." She sniffed a little. "Good. That's what I wanted."

The drive back was a silent one, giving him plenty of time to work out his next move.

Develop a plan of attack.

That's what it would have to be.

An attack.

Because Elise wasn't going to go down easily.

Yet another thing to draw him in. He liked working for what he had.

Liked putting in time and effort. Proving he was capable.

And nothing tested him like this woman.

The halls of the rooming house were quiet as he snuck her in, making sure no one would know she was anywhere but her room all night. The less Elise tried to come up with an explanation for tonight, the better.

Because while he had realized the possibilities in front of them, she clearly had not.

And that would work to his advantage.

He waited while Elise unlocked her door. Just before she slipped inside he caught her arm. "I'll see you in the morning, Babe." He stepped close, tipping her chin up as he leaned down to brush his lips across her forehead. "Sleep tight."

Then he turned and walked away. Using every bit of willpower he had not to run back and give her a proper kiss.

One that would prove all he knew.

All the potential between them.

All they could be.

As long as he could get Elise on board.

****

"WHAT ARE YOU doing here?" Elise's eyes were wide as they snapped up and down the hall just outside her room.

"Just keeping you from being a pain in your own ass." Abe straightened from where he'd been leaning against the opposite wall. "Put your shit back in your room."

Elise dragged her rolling suitcase closer. "No."

"Fine." He reached for it. "We can take it to my house then."

She jerked it out of reach. "No."

He lifted a brow at her. "What was your plan, Babe? To walk out the front gate?"

The shift of her features made it clear that was exactly what her plan was.

Yesterday this might have upset him.

Not today. He'd had time to think everything through.

Time to step back and take a deep breath.

Time to consider all he knew about Elise.

"Here's the thing, Babe." Abe moved close to her. "I'm done watching you punish yourself." He hadn't connected the dots until he saw her leg, but once he processed it all, he could see exactly what was happening.

Elise had unreachable standards for herself and when she fell short, someone had to pay for it.

And that someone was her.

He tipped his head to the room behind her. "So you can either put your shit back in there, or you can bring it to my house." He shook his head. "But you're not leaving Alaska."

"I am leaving Alaska." She swallowed, jaw clenching tight at the move. "I have a ticket." Elise tried to get around him. "And you're making me late."

Abe let her pass, watching as she marched down the silent hall. Giving her just enough time to think she was getting away.

"I'm not above kidnapping, Elise." He took slow steps in her direction. "You won't make it to that front gate. Might as well stop now."

She wasn't running again. Not from him.

Not from herself.

But Elise clearly wasn't on the same page. Her march continued down the hall and toward the walkway connecting the rooming house to the main building.

It was unsurprising.

He huffed out a sigh. "Fuck."

Now he had to kidnap her.

****

"FUCKING MEN." ELISE shoved her way out the doors of the main entrance to Alaskan Security, blinking fast at the emotion trying to break free.

The desire to channel that emotion into something else was strong. Almost overwhelming.

So she walked faster, trying to smother out the urge she'd been fighting for years.

Since the first time she dragged an open pair of scissors across her thigh, cutting out the pain that made her skin crawl and her stomach ache.

Replacing it with a tangible pain. One that had a reason. One that she could see. Identify.

It made things bearable. Allowed her to control the uncontrollable.

At least it used to.

She yanked the handle of the bag carrying all her belongings, dragging it closer as she moved faster along the smooth surface of the fresh blacktop she'd suggested putting down when the new gate was installed.

Elise checked over one shoulder, looking for any sign that Abe might be making good on his threat, even though she knew it was an empty one.

He was just trying to be the asshole he was. Get one last dig in before she wasn't around for him to jab anymore.

The fingers of her free hand went to the center of her forehead. The spot he'd kissed last night before leaving her alone to fester in the mess he'd made during an evening of contradictions.

And there was only one way to explain all of it.

Abe was the biggest asshole she'd ever met.

He wasn't satisfied at simply turning her down.

No. He wanted to drive that rejection deeper. Trick her. Lure her into a false sense of acceptance before cutting her down again.

And laughing about it.

But she was done being laughed at. Done being rejected for what she couldn't help.

54

As the trees started to close in at the side of the lane she walked faster, her pace turning to more of a run as she raced to put more distance between herself and the place she thought she might finally find happiness.

What a joke that was.

Alaska was just like everywhere else. Only colder.

And with more moose.

Elise made it to the gate, using her Alaskan Security badge for the last time to open it. She tried to let out a breath as she stepped through, thinking it would be easier to breathe.

It wasn't.

Not yet.

But it would be soon.

She checked the time on her phone as the gate closed, scanning the road for any sign of the Uber she'd scheduled.

Five more minutes.

It seemed like an eternity. Based on past experience it might be.

Elise crossed her arms, tapping one foot as the seconds ticked by, each one dragging out longer than the last.

She couldn't get away from this place fast enough.

A dark sedan turned onto the road leading to Alaskan Security. Elise checked her phone again, watching as the map showed the car coming her way.

It was time. Time to try again.

Time to take what she'd learned and be better.

Maybe eventually she'd get it right.

The four-door pulled up in front of her and the trunk popped. A very tall man dressed in all black got out of the driver's side. He gave her a smile. "Good morning."

Elise looked him over, taking a small step back as he came closer. "Morning."

The man was big. Fit. Decent-looking.

All things that should be considered good.

But the way he looked at her was odd.

The smile on his face seemed out of place.

"I can put your bag in the trunk." He took another step in, sending her feet back a little more.

"I can get it." Elise gripped the handle as she looked back at the gate.

It was closed. Locked tight behind her.

"Something wrong?"

She turned back toward the man, forcing a smile of her own. "Just making sure the gate closed all the way."

His cool gaze flicked to where her badge was still clutched in one hand. The move was fast enough she might have missed it if she wasn't watching him so closely.

"Not that I could do much about it if it wasn't." She managed a laugh that only sounded a little tight. "My badge is deactivated." She took a quick step, launching the rectangle of plastic over the gate, the weight of the clip attached to it helping carry it a decent distance to the other side. "Might as well leave it here."

"That wasn't a smart move." The man's voice carried a threatening edge that sent a chill up her spine.

56

And made her even more sure she'd done the smartest thing possible.

Because she might have been leaving them all behind, but the women inside were the best friends she'd ever had.

No one would get close to them if she could help it.

Elise turned to the man, standing tall, trying to do what she'd always done.

Bluff her way through.

Any softness the man's face held before was gone, replaced by hard angles and eyes colder than the Alaskan winter.

Lucky for her she was used to cold men.

He was on her before she could blink, grabbing her arms so tight it would leave marks.

If she survived long enough.

"Stupid bitch."

"I'm not stupid." She'd been called bitch enough times that it carried no weight anymore.

But stupid? That one she would fight.

"If I was stupid I'd be in that car right now." Elise braced her feet, ready to put up as much of a fight as she could.

"If you were smart you wouldn't be outside that gate." This time the man's smile was genuine. Like he was amused at her mistake and what it would cost her.

He shook her. Hard enough her teeth slammed together and her vision scrambled, the blur of movement clearing just as his hand came to her face, a dirty, wet rag smashing into her nose and mouth.

Don't breathe.

Don't breathe.

Don't breathe.

He pushed harder, digging the rough weave into her skin, holding tight as her lungs burned.

Unfortunately, she quickly reached the point where there was no stopping it. The air sucked in all on its own, pulling in a slightly sweet smell from the rag. Her head immediately started to swim as the fight drained right out of her.

The second breath stole a little more of her strength. Her awareness.

The third breath sounded funny.

Like a strange popping noise.

One that made the whole world start to fall. Like her body was weightless, caught in a never-ending freefall.

Her next breath lacked the sweetness of the last three. The air was cooler. Fresher.

"Good girl. Deep breaths."

Her eyes moved slowly, dragging from one side to the other as the familiar voice continued on.

"I need you to keep breathing, Babe." A warm touch slid down her cheek. "It's the only way you'll feel better."

The trees were so tall, their limbs stretching high into the sky she stared up at.

She was supposed to be in that sky.

Flying away.

"Help me get her up." The familiar voice was sharper now.

Her body started to move again, but this time it wasn't falling.

It was floating.

Elise closed her eyes, head rocking to one side as the world became louder.

"Open the door." The rough voice was right next to her ear now, the deep rumble of it tangible.

Then everything was silent.

Silent and soft and warm.

Peaceful.

Peaceful enough her eyes stayed closed in spite of the soft touch sliding down the side of her face.

CHAPTER 5

"IT WAS A misunderstanding."

"A misunderstanding?" Heidi glared at him from her spot in the center of the line of women facing him down. "What did you do?"

They thought this was his fault.

Good.

"I miscalculated." That was the understatement of the century.

He should have expected Elise to stubbornly stick with the plan she had. If for no other reason than to prove she could.

"You miscalculated?" Eva practically snarled at him. "What sort of fucked-up miscalculation almost got her kidnapped?"

"She wasn't almost kidnapped." The minute that prick stepped out of the car his fate was sealed.

"How much closer does it need to be to qualify?" Heidi's voice climbed with each word.

"They've got to get you in the car for it to count as an almost kidnapping." Shawn stood behind the girls. "If the door closes then it counts as an actual kidnapping."

"You assholes and your stupid rules." Paige, one of the women who moved to Alaska when Lennie and Elise came, rolled her eyes. "It's the dumbest thing I've ever heard of. Shot is shot and almost kidnapped is almost kidnapped." She shook her head at him. "But I guess go with whatever makes you feel better."

He'd been trying to keep his cool about this whole thing, but the longer he stood out here answering their questions, the more likely it was that Elise would wake up alone.

And probably a little uncertain.

"I'll let you know when she wakes up." Abe turned his back to them, hoping they'd take the hint.

"You better." Lennie stepped into his peripheral vision. "Cause if you don't, you'll be almost dead."

The threat caught him a little off-guard. Especially since it came from Lennie. She was the sweetest of the group.

At least he thought she was.

Looked like there were limits to her sweetness.

Abe tipped his head her way. "Understood."

He opened the door to Elise's room, stepping through and closing it behind him. It took a second for his eyes to adjust to the darkness. When they did he realized he'd stayed in the hall too long.

"You're awake." He moved toward the spot where he'd spent the past two hours, waiting for her to sleep off the effects of ether and adrenaline. He slowly eased onto his still-warm spot on the mattress. "How are you feeling?"

"Fine." Her answer came quickly.

"Fine?" It wasn't what he was expecting. "No headache?"

"I'm fine." She scooted up to a sitting position as he retook his place at her side. "Why are you in my bed?"

"Because Eli wouldn't let me take you to mine." It was his initial reaction. To take her somewhere else. Somewhere he could keep her safe. Keep her close. "He wanted you to stay here for a little while so he could keep an eye on you."

"I'm fine." Elise yanked at the front of the soft sleep shirt she wore. Her eyes immediately dropped. "What's this? Why am I wearing this?"

"The shirt you had on was ruined." He tried to keep the explanation simple.

No reason to tell her exactly what ruined the shirt.

Elise wrapped both arms tight across her front. "Why did they change it? I'm sure it was fine."

"It wasn't fine, Babe." He scooted closer, keeping his voice low and calm. "And I'm the one who changed it. I wouldn't let anyone else come in the room while I did it."

Elise's eyes moved away as her fingers wrapped tight around the upper part of her arm, covering the skin he now knew shared the same white lines as her thigh. "Oh."

"Here." He grabbed a bottle of water from the side table. "Eli says you need to stay hydrated." He twisted the lid off before holding it in front of her.

Elise stared at it a minute before finally taking it. "Thank you." She took a tiny sip.

"Not enough, Babe." Abe leaned back, assuming the same position he'd held while she slept. "Gotta get it down or Eli will give me shit."

"Maybe you deserve it." Elise took another drink.

"I'm sure I do." Abe watched as she swallowed down a few more long gulps. "I should have gotten to you sooner."

He should have stopped her before she made it outside the gate.

Then none of this would have happened.

"I'm fine." Elise tossed the covers back, whipping them off her body as she stood, going straight to the bathroom. She flipped on the light and closed the door.

He waited, counting the seconds, deciding how many he was willing to give her.

By seventy-five he was at the door. "Elise?"

The door whipped open. "I can't even pee in peace?"

"Of course you can pee in peace." Did she not realize what just happened to her was a big fucking deal?

She should be at least a little upset.

"I just want to be sure you're okay."

She lifted her brows at him. "I'm fine." Elise went past him. "What do you want from me?"

"I want you to acknowledge that someone just fucking tried to kidnap you."

"Why? So you can point out how stupid I was?" Elise went to the closet and yanked open the door.

"No." She wasn't being stupid. She was being headstrong. They were two completely different things. "But you should sure as hell want to talk about what just happened."

"No thanks." Elise turned toward the door, walking around the side of the bed to look into the small recess at the end of the closet. "Where in the hell is my stuff?"

That was going to be fun to answer. Especially in light of her current frame of mind.

"It's not here."

Her head snapped his way. "Not here?" Her eyes narrowed. "Where is it?"

"At a different location."

Elise was her own worst enemy, and there wasn't a doubt in his mind that if she could figure out a way to make it happen she'd try to leave again.

And until they figured out who attempted to take her today, that wasn't an option.

Which was convenient since he didn't plan on letting her leave regardless.

She walked right up to him, proving she was as physically fine as she claimed. "You can't just hold me hostage here."

"I'm not planning to hold you hostage here, Babe." He considered it.

But this place offered her little in the way of freedom.

Or privacy.

"I'm taking you to my place."

"Absolutely not." Elise shook her head. "No way."

"I'm sure it won't surprise you to know that Pierce isn't thrilled with what happened this morning." Abe

glanced to the door. "And neither are your friends."
He started picking up the items he'd lined down the dresser, his taser, knife, and cuffs, tucking each one back into place as he continued laying out the reality of her situation. "It took Heidi all of two seconds to find your plane ticket." He snagged his firearm last, strapping it into place before grabbing the keys to the SUV he drove to and from headquarters every day. "Staying at my house will buy you some time before you have to deal with that."

Elise eyed his pistol. "Is she mad?"

"Not mad." Abe shook his head as he tapped a message out on his phone. "Just scared."

Her attention jumped to his face. "Scared?"

"They're all scared." He sent the message before grabbing Elise's shoes from beside the door. "They're worried you're going to try to leave them again." He tipped his head toward the bed. "Sit."

To his surprise, Elise immediately dropped down. "I wasn't leaving them."

"Who were you leaving then?" Abe slid one canvas sneaker into place before tying the lace. He glanced up when she didn't answer.

Elise looked away, turning her head toward the wall.

"That answers that." He finished tying the second shoe and stood up. "Come on."

"Is this really necessary?" Elise wiped at her eyes. "That guy was probably just trying to get anyone he could." She shook her head. "Not me specifically."

"Unfortunately, even if that was true, it's not now." Abe held his hand out. "Most people like that take it personally when shit doesn't go the way they wanted it to."

"You're saying that because I didn't get kidnapped they will really want to kidnap me now?"

If only.

"I'm saying that one of their men died trying to abduct you." He stopped waiting for her to take his hand and reached down to grab hers. "And I'm sure that pissed them the fuck off."

"*I* didn't kill him." Elise dragged her feet as he pulled her up and toward the door.

"You're easier to kill than I am." He looked back at her over one shoulder. "No offense."

"How is that not supposed to be offensive?" Elise jerked to a stop when he cracked open the door to peek out.

"You should hope you're easier to kill than I am. If I was easy to kill then we'd both be dead right now." The hall outside was empty, probably due to the efforts of his own team. "Come on." Abe pulled Elise out into the hall and straight toward the garage.

Getting permission to take Elise off-site took some pretty hefty convincing, especially since he wasn't willing to disclose all his reasons for the request.

But putting her in a position where she was faced with a line of disappointed friends would bring on a huge amount of guilt and increase the chances that she would try to run again.

And this time he might not be as lucky.

"Why can't Rico just take me home?" Elise stuck a little closer as they moved through the garage, her eyes constantly moving, like she was waiting for someone to jump out at them any minute.

Which only made him more sure this was the right thing to do for her.

"I'll just go back to my old life." She was almost pleading at this point. "No one will even notice that I'm gone."

"First of all," Abe opened the passenger's door to the SUV, "Cincinnati is just as fucking dangerous as Alaska." Maybe more so. "Second, plenty of people would notice you were gone." He jerked his chin toward the interior of the Rover. "Get in."

"You're so fucking bossy." She flopped into the seat, crossing her arms.

"I'm so fucking bossy because you don't listen any other way." He grabbed the belt and strapped it across her chest. "And it's going to get you hurt."

Already did.

"I'm an adult. I don't need someone else telling me what to do."

Abe leaned down, leveling his eyes with hers. "I beg to differ, Babe." He couldn't stop his eyes from moving to the angry line he knew hid under the fabric of her pants. "You forget, I've seen what you tell yourself to do." He closed the door, taking a physical step back.

Hoping it would help make a mental one happen too.

He walked around the back of the SUV, rocking his head from side to side, trying to ease the tension building in his neck and shoulders.

Elise was still exactly as he'd left her when he got in, sitting stick straight, arms crossed, chin high, glaring out the windshield.

He pulled out of the garage, watching in the rearview mirror as a second SUV pulled out behind them.

The front gate now had an armed guard on duty, and Brock tipped his head in a nod as they passed. The gate stayed open as the second SUV followed them out.

"Who's following us?" Elise didn't move, but her eyes slid to the side mirror, watching the vehicle tailing them.

"Tyson and Jameson." Abe scanned the roadway as he turned toward the line of townhouses Pierce had constructed. His was the first one completed, but the rest would be ready for occupancy shortly, and considering what happened this morning, that was a concern.

"Why are they following us?" Elise's gaze shifted from window to window.

"I don't know if you heard," he came to a stop at the first crossroad, waiting until there was a gap large enough for both of them before turning, "but someone tried to kidnap one of our most valuable employees this morning."

Elise shifted in her seat, running her tongue along her teeth before tilting her head his direction without looking his way. "Thank you."

"Wow." He passed the grocery store within walking distance of his new home. "That must have been painful for you."

"I don't have a problem thanking someone when they help me." One of her blonde brows lifted. "And you helped me."

His goal hadn't been to help her. Not technically.

His goal was to end the man who thought he had a right to take her.

To touch her.

To handle her like he did.

"Are you sore?" The tension in Abe's neck pulled tight, forcing him to stretch against it.

That son of a bitch grabbed her like he owned her. Shook her like she wouldn't break.

Hadn't already broken a hundred times.

"I'm fine."

"Right." He rocked his head to the other side, stretching the muscles and tendons as far as they would go.

"What's that mean?" She finally looked at him, lips twisted into a deep scowl.

"Means I don't believe you." He pulled up to the heavy gate at the townhomes and punched in his code.

"I don't care if you believe me." Elise leaned to look up at the face of the buildings, her frown deepening.

"What's wrong?" He tried to find the spot where her eyes were fixed, but the angle of the SUV made it impossible.

She pointed toward the roofline of the unit next to his. "That gutter is sagging."

"I'm sure they'll fix it."

"They better." Elise's eyes moved along the windows and siding. "Otherwise I'll find someone else to build the next ones."

A little of the tightness in his body eased. "Thought you were leaving?"

"How can I leave?" Her head snapped his way as he pulled into the garage. "I'm being held hostage." She snapped her belt loose. "I might as well do something while I'm stuck here."

"You might as well relax for five fucking minutes." Less than six hours ago she was fighting a man twice her size. "You need a minute to deal with what happened."

"What for?" Elise shoved her door open before he had the engine shut off. "If you think I'm going to sit around and cry because of something stupid then you're an idiot."

"Something stupid?" He dodged the second SUV as it pulled into the other half of the two-car garage, going straight for where Elise was heading for the door leading inside. "I'm not sure if you realize this, but chances are good you wouldn't have made it out of that alive."

Elise spun to face him. "How many times has that happened to you?" She looked him up and down. "I don't see you sitting around crying." She pointed at Jameson as he got out of the passenger's seat of the second Rover. "He might though."

"Don't put me in the middle of your little lover's spat." Jameson went straight to the back end of the SUV and opened the hatch.

Elise let out a long, loud laugh. "I would never," she shook her head, "ever fu—"

Abe moved close to her, keeping his voice low as he backed her against the door. "Watch what you say, Babe." He leaned into her ear, grabbing the front of Elise's shirt with one hand, fisting it tight as he opened the door, using his hold to keep her from falling inside. "I like a challenge."

It was the truth.

And probably how this whole thing started.

Elise was quick on her feet and unafraid to speak her mind. She had a smart mouth and balls bigger than most of the men he knew.

And most the men he knew were mercenaries.

The woman had challenge written all over her.

"Come on." He pulled her toward the stairs.

"I don't need you to drag me everywhere." Elise wrestled against where he still held onto the soft shirt he'd picked out to replace the one covered in the blood of the man who'd made one too many bad decisions.

"Seems like you do." Abe continued through the house, past the kitchen and down the short hall leading to the main bedroom. "I've seen what happens when you get to do what you want."

"And this is your solution? To lock me up here?"

"Not just my solution, Babe." Heidi actually suggested locking her in one of the basement cells. "I'm not the only bad guy here."

"You're the only one I see." Elise snapped it out.

He shoved her into the room, slamming the door behind them as he finally let her go, the weight of the day pressing down on him from every angle. "I'm the bad guy?" He slowly walked toward her.

"Was I so bad when I shot the prick who thought it was okay to touch you?"

Elise backed away, uncertainty widening her eyes.

"What about when I made sure no one else found out what you do to yourself?" He needed to calm down.

Needed to walk away.

"What about when I made sure you didn't have to face down all of Intel at once? Tell them why you were at the gate in the first place." She could think he was an asshole all she wanted, but no way was he going to be the bad guy of this fucking day.

"I—" Elise was still backing away from him.

"You what?" He lifted his brows. "Might as well say it, whatever it is."

She bumped into the first bed he'd owned in years, her fingers pulling at the leg of the pants she wore.

No they weren't pulling.

They were digging.

Clawing at the spot he'd bandaged less than twenty-four hours ago.

"Stop it." Abe grabbed her arms, fighting her hand from the spot. "Stop."

"Leave me alone." Elise fought him the same way he'd watched her fight this morning. "Let me go."

She was surprisingly strong, using her whole body against him as she twisted in his grip, forcing him to get rougher than he wanted.

"I'm not letting you hurt yourself, Elise." He managed to get both wrists, but the second he did she yanked back, putting all her weight into the move. The frame of the bed made it impossible to get any sort of leverage that might keep them upright, so down they went.

Yelling and fighting.

Onto the bed.

CHAPTER 6

IT WOULD FUCKING figure.

Elise glared up at the man on top of her, the weight of his body pressing her into the bed.

"Are you done?" Abe was out of breath and it made her a little happy.

Something might as well.

He had her pinned. Arms over her head, both her legs clamped between his.

"If I let you go, are you going to try to kill me?"

The question made her look at the gun strapped to his side.

"Christ." Abe worked both her wrists into one of his hands. He pulled the gun from its holster and held it out. The inside of the handle fell to the floor with a heavy thud, then he shoved the gun back into place. "If you try to shoot me I'm going to be real fucking upset, Babe."

"I don't know how to shoot." She'd never even held a gun, let alone tried to shoot one.

All of Intel had been trained at this point, but so far she'd been lucky enough to escape that particular job duty.

Abe's eyes fixed on her face. "Why don't you know how to shoot?"

"Because I don't want to know how." It was her least favorite part about life at Alaskan Security. "I don't like guns."

"Of course you don't." He wiped his eyes with his free hand, digging his fingers and thumb into the sockets. "You have to know how to protect yourself, Elise."

"But they make me nervous."

"You make me fucking nervous."

"You say fuck a lot."

Abe's lips twitched. "I could say the same thing to you."

Her skin was immediately hot.

Maybe from embarrassment.

Maybe because of something else. "Shut up."

Abe eyed her for a second longer. "I'm going to let you up." His fingers relaxed just a little where they held her wrists. "If you come at me then I'm going to have to come up with another plan."

"You mean besides holding me hostage?"

"It's for your own good." Abe leaned back, using his grip to pull her into a sitting position. "And at least you're not locked in the basement at headquarters."

"What?" She scoffed. "You wanted to lock me in the basement?"

"Not me, Babe." Abe eased off the mattress one leg at a time. "My plan was always to bring you here." His eyes darkened just a little as they moved over where she sat at the end of the bed. "Maybe not under these circumstances."

Elise rolled her eyes to one side as the space around her started to register.

This was Abe's room.

His bedroom.

The place where he slept.

The place where he—

She cleared her throat as images she couldn't quite perfect worked their way into her brain. "Well I'm here." She forced her eyes to his. "Now what?"

Abe's nostrils barely flared as he watched her a second longer. Then he abruptly turned and went to the large walk-in closet. He came back a second later with some of her clothes. "You should probably take a shower." His gaze went to her hair. "I did what I could, but—"

"But what?" She grabbed the side of her hair and pulled it out. A few of the strands were a little darker than they should be. "What's in my hair?"

"I wouldn't think too hard about it." He went to the dresser and pulled out the top drawer. "Anything else you need is probably in here." He backed toward the door. "I'm assuming you know where the shower is."

Elise looked toward the bathroom. "Where are you going?"

"I'll be right outside." Abe opened the door. "If you need me just yell."

She grabbed the knit pants and shirt he brought and headed toward the room she knew had a waterfall shower that might wash away at least a little of the day's bullshit. "Are you offering to wash my back?"

"Not today." Abe's voice was quiet as he pulled the door closed. "Tomorrow's a different story."

"Sure." She snorted in the empty room, talking to herself at this point. "I'll hold my breath."

Elise peeked into the bathroom.

The bathroom she'd basically designed. Pierce had expensive taste and she'd had to reign him in, reminding the owner of Alaskan Security that these homes needed to be nice, but not so nice that they were too expensive to make sense. Pierce sold them to his employees at cost, but even that could add up when you wanted marble heated floors.

Elise flipped on the light, dropping her clothes onto the counter between the double sinks as she went to twist on the shower. Her hand stopped just over the knob.

All her toiletries were lined down the ledge, perfectly spaced, labels facing forward.

She turned the water as hot as she could stand, stripping down before stepping under the wide head suspended from the ceiling, letting the spray run over her head and down her body.

After washing her hair three times and scrubbing everything else until it was pink, she shut off the water and stepped out, grabbing one of the thick towels off the rack and wrapping it around her body. She squeezed the water out of her hair with one hand and sifted through her clothes with the other.

Pants.

Shirt.

Shit.

Elise opened the door to the bathroom and went to the drawer Abe left open. Her bras and panties were lined inside, each one folded perfectly.

The door behind her made a soft click as it opened.

"Looks like someone spent a lot of time with my panties." She snagged a pair of super-stretchy briefs and a pull-over cotton demi bra.

"I'm gonna need you to say that again."

She spun to face Abe, motioning to the open drawer. "My underwear. It's organized."

Abe stalked across the room, leaning to glare in at her unmentionables. The lines of his face hardened. "*Tyson.*" He spun away and stormed out into the hall, slamming the door behind him.

She peeked in at her panties. The neat rows and perfect folds certainly looked like the work of a man who couldn't let anyone else load a damn dishwasher.

And now she was barricaded in a house with him for the foreseeable future.

The bathroom was still a little steamy when she went back in to wiggle her way into the bra and panties. By the time she had her pants and shirt on Abe was back, looking just as sour as before.

And for some reason that made her very happy. At least she wasn't the only one who was miserable.

Right now she should be landing in Ohio, deciding what she would eat first.

Her stomach growled. Apparently it didn't realize their plans had been thwarted by a giant man with an Uber account.

"I used Uber to schedule that car." Elise combed her fingers through her hair as Abe watched her from the doorway of the bedroom. "I bet Heidi can hack into their system to see who it was."

"The actual driver showed up." Abe came into the bathroom and pulled open a drawer, pulling out a familiar wide-toothed comb. "He was confused as hell when I pulled a gun on him."

"I'm sure confused isn't the right word." Elise tried to grab the comb from him, but Abe pulled it out of her reach.

"He might have needed new pants." Abe gently turned her head toward the mirror. "We talked to him, but it was pretty clear he didn't know anything." He slowly worked the teeth of the comb down the back of her head.

"So they just sit around waiting to see if someone calls an Uber to Alaskan Security? That doesn't seem like a very efficient way to kidnap people." Elise tried not to focus on the slow drag of the comb through her hair, but it was impossible. Her eyes dropped closed as the soft tug and pull worked its hypnotic magic.

"Heidi's best guess is that they have a program that skims information and is set to search for specific words." Abe reached into the cabinet and came out with a blow dryer. "Alaskan Security. Probably as many of our names as they know."

She swallowed. They definitely knew her name now. "Do you think they know everyone's names?"

79

Abe's eyes lifted to hers in the mirror as he switched on the hot air and carefully moved it down the length of her hair. "Everyone who matters."

The hunger she'd felt earlier twisted, binding its way into a sickness that made her skin cold and her hands sweat. "You mean everyone in Intel."

"At least everyone in Intel." He worked through her hair systematically, using his fingers to smooth down the strands as he went. "Probably more."

"Do you think they know your name?" It was just curiosity that made her ask.

Nothing more.

Abe's lips lifted at the edges. "Careful, Babe. I'll think you're worried about me."

"It's self-preservation. If something happens to you then I have to dry my own hair." She glanced toward the door. "And I don't imagine Tyson or Jameson will be interested in filling that position."

"I think you'd be surprised what positions Tyson and Jameson would be interested in filling." Abe moved in a little closer, the front of his body nearly touching the back of hers. "Which means I'd have to take them down with me." He set the blow dryer onto the counter. "And I can't imagine Pierce would be thrilled at losing three of us at once."

She tried to listen to what he was saying, but suddenly every bit of her was focused on where his heat sank into her back. "Okay."

His hand came out to sweep her hair over one shoulder. "Okay?"

The word warmed the side of her neck, making the distraction she was fighting even worse. "What?"

80

Abe's nose ran along her skin, dragging slowly toward her ear. "I told you I would rather kill two men than let them stay here with you." His lips replaced his nose, moving as he continued to talk. "And you agreed."

Was that what just happened? "You're distracting me."

"Not yet, but I'm more than willing to."

"Willing to what?" It was nearly impossible to follow along as his hands slid up the sides of her body.

"Willing to distract you." His teeth scraped along the lobe of her ear, sending a shiver down her spine. "Would you like me to distract you, Elise?" One wide palm slid around her front, fingers splayed across her belly as it dipped lower.

What was happening right now?

If it was someone else in her shoes, she'd say Abe was suggesting sex.

But it wasn't someone else. It was her.

And, historically speaking, that meant she was reading the situation wrong.

Really wrong.

"What are you suggesting?" She watched as his hand dipped lower, teasing along the waistband of her pants.

"Not sex."

That made sense. She would be the only woman in the world who could have a man pressed against her offering favors that were of the non-sexual variety.

"I guess I'm hungry." Might as well get some good food out of this. "I'm not eating the leftovers though."

She deserved way more than leftovers at this point.

Abe's head tipped and his eyes lifted to hers in the mirror. "You want me to distract you with food?"

"Isn't that what you were offering?" He better at least give her some damn food. He'd taken her phone. Her computer.

Gotten blood on her favorite shirt.

And her hair.

She deserved some freaking fried rice or something.

Maybe a pulled pork sandwich.

Abe's eyes slowly skimmed down her body before coming back to her face. "No. That's not what I was offering."

"Well you weren't offering sex or food." She lifted her brows. "Not sure what else you can give me."

Abe stood a little taller behind her, but his hands didn't leave her body. He shifted closer, pressing tight enough even she could notice the contradiction he was sporting.

She tried to keep her eyes from widening.

And failed.

He specifically said *not sex*. Made it clear he had no interest in fucking her.

Again.

"I think we're having a miscommunication." His eyes narrowed a little as they moved over her face. "Somehow."

"I've made my position pretty clear." She'd offered him sex. Clearly and concisely.

He declined.

Now she was requesting food.

Not much left to interpret there.

"So you're saying I'm the issue?" He looked almost amused.

Which was more than mildly irritating. "Aren't you always?"

Abe fisted her shirt in his hands, gripping tight as he spun her to face him.

Elise grabbed the counter, doing her best not to let him knock her any more off-balance than she already was. "If you ruin another one of my shirts I'm going to be pissed."

"Technically I didn't ruin the first one." One arm snaked around her back, holding her tight to him.

Tight enough she was faced with his contradiction once again, but this time it was front and center.

It was great being so undesirable that a man could literally have a raging hard-on and still refuse to use it on her.

There should be a place in the Guinness Book of World Records just for her.

Least desirable female.

Abe's free hand came to her neck, fingers pushing up and into the hair he'd just finished drying. They laced tight. Tight enough she couldn't move her head without sacrificing a few. "And technically, *you* are the issue." He leaned in a little more, the arm across her back keeping her from rocking back. "Because you seem to be a little confused."

"I can't imagine how that happened." She held the counter tight as his lips came close to hers. "Considering you make things so clear."

It wasn't the first time she got caught in the muddied waters around a man. She'd missed important clues before, blinded by her complete belief that she understood the situation.

"I'm not sure how much clearer I need to be, Babe." Abe's lips brushed the corner of her mouth. "You're in my house. You'll be sleeping in my bed." The hand in her hair opened, fingers spreading wide along her scalp as his lips continued tracing a path around hers. "I found the best places to eat in Fairbanks." His voice was low and deep. "For you." His lips whispered across hers. "I killed a man for touching you."

"You killed him because he was trying to kidnap me." Her fingers burned where they held the edge of the counter, squeezing tighter with each pass of his lips.

Abe slowly smiled, the hand on her back sliding down the center of her spine. "Did I?"

"Yes." She was there. Sort of. She saw it happen. Sort of. "He was trying to take me and you shot him."

"I shot him because you are not his to take."

"I—" Elise clamped her mouth shut. There weren't any words to come out of it.

None that made any sense.

"That is why I wouldn't fuck you that night, Elise." Abe's head moved, tipping from one side to the other. "You weren't mine to take."

That sounded nice enough, but it didn't line up with the facts. "But you laughed."

"I definitely didn't laugh, Babe." His lips lifted into the same smile she'd seen in the flashing lights of the bar in Cincinnati. "But I sure as hell smiled." His hand pressed lower, curving along the line of her ass. "I thought you were finally figuring out what I already knew."

"What did you know?" She could barely whisper it out as his hand cupped against her, fingers sliding between her thighs as they eased toward the part of her that suddenly felt very achy.

"I knew that there was something between us." His touch brushed across her. "Something more than just fantastic fucking."

Thank Christ she was holding onto the counter. Otherwise she might have fallen down.

Collapsed right then and there.

Because of the sound of his voice.

The heat of his body.

The way he smelled. The way he sounded.

The drag of his fingers.

"So let me ask you again." Abe's gravelly voice cut through the haze blurring her brain. "Would you like me to distract you, Elise?"

Saying no seemed like a terrible idea. Terrible because she could really use a distraction.

Terrible because Abe might be a skilled distractor.

Terrible because if she said no then he might stop touching her.

"Yes." The word wasn't completely out before it was cut off, smothered out by his mouth covering hers, silvery stubble scraping her skin. His thumb pressed her chin, parting her lips so he could take her mouth completely, tongue sliding against hers as he hefted her up, resting her ass on the bathroom counter. Her knees parted as she tried to find balance, and Abe immediately stepped between them, one hand catching her thigh and pulling it around his waist.

Then he grabbed her, holding tight as her body swung away from the counter.

Both arms reflexively went around his neck, hanging on for dear life as Abe carried her out into the bedroom. She locked her ankles together as he leaned forward, pulling her body tight to his as her back hit the mattress. The hard line of his dick rubbed against her, making her suck in a breath.

A breath of surprise.

Shock.

Fear.

Abe's lips moved down her neck as his hand shoved into her pants, fingers immediately moving between her legs to tuck against the most intimate part of her.

She tried not to react.

Not to do something that might give her away.

Something that might stop whatever was happening right now.

Abe froze, his whole body going completely still. "Elise," his head lifted, eyes coming to hers, "what's wrong?"

"Nothing." She forced her legs to relax, trying to seem like everything was fine.

Because everything was fine. This was a normal thing. A thing most people her age did all the time. "Nothing's wrong."

The hand on her didn't move, just stayed cupped in place as his eyes moved over her face.

"Why did you stop?" She wiggled a little, thinking that might be the key to getting things moving again. "Don't stop."

"I stopped because I've known you long enough to realize something is wrong." Abe's hand eased away from her.

Because of course it did.

That's how this always went when she did manage to get to this point, which wasn't often.

"Nothing is wrong." How many freaking times did she have to say it?

"Then why did you tense up when I touched you?" He shook his head. "That's not nothing." The lines around his eyes hardened. "Has someone hurt you, Elise? Because I swear to God—"

"No one's hurt me." Not outside of the damage she'd inflicted herself. "I'm fine."

"Now I know you're lying." Abe rolled off her but he took her with him, keeping her close at his side. He tucked her head under his chin as one hand stroked down her hair.

The skin of her face was hot. From embarrassment. From guilt.

She couldn't let him think what he was thinking. Not when it wasn't even close to the truth.

"No one's ever hurt me." Maybe that would be enough to make him happy.

Enough to make him drop it.

"I think you underestimate how patient I am, Elise." His hand did a slow pass down her back before sliding up again. "I waited three months to touch you. I can wait three more."

Of all the—

Fine.

He wanted the truth.

He was about to get it.

Spoiler alert. He wasn't going to like it.

Elise shoved up, using the center of his chest as leverage as she moved toward the edge of the bed. Might as well get out of the way so she wouldn't get injured when he took off.

Which had happened before.

Twice.

"I'm—"

She squeezed her eyes shut, huffing out one final breath.

"I have not currently ever had sex."

CHAPTER 7

ELISE STARED AT HIM.

He stared back at her.

No way was she saying what it sounded like she was saying.

He must have missed part of the sentence. "I'm going to need you to repeat that."

"I'm a virgin." She tried to roll away, forcing him to move fast to catch her.

He barely managed to get his hands on her and pull her back. "I'm sorry. I'm just a little shocked."

"*You're* shocked?" She laughed. "How in the hell do you think I feel?" Elise's cackle went up an octave. "Do you know how men look at me when they find out?"

She didn't wait for him to answer.

"They look at me the same way you're looking at me."

"I'm not gonna lie, Babe. It's a little surprising." He wrapped one arm around her waist, making sure she stayed close. "But it's way better than what I was thinking."

For a second there he almost lost his mind.

Almost considered leaving Elise with Tyson and Jameson so he could hunt down whoever hurt her.

It was something that happened way too often, and he would take any opportunity to right one of those wrongs.

"So I guess that's it then." Elise stared up at the ceiling.

"That's what?" Abe reached up to smooth down her hair, working through the soft strands.

"Now you're not—"

A knock at the door cut her off, stealing her next words from him.

"I've got some intel." Tyson's voice carried through the door.

Of course he did.

"I'll be right back." Abe forced himself up and away from her, pulling the door closed behind him as he left.

Jameson and Tyson were set up at the dining room table, laptops open as they watched the cameras set up around the property.

"What's going on?"

"Heidi got an ID on the guy from this morning." Jameson spun his screen Abe's direction. "Small-time criminal. Decent rap sheet. Nothing too major."

"That explains the sloppy attempt." It was one of the reasons he'd been able to take the man out so easily. The guy was almost oblivious to what was going on around him.

Definitely not a professional.

"Oh." Elise came to a quick stop behind him, one hand coming to cover her mouth, her eyes fixed on the mug shot displayed on Jameson's computer.

Abe stepped between her and the monitor, blocking Elise's view.

She immediately went around him, going straight for the computer. "Who is he?"

Jameson's eyes went to Abe.

Abe nodded. He'd spent too long not giving Elise enough credit. If she wanted to know about this guy then he wouldn't stand in her way.

"His name was Jason Hixon." Jameson twisted the computer back in his direction. "Forty-one. Six-four. Two-fifty."

"Where's he from?" Elise leaned down to peer over Jameson's shoulder, getting close enough to make Abe grit his teeth.

He rocked his head from one side to the other.

"What's wrong?" Tyson grinned at him across the table. "You look stressed."

Fucking Tyson.

"I'm fine."

Elise turned his way. "Why do you get to be fine?"

"Because I really am fine." He stepped in right behind her, wrapping one arm around her waist as he repeated Elise's question. "Where's he from?"

Jameson looked his way, the expression on his face saying everything Abe needed to know.

"Shit." He was hoping it was some lingering asshole from their earlier problems. Maybe a vigilante looking for retribution after the convoluted mess that started and ended with Pierce.

"Where's he from?" Elise looked from Abe to Jameson and then back again. "Tell me."

Abe met her eyes, saw the fear in them.

Elise already knew. She'd put the pieces together.

"He's from Cincinnati."

She turned back to the screen, eyes locking onto the man staring back at her.

"Did anyone in Cincinnati know you were coming home?"

Elise shook her head. "No."

"Not even your family?" She had to have told someone.

Elise rubbed her lips together. "No."

He watched her face. Her expression. "Why were you going back there then?"

She lifted one shoulder. "Where else was I going to go?"

She shouldn't go any-fucking-where. "Heidi's got your computer."

And she was going through it with a fine-toothed comb, looking for any sign of how Jason Hixon knew Elise was going to be leaving Alaska.

Attempting to leave Alaska.

"I figured." Elise huffed out a breath. "She'll tell you the same thing I'm telling you." Her lips twisted to one side. "She knows I don't talk to my family."

He struggled to keep his cool but knowing that she'd leave everyone who cared about her behind to go back to a place where she had no one made him aggravated in a way he couldn't explain.

It bothered him on a deep level.

Like it might be another way for her to hurt herself.

"So maybe he didn't specifically know you were leaving." Abe scrubbed one hand across the stubble making his jaw itch.

"You said they were using some program to search for Alaskan Security." Elise glanced at the screen of Jameson's computer again. "Maybe he just saw that I scheduled an Uber."

"I'm sure that's what happened." Abe almost didn't finish the thought, but holding shit back from her felt wrong. "The question is *why* was he looking for Alaskan Security."

Attempting to abduct an employee of Alaskan Security was dangerous under normal circumstances, let alone to do it five feet in front of the gate.

That was basically a suicide mission.

Which meant the guy might not have had any idea what he was really getting into.

It made sense to hire from outside the state.

But the fact that the guy was from Ohio was more than a coincidence.

"Aren't there always people looking for Alaskan Security?" Elise was trying to work her way out of the middle of this, and he couldn't blame her.

No one wanted to be in the center of something that had the potential to blow up any second.

"Not smart people." Abe pulled out his phone and punched out a message to Shawn.

Just heard Hixon was from Ohio. Let me know when Heidi finds his connection to this.

It shouldn't take her long considering chances were good the connection was the company Mona and Eva used to own.

He tucked his phone back into place before turning to Elise. "Hungry?"

Her eyes dragged to Jameson's computer. "Sure."

"What sounds good?" He went to the drawer in his kitchen that held the menus from the best places he'd found to eat. Some were closer than others, but right now he'd get her anything she wanted.

"Whatever."

That wasn't good.

Abe held out the menus. "I thought you liked picking out food."

Elise shrugged one shoulder. "I'm sure you'll do fine."

"You trust me to order dinner?" He shouldn't be flattered by that, especially given the circumstances, but he was.

"You did okay last night." Elise went to the couch where they sat not so long ago.

When he thought he knew what his biggest hurdle would be with her.

But the curve balls kept coming his way.

"Let's hope I can be two for two then." He followed her to the sofa, grabbing the remote from the table and switching on the television as he went.

Elise snatched the remote as soon as it was within grabbing distance and lowered to the cushions, tucking one foot under her butt. "I'm going to pick what we watch."

"That seems fair." He dropped down beside her and spread the menus across the table while she flipped through the channels.

It might feel like a normal domestic night if not for the men stationed at the dining room table, watching for any sign that the people who tried to take Elise were stupid enough to make a second attempt.

"Anyone else have any preferences?" He picked out the pink folded paper he'd ended up ordering from more than the rest.

"Nope." Tyson leaned back in his chair, eyes staying on the screens in front of him.

"No raw fish." Jameson closed his computer and stood up, checking his side piece as he walked toward the steps. "I'm going to go do a walk of the grounds. Check for any weak points we need to keep an eye on."

Elise watched him go, her eyes lingering on the stairs long after Jameson was out of sight. "Maybe you should have locked me in the basement."

"That was never going to happen." Abe opened the trifold menu and scanned the options, settling on ordering his favorite for everyone. Keep it simple.

Thank God something could be.

He swiped across his phone and dialed the number for Sara Jane's. While he was ordering his phone vibrated in his hand, signaling Shawn's return message. The second he disconnected the call he went straight to his texts.

All of Intel is on it. They've been waiting for a break in this.

It was what they'd been trying to figure out since returning from Cincinnati. Rob and Kyle were bottom feeders, just like Chandler was. Intel had been trying to find out who was next up the food chain for three months, chasing down every lead they could find and always hitting a dead end.

Even Vincent and GHOST were stuck.

That meant they'd been in a holding pattern, waiting until there was something more to go on.

Unfortunately that something more involved Elise, tangling her up in a mess he'd prefer she stayed far away from.

Abe stared across the kitchen island to where she sat on his couch, curled up, eyes unfocused where they rested on the television.

Elise was all passion and fire. It should have drawn men in like fucking moths, ready and willing to succumb to the flames just to get close enough to touch her.

How in the hell did a woman like that make it to almost thirty without—

"What time do you need the food picked up?" Tyson glanced at his watch. "It's been five minutes."

Abe fought his attention away from Elise. "They said fifteen to twenty."

"I'll go meet up with Jameson and head out once I check in." Tyson grabbed the keys to the second Rover. "Need anything else while I'm out?"

His eyes slid back to where Elise sat. "I think we're good for now."

Hopefully that was true.

Elise was struggling even before Jason Hixon walked into her life. Fighting a demon he wasn't really sure how to wrangle.

At least what happened this morning was an issue he was familiar with. One he knew how to handle.

Tyson disappeared down the steps, locking the garage door on his way out.

Abe glanced around the quiet space.

There was no one to fight. No one to kill. No plan that would help him navigate the situation he was faced with.

He grabbed two glasses and the pitcher of water from the fridge, taking both into the living room area. "You need to drink."

Elise hadn't eaten in almost twenty-four hours, and chances were good she hadn't had anything to drink in just as long.

She took the glass he offered and immediately swallowed down a long drink. "Thank you."

"You're allowed to get anything you want here." He eased down beside her. "You don't have to wait for me to offer it."

She finished another long swallow. "Okay."

Abe stretched one arm across the back of the couch, studying the line of her profile. "Can we talk?"

"What do you want to talk about?" Elise traced her fingers down the side of the glass, marking lines in the condensation there.

"We have a few important things to talk about, but I think maybe we should start with your expectations."

That brought her attention his way. "My expectations?"

"That's right." He stretched out, kicking his feet up onto the table. "Your expectations."

She eyed him suspiciously. "My expectations about what?"

"About sex."

Elise's skin barely flushed. "I don't have any expectations about sex. Trust me."

"I think you do."

She laughed, short and sharp. "And what would those expectations be?"

"You expect a man to want to stick his dick in you and call it a day."

"I've got enough friends to know that's a bet that wins more than it loses." Her expression soured. "Usually."

"Depends on the kind of men you're after." Abe smiled a little. "And the kind of woman you are."

She sat a little straighter. "Are you saying I'm the problem?"

"Only if you think it's a problem that you scare the pussies and assholes of the world."

"Are you trying to argue that men won't fuck me because they're scared of me?"

"Confident women can be demanding in bed, Babe." He let one thumb stroke across her shoulder. "Definitely not the type that would be fine with a man dry rubbing her left labia for ten minutes, thinking it would get her off."

The flush on her skin deepened. "I was just trying—"

"You were just trying to get someone to rip the Band Aid off. I get it." Technically it made sense. Plenty of men shy away from an inexperienced woman because they can't handle the pressure. "I'm saying that's not an option readily available to you."

"Because I scare men." She definitely wasn't buying what he was selling, but that was because she still wasn't getting what he was trying to say.

"You scare the kind of twats who would have stuck it in you and walked away." He'd seen how hot Elise burned. No doubt that even if she did manage to get one of those pricks near a bed, he'd tuck his tail and run before his dick was even fully hard. "That means you're stuck with men who prefer their encounters a little more mutual."

She tugged at the sleeve of her shirt. "It shouldn't be so freaking hard to get laid."

She wasn't wrong. Even with Elise being intimidating, there still should have been a handful of guys willing to try their turn at bat. Especially when she was younger. "You might have gotten away with it in high school, but now you're dealing with people who know their place in the world."

Elise huffed out a little breath. "In high school I still thought purity was a girl's best friend."

"Your family big into the church?" That made more sense than anything he'd heard all day.

Chastity was a gift owed to a man. The most important thing a woman could bring into a marriage.

"Not so much *my* family." She shifted, tucking her second leg onto the cushion in a move that slanted her body closer to his. "My boyfriend's family." She chewed her lip. "We were together all through high school and college."

"All the times you could have had that Band-Aid situation handled."

"Right." Her eyes lifted to the ceiling. "He was the one who wanted to wait for marriage."

"How'd that work out for him?"

Elise glanced his direction before looking back down at her lap. "I'm sure his boyfriend appreciated it."

"Ouch."

"I'm happy that he finally felt like he could live his life the way he wanted." Elise fiddled with the hem of her pants. "He's a good person. I can't be mad at him for who he is."

"It would still be difficult to go through."

Elise shrugged it off, the way she did so many other things. "It was fine."

"All I can say is that if he made it years without touching you then he's definitely doing the right thing." Abe stroked down her arm then back up again.

"If not wanting to screw me is the determiner of sexuality then I think there's a lot of confused men out there."

"I didn't say men didn't want to fuck you." Abe slid his fingers through her hair. "I said they were scared to fuck you. Two totally different things."

Elise was quiet for a second. Her head tipped his way, but her eyes didn't follow. "Is that why you wouldn't fuck me? Because I scare you?"

"You don't scare me, Babe." He twisted her hair around his hand, using the grip to pull her eyes to his. "And I have no interest in fucking you and walking away." He leaned closer. "What you and I could have is too much for it to be a one-time thing." He brushed his lips across hers. "And I sure as hell don't have any interest in rushing it."

CHAPTER 8

OF COURSE HE didn't.

"Well excuse me for not wanting to wait until I'm eighty to finally get dicked." Elise tried to move away, but his hand in her hair held tight.

"Is that all you're interested in? Getting dicked?" He almost sounded amused.

"I'm glad you find this funny."

"Funny isn't the right word, Babe." Abe's hand gripped her hip, holding tight as he yanked her closer. "The word is appealing."

"You think it's appealing that I'm a virgin?" That would be a first.

"I don't give a shit about your virginity, Elise." His eyes met hers. "No offense."

"None taken, I guess."

"I find it appealing that you think the actual fucking is the most relevant part." He tugged her again, but this time his body pushed into hers, shoving her down to the cushions under him. "Which couldn't be further from the truth."

"That's because you've done the actual fucking." It was easy to think something was unimportant when it was readily available.

Like socks. They seem like a not-so-vital part of life.

Until you don't have them.

Then you had sticky, sweaty, blister-covered feet, and suddenly socks were the most important thing in the world.

Fucking was her socks.

"Based on that answer I'm going to assume fucking isn't the only thing you've never done." Abe's weight was surprisingly nice as it pressed her into the softness of the cushions.

"I've done things." She wasn't completely innocent.

She'd even managed to see a handful of dicks.

But not a single one of them ever made it inside her. At some point the man attached to them always decided she was not how he wanted to spend his evening.

"Like what?" His mouth was against her ear.

"Things." She wasn't going to lay out every sexual experience she'd ever had for him. Not unless he was willing to do the same. "What have you done?"

Abe leaned up, his lips twisted in a smartass little grin. "Remember when I said you scared the kind of men who would fuck you no questions asked?" His smirk widened. "That right there was the moment they'd grab their wilting dick and run away."

"Maybe I don't want questions asked."

"That's fine, Babe." His hand teased across her belly. "But that means we're taking baby steps."

She'd been trying to get laid for almost two years. Beggars shouldn't be choosers, but the thought of this dragging out forever made her want to scream.

Or maybe it was the rest of the day doing that. "Second base."

Abe stilled just a little. "Seriously?"

"If you're going to be a jerk about it then you can take me back to headquarters." She shoved at his chest, trying to move him enough that she could escape.

Run from the embarrassment.

The humiliation.

"I'm not taking you back." He shifted over her, making it even more difficult to fight his weight. "And you're going to have to simmer the fuck down about this." His body slid against hers, one of his thighs pressing between her legs. "No one's making this a big deal but you."

"That's because it *is* a big deal." It was a bigger deal than most people realized.

Ending up an old virgin made people think there was something wrong with you.

And maybe there was.

Maybe Abe was right. Maybe she was whatever the opposite of Medusa was when it came to erections.

One look at her and they all turned to mush.

"It's only a big deal if you let it be a big deal." Abe's hand skimmed across the skin of her stomach, sliding under the loose fabric of her shirt. "And

104

maybe it's a good thing. Maybe you should be glad you've been spared from all the selfish fuckers of the world."

"Are you arguing that you're not a selfish fucker?" She managed to get the question out, but it was difficult with the warmth from his palm teasing its way up her body.

"If I was a selfish fucker you wouldn't be a virgin right now." Abe's hand curved along the barely-noticeable swell of her breast. "I'd have taken you to my bed that night," his fingers inched in, "probably twice."

"You should have."

"Not a chance." Abe shoved one knee into the back of the couch, forcing her leg up toward his waist as his thumb raked across her nipple. "Fucking you would never be enough for me, Elise." He rolled it between his fingers, pinching it a little as he went. "I want more than that."

"More?" The word barely escaped as the twist and pull of his fingers shot straight to her core.

"More." His voice was rough in her ear. "I want everything from you."

His fingers plucked at her nipple one last time before setting it free, making her gasp at the loss of contact.

"I'm not going to fuck you until I'm good and ready to fuck you, Elise." Abe's lips were on her neck, mouth, tongue, and teeth sliding over her skin as the tips of his fingers worked into the waistband of her pants. "Not until I've made you come every other way I can think of."

Holy shit.

Maybe propositioning Abe was more terrible of an idea than she realized.

Maybe she should be the one to run right now. Metaphorical limp dick in hand.

Because this was sounding like way more than she bargained for.

"Has anyone made you come before, Elise?" His hand dipped lower into her pants, going straight under her panties.

"I thought second base made that pretty clear." She sucked in a breath as his hand cupped against her, the pressure of his palm coiling the ache there tight.

Abe nosed along her neck, taking the opening of her shirt with him as he moved lower. "Have you made yourself come before?"

Heat crept along her skin, but the urge to run was fading fast. "Have you?"

"Last night." There wasn't a hint of shame in his voice. "And again this morning."

Her thighs clenched a little at the thought of Abe doing that. Tall and strong, working his dick with the same hand tucked against her now.

"You like thinking of me like that?" Abe's hand moved just a little, his middle finger pressing against her just enough to slide between her labia. "Do you want to know what I thought of while I fucked my hand, Elise?"

"Yes." There was no point denying it.

"Your pussy on my face." His finger pushed deeper, sliding against the most sensitive part of her. "My tongue on your clit."

A strange sound escaped all on its own. Something between a whimper and a groan.

But it barely registered to her ears. All she could hear were the terribly dirty things Abe continued to whisper in her ear, his fingers stroking her clit in a perfect rhythm that made her hips try to work with it.

"That's my girl." His voice was a growl now. The sound of it almost feral. "Take what's yours."

Elise grabbed his wrist, holding it in place as her whole body started to shake. She rubbed against him, chasing the need he created, fueled by years of unspent desire.

Abe yanked down her shirt, the neckline dipping under one breast. His mouth was immediately on her, sucking the nipple he'd teased earlier. The deep pull went straight to where he touched her. It was too much to handle.

Too much to withstand.

She came hard and fast, holding onto him as her whole body rocked, convulsing from the overwhelming sensation. It was almost unbearable.

Almost unbelievable.

So unbelievable that she started to laugh, the sound jumping free before she could stop it. Both hands slapped over her mouth, trying to smother out the inappropriate sound.

Trying to stop one more embarrassing moment before it happened.

But just like all the rest, Abe was there to witness it.

And he didn't seem to realize she wasn't supposed to be laughing right now.

He worked one of her hands free, lifting the inside of her wrist to his lips. "Feel better?"

Elise rolled her lips together, trying to flatten them down as Abe waited for her answer.

His head suddenly jerked to one side, saving her from admitting that maybe she did.

"What's wrong?" She'd almost forgotten why she was here in the first place.

"Tyson's back with our dinner." Abe shifted, pulling her up with him as he moved upright. "You wait here." He grabbed a blanket off the back of the couch, flipping it open and wrapping it around her. "I'll go help him bring it up."

"What about—" Elise clamped her mouth shut, but couldn't stop her eyes from going to the hand that was just—

Was just—

Abe backed away, keeping his eyes on hers as he slid the fingers that made her forget at least half the contents of her brain between his lips.

Holy.

Shit.

What was she doing?

Messing around with a man twenty years older than her was supposed to be a means to an end.

She thought Abe would break the seal she was sporting and send her off into the world deflowered and finally on a level playing field.

But it was looking like the man might send her out ruined in the most true sense of the word.

As soon as he was out of sight she caught her head in her hands. "Hell."

This was one of many things she would love to be able to talk to her friends about.

Too bad she'd never told a single one of them the full truth about her previous engagement.

"Soup's on." Tyson's voice was loud and happy as he hit the top of the stairs. "Hope you're hungry."

Elise's stomach rumbled like it could answer the question for her.

Tyson carried a large shopping bag of food to the table, setting it down before reaching inside to pull out four large containers. He brought one to her as Abe came up the stairs carrying two twenty-four-packs of soda. Jameson brought up the rear, phone in hand, reading the screen as he went.

"How you doing?" Tyson passed over the food. "Hanging in there?"

She smiled. Tyson was one of her favorite guys at Alaskan Security. He was warm and kind and made amazing sweet tea. "I'm good."

"That's better than fine." Abe came in to pour more water into her glass. He held out a fork. "Glad something perked you up."

She held his gaze, flipping open her container. "It's probably just dinner."

One of Abe's brows slowly lifted.

She smiled. "I really like food." Her eyes dropped to what was in front of her.

Yeah. She for sure liked food.

The container was filled with chicken and noodles dumped over a pile of what appeared to be homemade mashed potatoes.

"Damn, Abe." Tyson sat down at the table, cracking open one of the sodas as he dug into his matching dinner. "You've really broadened your palate."

"I have." He didn't look away from Elise. "I try to taste something new every chance I get." His eyes dipped down her body, making his point clear enough she almost dropped her food.

"This is way better than that protein powder bullshit you tried to feed me for breakfast." Tyson was digging into his dinner, oblivious to the gauntlet she might have accidentally thrown down.

Accidentally.

Jameson came to sit on the couch across from her. He set his phone on the table between them. "Shawn has a few questions for you."

"How are you doing, Elise?" Shawn's voice was smooth and even as it came through the phone. As the team lead for Rogue, Shawn was in charge of coordinating the men and making sure everyone stayed safe.

As safe as any of them ever were.

"I'm good." She forced her eyes to stay on the phone even though she could feel the weight of Abe's stare. "How are you?"

"That's a complicated question." He paused. "The woman I love just threatened to murder half the men I work with if anything else happens to you, so that's concerning."

Elise smiled around the fork in her mouth.

"And the owner's wife offered to take down the other half, which is another issue I need to address." Shawn huffed out a breath. "So I'm calling to beg you to be safe. I haven't seen Eva or Lennie yet, but I'm assuming they will feel similarly to Heidi and

Mona. Please, for the love of God, keep your ass in that house."

"I will."

"I'm serious, Elise. If you leave that house I will haul you back here myself and let Heidi lock you in the basement."

"You guys keep acting like I didn't offer to stay down there with her." Heidi's voice was barely audible in the background.

"How in the hell did you get in here?"

"What do you mean how did I get in here?" Heidi was clearly annoyed. "And if you think I won't just walk out of here and tap your phone and listen that way then you've ignored at least half of my toxic traits."

Elise smiled a little wider. Heidi was one of the main reasons she'd finally learned to embrace her authentic self.

Tired to anyway. It was still difficult when the whole world wanted to make you think you were too much.

That you should be smaller.

Quieter.

Less demanding.

Softer.

Sweeter.

Shawn sighed. "Fine but sit your ass down and put your feet up."

Heidi was pregnant with twins and Shawn was ready to lose his mind over it. Every day he looked a little rougher around the edges.

It was interesting to watch a man who killed people for a living try to deal with the opposite scenario.

"Anyway," Shawn paused, probably to take a deep breath, "right now we're working under the assumption that what happened this morning might be connected to what happened in Cincinnati while you were there."

"Might be?" Heidi snorted. "It for sure was, don't let him try to sugar coat it."

"I'm trying not to scare her." Shawn was back to talking to Heidi.

"Have you met her? I think she'll be just fine." Heidi's voice came closer as something dragged across the floor.

"For the love of God." Shawn was moving around now. "Go sit in my chair."

"Perfect." Heidi was definitely smiling, the expression was right there in her tone. "Hey, Babes." Her voice came in loud and clear, like she was leaning right into the phone's speaker. "So there's this thing where you can scan the internet for certain words or phrases."

"Abe told me someone's probably doing that on Alaskan Security."

"Technically that's probably true." Heidi paused. "But that wasn't the case in this particular situation. I found the path and tracked it back to the initial search."

"Okay." Elise's eyes lifted to where Abe watched her.

Like he knew what Heidi was going to say next.

It made sense, considering Elise also knew what Heidi was going to say next.

And it formed a pit deep in her stomach.

"These people weren't searching for Alaskan Security. They were searching for you."

CHAPTER 9

THE URGE TO pick up Jameson's phone and throw it against the wall was almost impossible to ignore, forcing his hands into fists as he rocked his head from side to side, trying to work out the unspent rage.

He'd done it a million times in his life.

Breathed through his initial reaction to anything upsetting.

It was something he'd learned to control. To use to his advantage.

Because the feeling never went away. He just figured out a way to pack it up. Store it until there was a convenient time to let it out.

Like this morning.

But this time it wasn't so easy. This time the need to punish something was too strong to deny.

"I'm going to check the perimeter." Abe didn't wait for anyone to respond or even acknowledge his exit. He didn't dare breathe until he was out in the cool air of the night. It wasn't quite dipping into freezing temperatures when the sun went down, but it would be any day now.

And it couldn't come soon enough if this was how things were going to be.

Because he needed to cool off, literally and figuratively.

Abe glanced up and down the strip of blacktop running in front of the townhomes. The space was well-lit, thanks to the lampposts embedded in the concrete sidewalks poured throughout the large property. He decided to go toward the entrance first, following the walkway toward the main gate. The same fencing that surrounded headquarters lined the edges of this property, offering a level of protection that should put him more at ease.

But it wasn't the safety measures he was questioning.

The primary variable in this scenario was a tall blonde woman with no sense of self-preservation.

And he couldn't help but think it wasn't because Elise thought she was invincible.

The gate was secure as he passed, no sign that anyone might have attempted to tamper with it, thinking it would be a good idea to try to step foot on the property.

It wouldn't be. Especially not now.

Now he was itching to take down anyone who thought for a second they could touch Elise, let alone try to take her.

Abe rocked his head to one side, trying to force out the tension clawing at his shoulders and neck as he followed the fence line across the turned dirt.

The place would eventually have five buildings identical to the one he lived in. A family compound of sorts, complete with a playground, a gym, and a large community space featuring a kitchen and a theater room.

It would be the closest thing to a home he'd ever had, which was why he was the first one in line to purchase a unit.

So that even if he grew old single, he wouldn't do it alone.

Because up until recently, he was almost positive he would end up by himself.

Which was fine.

He liked his own company. Learned over the years how to spend time with himself. That a solitary life wasn't an unfulfilling life.

Which is probably what made it more difficult to find someone to fit into it.

He paused to look toward the backside of the single building set at the front-most part of the acreage. The large window in his living room sent a glow out into the darkness, but the height kept him from being able to see anything but the vaulted ceiling.

It still needed a blind. Something to make sure no one got any bad ideas.

He sucked in a deep breath, hoping the chilly air would cool the heat still brewing in his chest over the discovery that Elise was the intended target this morning.

Made him wish he could go back in time and shoot that bastard a few more times.

A quiet sound stopped him in his tracks and sent his hand to the pistol strapped to his hip.

Abe held his breath, waiting.

Another rustle sent him spinning toward the scrubby pile of cleared brush, stacked and waiting to be hauled away. He pulled his weapon, pointing it in the direction of the barely-perceptible movement.

"If you come out now I might not shoot you." *Right away.*

There was no answer, just another crinkle of the drying vegetation hiding whoever was about to be on the receiving end of the wrath he was itching to dish out.

"I'm not fucking with you today. You can either come out now, or I'll drag your dead body out myself." His finger barely squeezed, ready to make good on the threat.

But the next sound he heard was not what he was expecting.

The soft squeak tilted his head, moving his line of sight to the left of his drawn weapon. Abe squinted at the brush and the bit of it that seemed to be moving.

Another quiet squeak dropped his pistol to his side. He slid it back into the holster before crouching down, trying to get a better look at what might be hiding in the twisted branches and browning leaves.

A small orange ball of fur shot out, bouncing a few feet in his direction before stopping, the little body twisting to one side, tail up, back arched.

The kitten let out a hiss.

"Fair enough." Abe did a quick scan of the area around them. "I did almost shoot you."

The tiny kitten stared at him a second longer before bouncing to one side working its way behind his back. It crept closer, nose leading the way as it sniffed the air in his direction.

Abe slowly moved one hand in the kitten's direction, watching while it inched in, pink nose coming right to his skin and taking a few breaths.

Then it bit him.

Abe grinned, catching the little furball with one hand and holding it out as it tried to fight its way free. "I think I know someone who'll love you." He scanned the lot as he walked back toward the townhomes. "You'll be two damn peas in a pod."

Jameson was stationed at the front of the building when he rounded the corner. His dark brows lifted when he saw what Abe carried. "I don't think that thing's a threat."

"You haven't seen his claws." Abe used his free hand to unhook one pawful of daggers from the skin of his knuckle.

He went in through the garage door, closing it behind him before taking the stairs to the main floor. Elise was curled up on the couch, the blanket he'd given her earlier wrapped tight around her body as she stared at the television. Tyson sat at the dining room table, watching the feeds from the security cameras. He lifted a black brow at Abe but didn't say a word.

Elise looked his way, her eyes immediately going to what was in his hand. She immediately sat up. "What is that?"

118

"Vicious." He winced as the kitten tried to chew a chunk out of his thumb. "I found him in the brush pile in the back."

Elise got up, the blanket falling from her shoulders as she came his way. "It's so little." She reached for the tiny animal.

Abe pulled him away. "He's a biter."

"He's just scared." Elise managed to get her hands on the orange tabby, her expression immediately going soft. "*Aren't you*?"

Abe let her wrestle the bundle of fur and ferociousness from him. "I'll go get some Band-Aids. You're going to need them."

"No, we won't." Elise cuddled the kitten close to her chest. "*He just scared you, didn't he*?"

Apparently the cat wasn't completely feral, because when Elise tucked him under her chin he didn't go for her jugular.

"Are you thirsty?" Elise bounced a little as she walked toward the kitchen, going straight to the fridge. "You want some milk?" She stood in front of the open appliance. "Where's your milk?"

Abe went to point at the carton in the door.

Elise's eyes rolled his way. "Almond milk?"

"Lactose intolerant." He closed the door. "But I'm pretty sure I have something he'll like even better." He opened one of the cabinets and pulled out a pouch from the line he always kept on hand.

Elise stayed at his side while he grabbed a small bowl and ripped the pouch open, using a fork to scoop out some of the contents. Her mini-me purred the whole time.

Like he hadn't just tried to gnaw off an appendage.

"Here." He set the bowl of tuna on the floor.

Elise bent down to put the kitten next to the bowl, then she sat down right beside him. "He's so little."

"Don't tell him that." Abe grabbed another bowl and filled it with water. "He'll tear you apart." He lined the bowl next to the tuna.

Elise caught his hand before he could pull it away. "Oh my gosh, what happened?"

"Tough guy there tried to eat me."

Elise stood up, keeping his hand in hers the whole time. "Well what can you expect?" She switched on the faucet. "He probably took one look at you and crapped his little kitty britches." She waved her fingers under the stream of water, adjusting the handle a few times before shoving his injured hand under the warm water. "You can't walk around with every weapon known to man strapped to your body and expect it not to intimidate everything in your path." She pumped some soap into her hand and started to work it across the fine lines dug into his skin.

"I don't intimidate you."

Elise's movements barely hitched. "That's not true." She turned his hand over to inspect his palm. "It's just not as acceptable for me to go around scratching and biting people."

"Does that mean you don't plan to scratch or bite me?" He leaned into her ear. "That's disappointing."

"I think we might have an issue." Tyson leaned closer to one of the monitors, his brown eyes narrowing on the screen.

Abe pulled his hand from between Elise's palms, grabbing a kitchen towel as he went to stand behind Tyson, watching over his shoulder as Tyson backed up the feed. He pointed to a car rolling past the property. "That same sedan has come past four times in the past two hours."

Fucking fantastic.

"Does that mean I should go back to headquarters?" Elise stood just behind him, her new pet cradled in her hands.

Taking her back was a risk in and of itself. Being on the road could be just as dangerous at this point. "Call Shawn."

Abe pulled out his phone and punched Jameson's name. He picked up on the second ring. "How's your little friend?"

"He's fine." Abe reached out to scratch the kitten's head. "But we might have a potential interested party."

"That's exciting." Jameson's steps were barely audible as he started to move. "Where?"

"Outside the property. Drive by. Four passes."

"That was fast."

It was. Too fast.

"They must have already connected this property to Alaskan Security."

Heidi had done her best to ensure there wasn't much to follow between the two entities used in the purchase and sale of the units, but she could only do so much.

121

"We always expected we'd have to monitor this property like headquarters. Now we know it's time." Jameson was cool and calm, laying out everything Abe already knew.

But still didn't want to hear.

He wanted to think he could put Elise someplace safe. Somewhere no one would find her.

"Did you talk to Shawn?"

"Not yet." Abe glanced at where Tyson was filling the team lead in on the discovery. "Tyson's telling him now."

"Looks like we're about to have a party then." Jameson was quiet for a minute. "I don't see any issues right now. I'll hold my position until backup arrives."

"Thanks." Abe disconnected and went to where Elise sat on the couch, looking a little pale and a whole lot exhausted. "You should go to bed."

It took her eyes a second to find him. "Is it safe?"

This morning rattled her, even if she refused to admit it. "No one is going to get to you. I promise." He reached one hand her way. "Shawn will send more men over. No one will get on the property."

"But if they're here then there's less to make sure headquarters is safe." She pulled the kitten closer, nuzzling the sleeping feline's long orange fur.

"We always expected we would have to keep this place secure. That's why Rogue and Stealth are both still stationed here in Fairbanks. We have more than enough men to secure both locations." Abe bent, intending to scoop her up as an odd ping rapped against the large window beside them.

122

He dropped onto Elise, wrapping her in his arms and taking her straight to the floor as another ping splintered the glass he thought was high enough not to be a problem.

The lights went out, making the red glow moving across the wall easy to spot.

"Keep her down." Tyson's voice was quiet as he moved past them toward the window.

"No—"

Abe clamped his hand over Elise's mouth. "You've got to be quiet, Babe. Let him work. Tyson knows what he's doing."

Elise whimpered as Tyson shot off three rounds through the already ruined glass.

"Move." Tyson's direction was short and sharp.

Abe immediately hauled Elise up from the floor, keeping her low as he dragged her toward the stairs leading to the third floor. He yanked open the door to the closet at the top of the stairs. It was just big enough to fit a small family. He pushed her in and punched the button to turn on the screen inside. "Stay here. Keep the door locked."

"What?" She grabbed him. "Where are you going?"

He slowly smiled. "To have a little fun." Abe pulled her in, taking her lips in a quick kiss before pushing Elise and the kitten back into the safe room and closing the door. He looked up at the camera mounted just outside. "Lock the door, Elise."

There was a long pause before the deadbolt inside flipped into place.

He winked. "I'll be back."

Then he raced down the steps, drawing his gun as he went. The main floor was still mostly dark, the only light coming from the glow of the monitors still open on the table. There was no sight of Tyson, which meant he must have gone outside to serve as backup for Jameson. Abe stood on the main level, positioned between the two staircases where he could have eyes on any possible access to the townhouse. As much as he wanted to go find whoever tried to take a shot at Elise, he had to trust Tyson and Jameson to handle that.

The silence seemed to go on forever, each second dragging out until he was itching to move.

Itching to go see what was happening.

When his phone vibrated in his pocket, he let out a breath. He dug it out and connected Shawn's call.

"Rico, Brock, and Wade are headed your way. They should be entering any minute."

Abe holstered his pistol. "Did Tyson hit his mark?"

"Negative." Shawn sounded as disappointed as Abe was.

Probably because he now had to go tell Heidi that someone tried to shoot her best friend.

"We need to go full-gear on this." He glanced down the stairs as Brock and Wade came in through the garage door.

"Agreed. I'll send someone over with everything shortly." Shawn paused. "There's been some discussion about the main contact point on this."

"Heidi can't be the contact point." Heidi was very skilled at a number of things, but being a mission contact point was not one of them. "I'm fine if she wants to sit in, though." Abe tipped his head at Wade and Brock as they moved past him. "I can imagine this is difficult for her."

"Elise is her best friend."

"I know that."

"It's not that she doesn't trust you."

"I know that too." Abe took the stairs to the upper floor two at a time. "I'm not taking it personally." He trusted the men around him.

But if he couldn't be here he would be going out of his mind.

Abe stared at the camera just above the safe room. "Open the door, Babe."

"You put her in the safe room?" Shawn sounded more interested than surprised.

"Yup."

"How'd it work?"

Each of the units on the property was equipped with one. It was an unfortunate requirement for the life they lived.

"Depends on if she decides to come out of it." Abe lifted his brows at the camera as he waited.

"We might need an override." Shawn was probably thinking the same thing he was thinking.

Heidi was similar to Elise. Strong-willed. Opinionated. The main difference was that Heidi embraced what she was, while Elise still seemed to struggle with accepting what made her special.

"We're definitely going to need an override. I'll let you know when we're ready to go online." Abe disconnected the phone and slid it into his pocket, keeping his eyes on the camera. "Babe." He thumped his fist against the plane of metal between them. "Open the door."

A second later the lock flipped and he pushed the heavy door into the room. Elise tapped the screen of the monitor, closing out what she was doing.

"That was fast." Abe turned off the light in the small room and shut down the tablet-sized computer that connected to the same system Alaskan Security used, making it possible to reach anyone in the company with a touch of the screen. "Who did you call?"

"Heidi." Elise stroked across her kitten's back. "But everyone was there with her."

"How are they doing?"

"Okay I guess." Elise chewed her lip. "I think they're mad at me."

He pulled her close. "They're not mad at you for leaving, Elise." He rested his lips on the top of her head. "They're upset that they weren't there for you when you needed them."

"That wasn't their fault."

"You're right." Abe was careful not to crush the tiny kitten between them as he held her. "Which means you can expect them to be up your ass from here on out."

She snorted a little laugh into his chest, breathing deep a few times before rolling her head his way. "Did you get to kill anyone?"

CHAPTER 10

CALLING HEIDI WAS a bad idea.

Normally she wouldn't have done it. Normally she would have avoided dealing with the situation she created for as long as possible.

Hopefully forever.

But Abe was out there. In the dark.

And people were shooting.

"I couldn't see what was happening." It was a terrible thing being trapped in there with no clue about how awful things outside the room were.

"I'll show you how to pull up the surveillance feeds tomorrow." Abe held her close as he led her toward the stairs. "But right now you need to get some rest."

"Rest? Someone just shot through the window at me." She was trying not to panic, but it turned out she had a low threshold for being almost killed.

Once a day was all she could handle.

"And it won't happen again." Abe paused when they reached the main floor, his eyes going to the hardwood under his boots. He scooped her up before her bare feet left the last step, carrying her across the room. "We need to clean up the glass."

"On it." Wade went to the small closet off the kitchen and pulled out a broom. "Brock's out digging through the unfinished units looking for something to cover the window."

Elise stared at the holes cracked through the glass as Abe walked toward the bedroom. "Those windows are expensive."

"I've got insurance." Abe angled her through the door, flipping on the light as he went inside.

"Does it cover attempted murder?" There probably weren't too many policies that covered that.

Abe gently set her down on the bed before straightening.

Elise stared up at him, her already upset stomach dropping to her feet. "Oh God."

"What's wrong?" He turned to look behind him.

She swallowed down the amazing dinner he'd ordered as it tried to vacate her premises. "Your head." One hand went over her mouth as the other pointed to the tiny trail of blood drying down his temple. A line that almost looked like a scratch cut across the side of his head.

But it wasn't a scratch.

It was a graze mark.

"The bullet almost hit you." The panic she'd been fighting found footing and dug in. "You almost—" She rocked in place, trying to fight the overwhelming emotion clawing at her insides. She needed to stop it.

Smother it out.

128

It was too much to handle.

Too much to feel.

"Elise." Abe grabbed her, his hands firm where they held her wrists. "I need you to breathe, Babe."

"I can't." She'd been here countless times before. She fought against his hold. "Let me go."

She needed to drown the ache. Cover it with something else. Something that was stronger.

Something that was safer.

Pain.

"I'm not letting you go." Abe's face was close to hers. "It's not happening."

Elise yanked as hard as she could, using her whole body as she tried to get loose.

Pain would make it all better.

Pain she could handle. Pain had a reason. A source.

A solution.

She managed to fight herself free and scrambled up the bed, trying to put as much distance between them as possible.

But Abe moved with her, fast enough that she didn't stand a chance.

His arms came around her from the back, pinning hers across her chest as he hooked one leg around both of hers. "Breathe, Elise."

"No." She didn't want to breathe. She wanted to fix the ache inside. Cut it loose.

Carve it out.

"Leave me alone."

"That will never happen." Abe was calm as he tightened his grip on her.

"Let me go." Frustration mixed with the ache, making it all so much worse. "I hate you."

They were the magic words that cut people off with one swift slice. They'd worked before, and they would work now.

"You don't hate me." Abe didn't even flinch. "If you hated me you wouldn't be upset right now." He continued to hold her tight. "You'd be happy I was almost out of your life."

Elise squeezed her eyes shut. "Stop it."

"No." It was the first sharp word he'd spoken. "You've got to stop shutting it all out, Elise." His arms held her even tighter. "You've got to let yourself feel life. Even when it hurts."

"You don't understand." He didn't know just how painful life could be.

Just how devastating.

"I do, Babe." His voice was soft again, a low, soothing rasp in her ear. "More than I think you realize."

The hole in her belly deepened, aching more with each passing second, threatening to swallow her up. Take her down into depths she'd never escape from. "I don't care."

She couldn't hear what happened to him. What made Abe think he understood her pain.

Because maybe he did.

And that would be unbearable.

Something rough scraped against her nose. A tiny swipe of sandpaper that drew her out of the darkness trying to engulf her.

It happened again, the odd sensation a beacon she could follow through the walls closing in.

A soft touch pressed her cheek, rubbing her skin, opening her eyes.

The orange tabby scrubbed his head against her face, purring louder than his little self should be able to accomplish.

Elise stroked at him with her fingers, sliding them down his velvety fur. Her eyes focused on the beds of her nails.

Fresh blood stained the free-edge and smudged the surface.

"It's okay." Abe's hand covered hers, hiding the evidence of yet another failure. "We'll take care of it in just a minute."

She stared at his hand on hers, so solid and steady. "Why are you doing this?"

"Lots of reasons." He rested his forehead against the back of her skull, breathing deep. "But mostly because of you."

It was one more thing she couldn't bear to hear him explain, but this time it wasn't because of the ache it might cause.

This time it was because she was smart enough to know it was pointless.

"You can let me go now." Elise tried to wiggle free. "I don't need you to hold me anymore."

"Maybe it's not for you." His mouth pressed against her scalp. "Maybe it's for me." Abe's thumb stroked against her skin. "I can't handle watching you hurt yourself, Elise."

"No one's making you watch." She'd gone years without anyone knowing what she did in the quiet of her room.

Long enough she thought her secret would be safe. Long enough she thought it could be behind her. Locked away with all the pain it spared.

"Can I ask you a question?"

"No."

"Is that why you stayed with the man you were engaged to for so long? Because you knew he would never see them?"

Elise stared at the wall. "No."

"Are you sure?" He smoothed down her hair. "Is that why you looked for men who would be willing to fuck you, no questions asked? Because you didn't want anyone asking if you were okay?"

"I'm fine."

"You're not." Abe tucked his face close to hers. "But I will tell you something that might make that a little easier to deal with." He pulled the hand he held to his lips, brushing them across her blood-tinted skin. "No one is."

"You're fine."

He chuckled. A sound that rumbled from his body to hers. "I kill people for a living, Babe. If that's not the definition of 'not fine' I don't know what is." His body shifted on the mattress as he moved up and over her. "Come on." Abe rolled her with him, up and off the bed. "Let's get you cleaned up so you can go to sleep."

He stood her in front of the bathroom sink, cleaning her hand the way she'd cleaned his not so long ago. Once all the blood was washed away he turned her to face him and dropped to his knees. "I don't think these pants are fixable, Babe." One finger went to the hole she'd managed to dig into

132

the thin fabric without really realizing it. "And I think we should bandage this." He stood and went out into the bedroom, coming back a few seconds later with a pair of shorts. "Put these on." Abe passed them over before turning his back.

Normally she would argue, but right now she was so tired. Tired in a way that sleep might not fix.

So she pushed down the ruined pants and pulled on the shorts. They didn't have a drawstring, and the waistband was too big to grab onto her. "They won't stay up."

Abe turned, going back down to his knees. "You don't have to wear them long." He pushed up the leg, holding it out of the way as he inspected the spot she'd managed to reopen. He leaned to reach for the cabinet and the fabric fell down to her knee. He pulled out a first aid kit and moved the fabric again, trying to hold it with one hand while he took care of her self-inflicted injury with the other.

"Here." Elise dropped the shorts, letting them slide down to the floor.

It's not like the man didn't already know enough about her to be a problem. Why did it matter if he saw her panties too?

Technically his hand had been in them.

The reminder made her skin a little warm as she looked down at him, his hand moving so carefully across her skin.

Abe treated her like she was fragile, which had never happened before. Most people thought she was unbreakable.

Maybe because that's what she wanted them to think.

It was what she wanted to be true.

Abe's touch was gentle as he cleaned up the smudges of dried blood, slathered on a healing ointment, and taped on a bandage.

"Thank you."

"You don't have to thank me for taking care of you, Elise." His hand splayed across her thigh, the pad of his thumb sliding over the rows of silvery scars no one else had ever seen before.

"Are you sure? Because I think that's what most people do."

"We're not most people, Babe." His free hand lifted, skimming up her other leg to the matching collection of lines there. "How many are there?"

"I don't know."

His eyes lifted to hers. "I think you do."

"Two hundred and twenty-one." She ignored the sense of pride trying to move in.

Trying to make her think what she did was good. Healthy.

That those two hundred and twenty-one lines were proof that she conquered all the things they represented.

All the pain they smothered out.

"Is that counting this one?" He leaned in to brush his lips across the only line she'd made since coming to Alaska.

The only line she wasn't counting.

Because it failed her.

Or she failed it.

Either way, it was proof she wasn't what she tried so hard to be.

Strong.

134

Resilient.

"No."

Abe's lips made another pass across the neat rows before moving to the other side, the stubble of his cheek scraping her skin as his mouth passed back and forth.

Like he intended to trace each and every one.

As if he thought it would make a difference.

Change the past.

Erase the pain.

But that was the lesson she learned early and hard.

Pain never went away. That's why you had to bury it.

And it worked, as long as you dug deep enough.

He slowly stood, his gaze serious as it moved over her face. His hands came to her neck, curving around it before sliding higher to cup her face. His lips had barely touched hers when a savage scratching noise dragged his attention to their feet.

The kitten was attacking the black leather of his boots, going at them with claws and teeth. "Your cat might hate me."

"He doesn't hate you." She reached down to scoop up the kitten. "He just thinks you're a pain in the ass."

"I saved him from spending the night in a pile of wood."

"He doesn't know that." She carried the tiny cat into the bedroom. "He thinks you took him from his comfortable little hideaway and dropped him in the middle of people trying to kill each other."

Abe frowned at the kitten as she set it on the bed. "Fair enough."

Elise went to the closet where Abe found her clothes earlier, her feet skidding to a stop on the plush carpet. She looked around the space.

"I like things organized." He stood behind her.

"No shit." She went to where her clothes were lined down wooden hangers. "Why are all my clothes here?"

"I wanted you to be comfortable." He leaned against the door jamb as she pulled a pair of joggers free. "I thought maybe it would help to feel like you had space that was your own."

"I'm not sure much will help given the circumstances." Elise stepped into the pants, her eyes going to the dark red line etched across the side of his head.

"Don't look at it." He reached up and grabbed a black knit hat from the shelf, tugging it down over the silvery hair on his head.

"I still know it's there."

His eyes dropped to where her pants hid the bandage he'd just put on her. "I guess that makes us even then."

Only he would think a scratch and a bullet graze were equal. "You were shot."

"Definitely not shot." Abe backed out of the closet. "This doesn't even count as an injury."

"Is all this written in the handbook?" Their completely arbitrary designations were ridiculous.

"There's no handbook for what we do, Babe." Abe went to the bed and pulled back the blankets.

"You need a chart or something." Elise dropped to the mattress, her toes sliding over the smooth sheets. "We could hang it in the breakroom."

"Maybe that's what you can work on tomorrow." He pulled the covers over her before leaning down to press a kiss to her forehead.

"I'm sure I can squeeze it in between the kidnapping and murder attempts." Her job at Alaskan Security seemed low-risk. She was the freaking office manager for God's sake.

Who kidnapped the office manager?

Her knowledge of what went on around the place was focused on what food needed to be stocked and how many pens they went through a month.

Abe looked down at her, his hands pressing into the mattress just beside her shoulders. "What's wrong, Babe?"

"This is stupid." She pulled the covers higher. "All of it."

"I don't disagree." He smoothed his fingers down the side of her face. "But the more stupid they are, the faster we'll take them down."

The kitten purred his way up to the crook of her neck, spinning in place a few times before curling right against her. "If he's going to stay inside we will need a litter box."

"On it." Abe lifted a brow. "Anything else?"

"Maybe some food." She yawned as the weight of the day lowered her lids. "And some toys."

"It'll all be here when you wake up."

Her eyes jumped open. "Where will you be?"

Abe's lips eased into a slow smile. "Close."

137

CHAPTER 11

"IS SHE ASLEEP?" Wade glanced over the top of the screen in front of him.

"Seems like." Abe went to where Brock and Rico were screwing a sheet of plywood over the lower half of the broken window. "How's it going?"

"This will work for now." Brock leaned into the drill as the tell-tale squeak of screw into stud proved he hit his mark. "But the whole window will need to be replaced before it gets too much colder."

Rico stood back to survey their handy work. "We'll bring the second piece in once Dutch has us up and running." He tipped his head to where an earpiece and a vest sat on the table. "Check-in's happening in ten minutes."

"Good." The sooner they were online the better. He tucked his earpiece into place before strapping on his vest, making any necessary adjustments to the rest of his gear.

"Tyson found the spot they shot from." Wade's attention was fixed on the screens. "They must have had one hell of a long-range weapon."

"Great." Dealing with someone dumb enough to try to take Elise from right in front of Alaskan Security in broad daylight was problematic enough. Add in that they might be well-armed and things got a whole lot trickier.

"You know what that means." Wade glanced his way.

"Yup."

"Means they weren't trying to hit Elise."

"Yeah. I got that." He looked toward the bedroom door. "Can we keep it down a little?"

"You don't want her to know they weren't trying to kill her?" Wade's brows came together. "Isn't that a good thing?"

Definitely not. "I don't want to give her more to think about right now." Abe snagged the magnetic pad of paper from where it hung on the front of his fridge. "I need someone to go get a few things." He listed the items Elise requested before adding a couple of his own and tearing the sheet off.

"I'll go." Rico took the list and gave it a quick scan. His eyes lifted to Abe. "This is an interesting list, *Amigo*."

"I lead an interesting life."

Rico grinned at him. "It's about time." He grabbed a set of keys from the counter. "I'll be on when Dutch is ready."

Abe pulled off the cap he'd shoved onto his head and went to the kitchen sink, bending over the basin to tuck his head under the faucet, scrubbing one hand across the stinging line he hadn't known was there until Elise saw it.

And melted down.

He wiped the water off with a kitchen towel, pressing it against his head to stop any new bleeding.

"Damn." Brock rested one hand on his hip. "Doesn't get much closer than that."

"Yeah." Abe sat down next to Wade. "Might want to put a blind up in yours before you move in."

"Pierce is already planning to put up another fence. One that's taller and solid." Brock went to the fridge and pulled out a can of the soda Tyson brought earlier.

"The neighbors are going to think we're the militia." Abe pulled the towel away, checking to see if the bleeding had stopped.

"I mean," Brock came to inspect his head, "how wrong would they be?" He moved a little of Abe's hair. "I think you're good."

"Thanks." He glanced toward the bedroom right as Dutch's voice came through the line in his ear.

"Good evening, ladies and gentlemen. I'll be your captain tonight and for the foreseeable future."

Wade lifted a brow in question.

"Heidi's here." Abe didn't need to hear her voice to know Elise's best friend was on the line.

"Of course Heidi's here." The in-house hacker sounded as thrilled as he was with the evening's events. "How's Elise?"

"She's sleeping." He adjusted the vest strapped to his chest. "With the cat."

"Is that some sort of euphemism I don't know?" Heidi paused. "Ew. Don't Google that."

"If anyone ever looks at your search history they're going to have a lot of questions." Jameson's voice came through loud and clear.

"Good thing I know how to erase shit like that." Heidi's words weren't as fast as normal. She had to be exhausted. "Now shut up so Dutch can do roll call."

"Yes, ma'am." Dutch started with Abe, working his way down the list of men currently assigned to the townhomes, pausing for confirmation after each one.

"It looks like everyone is on-site except for Rico, is that correct?" Dutch was the eyes and ears connecting them all, watching their backs, and feeding them information during ops.

Which this now was.

"Correct." Rico answered. "I'm out buying kitty litter and two-percent milk."

"Kitty litter?" Dutch was obviously confused.

"Abe found a kitten out back." Tyson's voice held a smile. "You shoulda seen him jump when the thing came at him."

"It's feral. What do you want from me?" Abe stood up from the table, the need to inspect the property himself taking him down the stairs. "I'm heading out to do a perimeter check."

"Tyson and Jameson are at the southeast corner, checking the fence for any signs of tampering."

"You think someone tampered with the fence?" He stepped out of the garage and scanned the line of pointy metal pickets surrounding the property. It was strong enough that the only way to get through was with a welder and at least ten minutes of uninterrupted time. "How would we have missed that?"

"Just because we weren't looking at them doesn't mean they weren't looking at us." Heidi yawned. "They've had three months to watch and plan."

"So you think this started when we got back?" Abe followed the fence, moving in the opposite direction of Tyson and Jameson, looking for any sign someone tried to find a way into the property.

"I think this started before you even left Ohio." Heidi paused. "I think this started the second they found out you had that laptop."

"I don't have that laptop. I sent it straight to Vincent." He'd taken the computer being used to download video feeds from the women's bathroom at Investigative Resources and sent it straight to the head of GHOST, thinking Vincent and his team would be better suited to do an analysis on anything it contained.

"But they don't know that. All they know is you took that computer and gave the cops a different one."

"That explains why they tried to shoot you." Tyson grunted a little. "Everything back here is still holding strong."

"Shooting me won't get their computer back." Abe grabbed each metal bar, yanking to make sure it was solid before moving to the next one.

"Not necessarily true." Heidi yawned again. "Anyone not completely familiar with Alaskan Security might not have realized how shooting you would have played out. They might have believed it would afford them an opportunity to investigate your house."

"So why didn't they do it when I was here by myself for the past two weeks?" Abe hit a bar that shifted just a little when he put pressure on it. "Shit."

"What's the issue?" Dutch was immediately on alert.

"I found a loose spot." Abe gripped the squared-off bar and twisted, trying to find the weak point. "This one has a little give to it."

"He's about halfway back the west side." Dutch seamlessly directed Tyson and Jameson to where Abe was shining his light on the post, looking for what might be causing the issue.

Tyson pulled out his own flashlight, switched it on, and shoved one arm through the gap between the bars. He angled it down the length. "There's the issue."

A line of melted metal was cut halfway through the post.

Tyson took a series of photos of the defect before sending them to Dutch.

Abe wiped one hand down his face. "Hell."

"Tomorrow we need to check the entire fence line for any other signs of damage." The sound of typing carried through as Dutch continued. "I'll set up for the fence company to come back out and repair anything we find."

"Do we trust this fence company?" Abe looked toward the townhomes. "And what about the construction crew?"

"They were thoroughly vetted."

143

"By who?" Abe continued moving down the line of the fence, looking for any additional spots.

"By me and the woman sleeping in your bed." Heidi came at him with the same snark her best friend usually led with.

"We're going to need you to follow up on that, Rucker. Find out anything you can on them. We can't be too careful right now." Dutch put the request much more eloquently than Abe would have.

"I'll do it right now." There was a muffled sound on the line, then Shawn's voice came through. "She won't do it right now. Right now, she's going to bed."

"No problem. Until Heidi's had the chance to clear the fencing and construction companies, their access to the properties will be restricted." Dutch continued on. "We will also be sending over a few members of Shadow to help with monitoring."

"That's fine." Abe found another loose post. "We've got another compromised spot in the fence."

"We can't do anything about it tonight." Dutch pointed out a truth he wasn't thrilled to accept. "Tonight we just need to hold the perimeter and keep the property contained."

It wasn't an easy pill to swallow. "Maybe I should bring Elise back."

"You really want to get her out on the road at night?" Brock brought his two cents to the conversation. "I'm telling you, it's not as simple as it sounds. Right now, our best bet is to leave her where she's at. We've got to be here anyway. Might as well let her sleep."

"You should probably try to get some sleep too." Tyson tipped his head toward the fence. "Jameson and I will finish checking this."

He didn't want to sleep. He wanted to hunt down the men involved and cut them off from this life.

It would be clean.

Efficient.

And it would solve most of the problems he was facing right now and give him time to handle the rest.

"Just go." Jameson jerked his head at the townhomes. "She'll feel better if she knows you're in there with her."

Where will you be?

He hadn't let himself linger on her question at the time. There was too much to do and wondering why she asked would make him want to stay with her.

"I'll be available." He turned and stalked back toward the building, going past where Brock stood just outside the garage and in to where Wade sat at the table, still watching the monitors. "Anything?"

Wade shook his head. "It seems quiet. My gut says they're done for the night." He dug one hand into a bag of chips.

Abe eyed the chips that definitely didn't come from his cabinet.

"Don't look at me like that." Wade shoved a handful into his mouth. "We came here fully-equipped."

Heavy steps on the stairs sent him turning around as Rico came up to the main floor hauling an armload of bags and a large plastic litter box. "I don't remember putting that much on my list."

"Your list didn't take the shit in your kitchen into consideration." Rico dropped the bags onto the counter as he set the litter box on the floor. "If you think you're going to talk her into staying here, then you're going to have to buy some real food." He dug into one of the bags and pulled out a box of nut-topped ice cream cones. "She's going to take one look at the almond butter and chia seeds and run the other way."

"Almond butter is good." Abe snatched the box of ice cream and tore the end flap open. "And chia seeds are great for digestion and inflammation."

Rico dug into the open box, pulling out one of the cones and tearing into it. "Yeah, but they don't taste like ice cream."

Abe fished out a treat of his own before shoving the rest into the freezer. He peeled open the wrapper and took a bite of the nutty, creamy top.

Rico watched him with a smile. "I'm happy to see you enjoying life a little."

"I enjoyed it before." He'd lived life on his own terms. Done any and everything he'd wanted to.

"Let me rephrase." Rico bit off some of his ice cream, tucking it to one side as he continued to talk. "I'm happy to see you relax."

Wade snorted. "It's probably age."

"Kiss my ass." Abe tossed his wadded-up wrapper at Wade's head. "I can fucking run circles around you."

Wade smacked the wrapper mid-air. "It's all those chia seeds."

"There's only one person you need to run circles around, my friend." Rico looked toward the bedroom door. "And I think that one will be a challenge."

Abe took another bite of his first ice cream in years. "She's a handful."

Rico grinned. "Those are the best kind." He licked around the edge of the cone. "Nothing better than a woman who's not afraid to put you in your place."

"She definitely has no problem doing that." Abe crunched into the sugar cone. "These are better than I remember them being."

"Everything's better when you haven't had it in decades." Rico shot him a wink. "Remember I said that."

"Decades?" Abe held both arms out. "You act like I'm a goddamned monk. Just because you haven't seen it doesn't mean it hasn't happened."

Wade cringed. "No one wants to see it."

"You're still not as bad as this one was." Rico pointed Wade's way with what remained of his cone. "Bess ruined him in one night."

"It was a good night." Wade grinned as he popped in a few more chips. "Definitely worth the suffering."

Abe lingered a little longer, taking his time finishing his snack. Usually he felt out of place when his teammates started talking about the women in their lives. Their relationships.

Their plans for the future.

Not because it bothered him. His life was just so different from theirs. Much more…

Solitary.

In a good way.

He'd been happy being alone. Fulfilled and satisfied with the life he led.

But maybe he could be just as satisfied and fulfilled unalone.

Abe dusted his hands off. "I'm going to go shower and try to get a little sleep." He glanced at the clock. "I'll be back out in time to take the next shift."

Rico went to one of the sofas and stretched out across it. "See you in a few hours."

Abe grabbed the litter box and the bag of litter tucked inside of it, along with a bowl, and headed across the room. He eased the door to the bedroom open, trying his best to be as silent as possible.

Elise's kitten hissed at him from its spot on the bed.

He leaned to scoop it up as he passed, managing to avoid most of the claws and teeth directed his way as they went into the bathroom. Once the door was closed he flipped on the light and set the kitten on the floor. "I'm just trying to help you."

The top of the box snapped off, making it easy to pour in the granular litter. Abe clipped the top back into place before sticking the furball inside. "There you go." He pushed the box into one corner and turned to do his own business, glancing over his shoulder at the orange tabby. The cat walked around the box for a second before stopping in one corner. His tail went stick straight as his back end dropped down.

"Good job." Abe finished up, stripping down as the kitten jumped out of the box and started sniffing around the room.

He switched on the shower, climbing in before it was fully hot. Five minutes later he was scrubbed clean and drying off as the cat licked at the water sliding down his leg. "Sorry, buddy." The bowl he brought in sat on the counter, but he'd forgotten to fill it with water. Abe tossed his towel over one shoulder as he rectified the situation, setting the filled bowl onto the floor. "There you go."

The kitten immediately started to lap at the water, continuing to drink as Abe opened the door and went into the bedroom.

Elise jumped to a quick stop, both her eyes widening as they moved down his front. The light from the bathroom was still on, offering more than enough of a glow to illuminate his naked form.

"Everything okay, Babe?" He pulled the towel from his shoulder and used it on the water dripping from his hair.

"Um—" Elise focused right on his dick. "I was just—"

Abe tossed his towel toward the hamper in the corner. "Just what?"

He was still unclear on just how much actual experience she had. How familiar she was with her own body, let alone a man's.

"Just—" She licked her lips then rubbed them together. "I was just—"

He might have to help her along. "Just looking for your cat?"

"Mm-hmm." She still hadn't looked away from the line of his cock, which was fine.

But at a certain point, he was going to react to her blatant perusal. "He's in the bathroom." Abe stepped around her, going to the row of drawers that held his socks and underwear. "Rico brought him a litter box."

"That was nice of him." Elise turned, her eyes following him as he moved.

"It was." Abe pulled out a pair of boxer briefs, turning to offer Elise one last look as he pulled them on.

She took full advantage, not even blinking until the elastic waistband was completely in place.

"You should go back to bed." Abe grabbed the kitten from where it was circling Elise's feet.

Elise eyed him as she climbed back under the covers. "Are you going to bed too?"

"I am." He set the kitten on top of the blankets before sliding under them himself. He stretched out on the free side of the bed, tucking one hand behind his head and reaching out with the other to stroke Elise's hair. "Go to sleep."

She let out a long breath. "Okay."

CHAPTER 12

ELISE STARED DOWN at the kitten as he bounced out of the litter box for the hundredth time. "We're not leaving until you pee."

Abe would shit a brick sideways if the cat pissed in his house. The place was brand new. Clean and shiny.

Outside of the broken window and the resulting glass all over his hardwood.

Yesterday was...

A freaking nightmare.

Mostly.

Elise grabbed the cat and stuffed him back into the litter box. This time he finally started sniffing around, digging a little before squatting down.

"Thank God." She went to the sink and snagged her toothbrush, running a little water on it before adding on a swipe of paste and scrubbing away the morning breath. Luckily she'd woken up alone, which meant the only one who'd had to deal with it was the cat.

Elise tucked her chin, head jerking toward the litter box as one hand came to cover her nose. "Holy hell." She flipped on the fan, trying to suck out the stink coming from the plastic box.

The kitten jumped out and gave her a squeaky meow.

Elise kept her nose covered as she continued to brush her teeth. "How do you smell so bad?"

"Tuna."

Abe's voice sent her spinning toward the open door.

He stepped into the room, one hand coming to cradle her skull as he pressed a kiss to her forehead. "Good morning."

"Is it?" Elise mumbled around her toothbrush before spitting in the sink.

"Better than yesterday morning." Abe grabbed the tabby from the floor. "Have you named him yet?"

"I haven't really thought about it." She did a quick mouthwash rinse before shutting off the light. "I've been busy trying not to get killed."

"I appreciate that." Abe stepped in her path as she tried to walk out. "We have a full house."

"I figured." She attempted to get around him, but he continued to block her. Elise lifted a brow at him.

"Someone tried to cut through the fence."

Of course they did. Why wouldn't they? "Last night?"

"No." Abe's head barely tipped to one side. Like he was listening for something.

She stepped closer to him, ready to shove him out of the way of any projectiles that might come shooting through the room.

Abe immediately wrapped one arm around her, pulling her into his relaxed body as he reached for his ear.

"Copy. I'll get her set up."

Elise leaned, craning her neck to look up at his ear.

Abe turned his head, making it easy for her to see the earpiece tucked into place. He pressed at it. "Dutch and Heidi have a few questions they would like for you to answer."

That didn't sound good. "Okay."

"It will be on a video chat." Abe's lips lifted. "I think Heidi wants proof of life."

"I talked to her yesterday." Elise grabbed the kitten. "What does she think's going to happen to me?"

"Considering you're living in my house?" Abe pulled the door open. "She's probably worried you're going to starve to death."

"Isn't protein powder a complete meal?" She walked out into the main living area and was greeted by something that smelled nothing like protein powder.

"That probably depends on who you ask." Abe focused on where Brock stood at the cooktop stirring something.

"Morning." Brock shot her a wink. "Hungry?"

"Definitely." Elise peeked into the pot, confirming the savory scent of sausage was what hung in the air.

"You like biscuits and gravy?"

She was more of a sweet breakfast eater, but biscuits and gravy definitely ranked above a protein shake, so she wasn't going to complain. "That sounds perfect."

Abe caught her elbow, taking her toward the table where Jameson sat in front of a computer, clicking through the screens.

Jameson pushed the laptop back from the edge before standing up. "We're almost ready."

Abe dragged a second chair in beside the one Jameson vacated. He adjusted them so they were evenly spaced in front of the screen. "Go ahead and sit down." He lowered beside her as the screen flashed to life.

Heidi smiled out at her. "How's it going?"

"I'm still alive, so I feel like that's a win."

"Been there." Heidi's screen shifted to one side as the other half of the monitor populated with Dutch's face.

"We talked about this, Rucker. You can't start without me." Dutch looked tired. Like he might have been up all night.

Probably had.

"No one started anything." Heidi appeared slightly more well-rested than Dutch did, likely due to the fact that she had Shawn to drag her to bed. "Unwad your panties."

Dutch swallowed back a healthy amount of coffee before leaning back in his seat. "We need to talk about what happened in Cincinnati."

"Shouldn't you talk to Lennie too? She was there with me."

154

"I'm not talking about what happened this summer." Dutch picked up a file and flipped it open across his desk. "I want to talk about your time working for Investigative Resources."

"Oh." Elise glanced at Abe. "Okay."

"Specifically, I want to know who dealt with the maintenance on the offices." Dutch was more intimidating than he'd been before.

She'd been in sort of a different orbit than anyone else at Alaskan Security. Her job functioned in a much different way than everyone else's, keeping her far from most of the scarier aspects of the business.

"Well," Elise smoothed down the kitten's back, "it was a leased property, so most of the issues were handled by the company the owners of the building had under contract."

"Do you remember the name of that company?"

She did, actually. "JD's Property Management. The owner's name is Josh Devereaux."

Dutch picked up a pen and started writing. "How many times would you say they were in the offices while you worked there?"

"Gosh. Not many." She thought back. "We had an issue with a faulty outlet. One of the sinks started to leak." Elise shifted in her chair. "He came once because there was a squirrel stuck in the women's bathroom, but we ended up having to call an animal control company because he didn't have the equipment to catch it."

"He. Who's he?"

"Josh." Elise tried to sit still. "He was the one who always came out when I called."

"Okay." Dutch finished writing and glanced up at the screen. "The sink and outlet issues, what was the location of those?"

"The women's bathroom."

"So everything that happened was all within the women's bathroom?"

"Yes." Oh.

Oh.

"Gross." Heidi took a long drink from the water she always had with her.

"I can't believe those pervs liked to watch women pee." Even if they didn't use the site primarily for that function, there were still so many options to create content.

Options that didn't involve toilets.

"I've heard of stranger kinks." Dutch turned to type on a computer angled off to one side. "I used to know a guy who liked to get kicked in the nuts."

"I know a few guys I'd like to try that out on." Heidi's eyes moved on the screen as her fingers worked across the keys. "I just sent you the link to JD's." Her blonde brows suddenly lifted and her mouth turned down into an appraising line. "I don't remember him being that hot."

Abe's eyes slowly came Elise's way, making it even more difficult not to squirm in her seat. "He was all-right looking I guess."

"All-right looking?" Heidi snorted. "This guy has dimples on his dimples." She shook her head. "Hopefully we don't have to kill him."

"Why would we have to kill him?" Elise asked the question too fast, showing her hand.

"I mean, initially because he might be connected with the people trying to kidnap you." Heidi grinned out at them as her eyes came back into focus. "But I'm thinking there's more reasons on the list now."

"One more question." Dutch was still working at his computer. "Do you remember the name of the company you called to handle the squirrel?"

"No." Elise quickly corrected. "But only because I'm not the one who called them."

Dutch's gaze leveled in her direction. "Who did?"

"Chandler. He said he knew someone."

"I bet he fucking did." Heidi's face twisted to a scowl. "I really wish I coulda been the one to kill him."

"You're probably not the only one." Dutch was back to working on his laptop. "I'm sure our new friends are feeling the same way right now."

"You think since they couldn't get Chandler they're trying to come after us?" Elise started to scratch at her leg, scraping her nail across the spot Abe bandaged last night. Before she could make three full passes, Abe's hand slid into hers, his wide fingers making it impossible for her to continue digging.

"I don't think they're trying to get revenge, if that's what you're asking." Dutch turned to fully face their screen. "I think they're trying to save their own skin at this point. They know someone has the computer Abe sent to Vincent, and they're trying to figure out how to get their hands on it."

"If Vincent has the computer then shouldn't he be able to tell who was involved?" It seemed pretty cut and dried. "Isn't that why he got it in the first place?"

Dutch wiped across his jaw. "I know it seems simple, but it never is."

"If the people involved in this are connected to something else going on then Vincent won't tell us shit." Heidi huffed out a breath. "And all these dicks seem to be in the middle of five different things."

"Like Chandler." Chandler always made her wary. The guy gave off bad vibes for a reason she couldn't quite explain.

Not until she found out he was trying to screw over the women she worked for and exploit the ones she worked with.

"Chandler was small-time. He wanted to be big-time, but he didn't have the connections yet." Heidi paused for a second. "The guys we're dealing with now are bigger."

"Bigger means more dangerous."

Heidi tipped her head in a nod. "Yup."

"And so far they've tried to kidnap me and shoot me." Elise slapped on a smile. "I'm excited to see what comes next."

"We're not fucking finding out." Abe's voice almost surprised her. He reached for the computer. "Are we finished?"

"For now." Dutch tossed his pen onto the desk. "Thanks, Elise. I'll let you know if I have any more questions." His window disappeared.

"Is he feeding you?" Heidi glared out at Abe. "I know he and Shawn like to eat the same shit."

"Brock's making biscuits and gravy." Elise glanced up at where Brock stood at the stove, stacking biscuits onto paper plates.

"Well thank God for that." Heidi's expression softened a little. "No offense, Abe."

"I get it. Everyone thinks I'm going to starve her."

"Not starve, specifically."

Elise smiled, hoping to reassure her friend. "I'm fine. There's plenty to eat here."

Abe's thumb dragged across the skin of her hand. "Plenty."

Elise tried not to react but heat still crept across her skin at the not-so-subtle suggestion.

"Gross." Heidi lifted her hand in a little wave. "I'll let you get to your biscuits and gravy." She wiggled her brows. "And whatever he's eating."

Heidi's face disappeared, and the logo for Alaskan Security repopulated the screen.

"Still hungry?" Brock put a plate of biscuits and gravy down in front of her.

"Sort of." Elise fought on a smile for him as she set the kitten down on the floor. "Thank you."

"No problem." Brock passed her a fork. "Hopefully Dutch didn't ruin it for you."

"Dutch didn't ruin anything." Elise stabbed at the biscuit with the tines of the fork.

She'd worked so hard to be an asset at Investigative Resources. Now to find out she might have let in someone who put so many of her coworkers in such a terrible position was painful.

And it made her question everything she'd done at Alaskan Security.

She'd helped narrow down the companies who bid on the fences that weren't as solid as they were supposed to be. She was the one who chose the large window, not for a single second thinking of what would happen if someone was outside lurking.

Who knows what other mistakes she might have made.

"Come on." Abe snagged her plate, carrying it as he led her back to the bedroom, using one finger to flip on the lights as they went inside. He bumped the door closed. "I tried to put them off." He pulled her to the bed with the hand still wrapped tight around hers. "But Dutch wanted to do it as soon as possible."

"I'm glad we didn't wait." Elise dropped to sit at the edge of the mattress. "If I let someone into Investigative Resources then they need to know that."

"That's what you got out of that conversation?" Abe set the plate on the nightstand before crouching in front of her. "You aren't responsible for every bad thing that happens, Elise."

"I was in charge of the offices. I should have been the one to pick the people who came in." She should have put her foot down. "I knew Chandler was an asshole. I should have—"

"You should have known he was bringing people in to plant cameras in the women's bathroom? How in the hell should you have known that, Elise?"

Somehow. "I should have at least questioned it."

"Eva and Mona were there too, and they sure as hell had more power than you did. If you're guilty then they're guiltier."

Elise scoffed.

Abe tipped his head. "See how it sounds?"

He wasn't understanding what she was trying to say. "It was my job—"

"Bullshit."

"I was supposed to—"

"More bullshit."

She glared at him, pressing her lips together. Fine. If he was going to be a pain in the ass about it then she would just keep her fucking mouth shut.

"That's better." Abe looked at the untouched biscuit. "Are you going to eat your breakfast?"

"I'm not hungry." She clamped her mouth shut, going back to glaring at him.

"You're sexy as hell when you look at me like that, Babe." Abe's hands slid up her thighs. "There's something about you being pissed at me that makes me want to prove you don't hate me as much as you think you do."

"I don't hate you."

"That's unfortunate." Abe's hands moved up her hips and past her waist. "Not even a little?"

"It's early."

He smiled, the expression moving over his face slowly. "So there's hope then."

"Weirdo." She leaned toward him. "Is that your kink? A woman who hates you?"

"Definitely not." He wrapped one arm around her waist, holding tight as he hauled her to the center of the mattress. "My kink is you, Babe."

161

Elise snorted out a laugh. It was ridiculous to even pretend that was true. "You're even more boring than I realized."

"Then it should make perfect sense." He nosed along her neck. "Because you are as far from boring as it gets."

"So you're hoping for guilt by association?"

"Something like that." The weight of his body was solid as it pressed down onto her. His hips worked between her thighs, adding a level of friction and pressure that warmed her insides immediately.

Abe's lips passed across hers. "I like a challenge, Elise. I crave it."

"That explains how you manage to drink protein shakes when you could be eating biscuits and gravy."

He smiled against her mouth. "I'm done with protein shakes. I have a new favorite thing to eat for breakfast." His fingers hooked into the waistband of her pants, dragging them down her hips, his body moving with them, stealing that wonderful weight and pressure.

"What are you doing?" She barely made it up to her elbows. His mouth was on her before she could manage to complain about the loss.

Which turned out to be not as much of a loss as she thought it was.

As good as what he did with his fingers felt, this was a whole different level. The stroke of his tongue was smoother. Softer.

Wetter.

And then he sucked.

Not a lot.

Just enough to send her hands flying to his head, fingers digging into his hair as he lapped at her clit, setting a perfect pace that made anything she'd ever been able to accomplish on her own seem like freaking amateur hour.

His hands gripped her thighs, opening them wide as his lips and tongue worked her flesh, making her forget about everything except what he was doing to her.

Where he was taking her.

What he was giving her.

An offering of one-sided pleasure.

Again.

And she was greedy enough to take it. No questions asked.

His fingers moved against her, sliding up her slick skin to open her wide, baring the most sensitive part of her for his unrelenting and perfect torture.

"Abe." Elise gripped the blankets with one hand and his hair with the other, holding on to anything as the world spun around her. All the sadness. All the pain. All the fear fell away, leaving nothing but sensation.

And something else.

Something she couldn't quite put her finger on as it teased through the cloud of pleasure fogging her brain.

Abe's finger moved lower, circling slowly before easing into her body. It fucked her slowly, shallowly. Tempting her with what was to come.

"Yes." Elise dug her heels into the bed as he pushed deeper. "More."

He shifted a little and the pressure increased, filling her a little more. Enough to make her clench around him.

Abe groaned against her pussy and the deep rumble almost seemed to vibrate. The added sensation took her down, dragging her faster than she thought possible, her body rocking with the waves as they took over, crashing against her.

Inside her.

Stealing her breath and her strength.

Abe's lips skimmed up her body, moving across her skin as he shoved her shirt up, to suck at a puckered nipple. The pull of his mouth shot straight to her still-throbbing pussy, making it clench tight, the sensation pulling in a sharp gasp.

Abe's fingers replaced his mouth, working the nipple as he leaned into her ear. "I definitely have a new favorite breakfast."

CHAPTER 13

"SHE UPSET?" BROCK watched as Abe slid Elise's breakfast into the microwave.

"Just overwhelmed." It wasn't a lie. Technically Elise was overwhelmed. Just not currently by the issues that brought Brock and the rest of the men to his home.

"She's not as used to this kind of shit as the other girls. Even before they came here they were used to people being crazy assholes." Brock finished loading up the dishwasher and leaned down to stare at the buttons. "How do you start this thing?"

"No clue." Abe grabbed the plate from the microwave as soon as it beeped. "I've never used it."

"We're going to have to have a talk." Brock punched a couple buttons and the appliance made a noise that sounded like rushing water. "Because you can't have a woman like Elise and not know how to cook."

"Sure I can." Abe opened the fridge and pulled out a bottle of hot sauce. "That's what restaurants are for."

"You'll spend a fortune."

Abe grinned. "It's one of the perks to being an old man." He backed toward the bedroom. "I can afford it."

While his friends were pairing off and getting married and having families, he was out living his life.

And it turned out living your life was a hell of a lot cheaper without marriage and kids.

By the time he connected with Pierce he was set for life, thanks to a career made up of doing the kinds of things most people shied away from.

"What are the other benefits?"

Abe rested one hand on the doorknob. "Stamina."

Elise was still laying on the bed, one arm draped across her eyes, clothes still a little askew from where he'd pulled them into place before going to reheat her breakfast.

Hopefully she'd be hungry now. She'd only eaten once yesterday, and even then hadn't finished the meal.

She peeked out at him. "What's that?"

"I warmed your breakfast up."

"Oh." She sounded a little disappointed.

"Were you hoping for something else?"

"No." Elise shifted around, using her hands to maneuver her body into a sitting position. "Not specifically."

"Not a big fan of biscuits and gravy?"

She reached for the plate. "It's not that."

"What is it then?"

Elise took a little bite. "I just usually like it better for dinner."

"You eat biscuits and gravy for dinner?"

She frowned at him. "There's no rules about what time you can eat breakfast foods."

"Most people would probably disagree with you."

"That's pretty normal." Elise took another little bite. "Most people always disagree with me."

"I don't think that's necessarily true." Abe stretched out on the bed beside her. "I think you're just willing to argue with the kind of people who think they're always right."

She turned toward him, lifting one brow. "Like you?"

He smiled. "Like me." He watched her take a couple more small bites. "So what do you normally eat for breakfast?"

Elise pursed her lips, peeking his way as she dug at the biscuit. "Not savory stuff."

That made sense. "So you're the reason for all the Danishes in the break room."

"I'm not the only one who eats them." She set the plate on her lap. "Most of your friends are also fans of the new addition."

"Most of my friends will eat literally anything you put in front of them." He watched them do it, knowing their days were numbered. "Wait till they hit forty. Then see what happens."

Elise smirked a little. "Is that what happened to you? It was all fun and games until forty?"

"It's still fun and games." He didn't want Elise to think too much about his age and the vast gap between them. "Now the fun just includes more egg whites."

She laughed and the sound caught him a little off-guard.

He'd never heard it before.

And now he had one more high to chase. One more challenge to fuel his days.

"So what I'm hearing you say is that I need to get some Danish." Abe pulled out his phone and opened up the shopping list he used to make sure he always had everything he needed. "What else does a woman like you eat when she's not dining at the finest establishments Fairbanks has to offer?"

"I can't tell you." Elise took one final bite of her breakfast before setting it aside. "You'll judge me."

"Have I ever judged you, Elise?"

She studied him for a second, her eyes moving over his face as she thought the question through. "No."

She sounded surprised by the answer.

"Unless you want to get stuck eating what the rest of those savages out there bring in, you should probably tell me what you want." He typed Danish onto the list that already included almond milk, egg whites, and turkey sausage.

"Well," Elise leaned over his shoulder to look at the screen of his phone, "maybe some turkey snack sticks."

He typed her addition. "Are those like Slim Jim's?"

She chewed her lip. "Sort of."

"Got it." He moved to the next line. "What else?"

"Cheese."

"What kind?"

"All kinds." She gave him a nose-wrinkling smile. "I'll eat whatever you get."

"All kinds of cheese." He read as he typed. "You want crackers too?"

Elise nodded. "And tortillas."

"What do you put in the tortillas?"

"Cheese."

"Just cheese?"

"It's easy." Elise scrunched her face up. "I don't really cook."

"Good. Me either." Abe added tortillas and crackers to the list. "Once this is all over we can go shopping and you can show me exactly what you like."

Elise was quiet for a minute, making him think she was mulling over the implication of his suggestion. Right now she was here because she had to be, but once that requirement was passed, he didn't intend for anything to change.

And once she realized that Elise was probably going to freak out a little.

Or a lot.

"Do you think it will be a long time?"

"I hope not." He'd gone decades without coming across anyone who fit into his life. Having to deal with fears about her safety now that it had finally happened was inconvenient to say the least.

Elise huffed out a little breath. "Okay."

"I know it's stressful." Abe reached out to rest his hand on her leg, covering the lines he knew hid there.

"It's not just that." Elise stared at where he touched her. "I just can't sit here all day doing nothing."

"What do you want to do?"

Elise reached out to trace along his knuckles with the tip of one finger. "Someone needs to handle the grocery order for headquarters." She tucked her hair behind one ear. "And Pierce's office is probably out of scotch."

"You want to work?"

"I can't do everything from here, but I could at least keep things running." Elise shrugged. "It would give me something to keep my mind off everything."

"I'll figure something out." Heidi had Elise's laptop and phone so she could look for any signs that either had been hacked, so it would have to be a new computer that had more security measures in place.

But if anyone could come up with a way to make that happen, Heidi could.

"Do you want anything else?" Elise hadn't asked for much and as time went on that told him more and more.

She hadn't called anyone to tell them she wouldn't be arriving in Ohio, which meant what she'd claimed was true.

No one knew she was coming.

No friends.

No family.

Elise shook her head. "Not that I can think of."

She was as undemanding of a person as he'd ever met, which was less of a surprise to him than it would have been two days ago. Elise was opinionated and willing to speak her mind, but when it came down to it, she was sneakily easy-going.

"You need a hobby, Babe." Abe leaned in to press a kiss to her cheek. "Maybe two."

"I have a hobby. It's working."

"Work isn't a hobby." Abe rolled up to a stand and went to the door.

"I'm not really a hobby person." Elise slumped down a little. "Creativity is boring."

"Hobbies don't have to be creative. None of mine are."

Elise lifted a brow. "You have hobbies?"

"Of course." Abe tucked his phone back into his pocket. "What did you think I did in my free time?"

"I didn't really think you had free time."

"I have a little." She wasn't completely off-base. When he took the position at Alaskan Security, it was clear it would be more of a lifestyle than a job.

Which was fine with him.

Alaska was one of the few places he'd never been, and it offered a number of challenges he couldn't wait to tackle. The weather was harsh. The terrain was unforgiving.

Then there was the job itself.

Being on Team Rogue granted him very few boring moments, which was how he preferred to live.

171

Elise's eyes skimmed him, full of skepticism. "So what are these supposed hobbies?"

"Come on and I'll show you."

She hesitated for just a second, but soon Elise was swinging her feet off the side of the bed and following him out into the common area of the main floor. Brock was nowhere to be seen, but Jameson was at the table, watching the property through the camera feeds.

"Anything interesting?" Abe paused for a quick scan as he passed.

"Not outside the issues with the fence." He pointed to where Tyson and Rico were out tying red flags onto each of the compromised sections.

"Isn't that a bad idea?" Elise leaned in, watching the men work. "Now they won't even have to look for the spots they made if they want to try to get in."

"They're not going to try to get in that way." Abe rested one hand between her shoulder blades. "They couldn't get through the fence fast enough for it to be a possible entry point."

Her eyes pulled from the screen to come his way. "So the fence wasn't faulty?"

"Not at all." Abe pointed down the row at each of the locations they'd tried to gain entry. "Not a single one was cut completely through. The fence held up better than we hoped it would."

"Really?" Elise seemed relieved.

"Really." Abe stepped away from where Jameson continued to keep a close eye on the area around them. "Heidi is doing a second background search on the company that installed it, but right now it looks like they will be back out soon to make any necessary repairs." He used the hand on her back to angle Elise toward the stairs leading to the bottom floor.

"I thought maybe the fence wasn't put in correctly." Elise's steps were soft as they moved down the treads. "Or maybe the company might have been involved."

"As of right now I don't think that was the case." Abe flipped on the light in the large room that took up most of the finished space on the bottom floor. "Which is good, because it sounds like Pierce is hoping to add a second fence here and it will be convenient to be able to use the same company."

"He doesn't have much time." Elise leaned to peek inside the room. "The ground will be frozen soon."

"I don't see this being something Pierce is willing to wait on, especially considering how many of us will be here." He was the first of the team to move into his unit, but it wasn't supposed to be by much. "Brock and Eva were supposed to move in this weekend and Wade and Bess weren't far behind them."

"Do they still want to live here?" Elise stepped into the room, her bare toes pressing into the padded flooring as she walked.

"Of course they still want to live here." Abe followed her in. "This is how our lives always are, Elise. We just have to learn to live with it." He watched as she pushed at the heavy bag hanging from the ceiling. "And technically this is the second safest location in the state."

"Are you counting GHOST headquarters in that?"

Damn she was fast. "Fine. We'll call it the third safest location in the state."

"Isn't there a military base close by?" Elise put a little more weight into a second shove.

"They frown on the military shooting people just for coming onto base."

Her eyes came to him. "But they don't frown on you doing it?"

"There's a limited number of reasons a person would try to come onto Alaskan Security's property." Abe went to the corner of the room. "It affords us more of a shoot now, ask questions later policy."

"What about people who don't like to carry guns? What sort of policy do they get?" Elise jabbed an elbow into the red bag, smiling a little as it swung away from her.

"People who aren't comfortable carrying guns shouldn't carry them." Abe snagged a couple items from a shelf before going to where Elise was toying with his boxing bag. "It's too risky." He reached for her. "Give me your hand."

Elise immediately did.

"Carrying a gun is a huge responsibility. To you and to the people around you. It's not something you should do if you're not comfortable with it." He went to work layering a handwrap around her palm and knuckles. "It's too easy for someone to use it against you."

174

Elise flexed her wrapped hand, turning it from side to side as he went to work on the other one. "What are these for?"

"These are so you don't tear your hands up."

She eyed the bag. "You want me to punch it?"

"Punch it. Kick it. Shove it. Whatever makes you happy."

"You think hitting something will make me happy?" Elise punched one hand into the opposite palm.

"Why wouldn't it? I bet you've got some anger to take out." He stepped to the back of the bag, bracing it with both hands as he leaned into it. "Try it out."

"With you standing right there?" Elise peeked around the bag at him. "What if I miss and hit you?"

"Won't be the first hit I've taken."

Elise's lips tipped in a frown. "Is that supposed to make me feel better?"

"No." He wiggled the weighted bag. "But I bet punching this will."

She sighed and stepped closer, resting the knuckles of one hand against the bag, like she was trying to get her aim just right. Then she pulled back and gave it a little whack.

"I'm pretty sure you can do better than that."

"You're making me nervous." Elise backed up like she was ready to abandon ship already.

And he didn't want that to happen. Not when this might help her get out everything she pretended wasn't inside her.

"Maybe this is something you will enjoy doing by yourself." Abe went for the door. He pointed at the stereo in one corner. "There's music there if you want it." He backed out of the room, pulling the door closed as he went.

He went straight up the stairs to the kitchen to mix up one of the shakes everyone loved to give him shit about, sending it through the blender with a few cubes of ice and a banana that was almost at the end of its life. While he drank it he went to the bedroom and made the bed, before collecting the laundry and getting a load started. As he was resituating the kitten's bowls at the end of the kitchen island, Jameson started looking around.

"What's wrong?" Abe stood, listening for what Jameson was concerned about.

"What in the hell is that sound?" Jameson moved toward the boarded-up window, walking around the room as he searched for the source of the thumping noise.

"I showed Elise the punching bag." Abe tipped his head toward the stairs, smiling at the consistent hits as they kept a steady pace. "Sounds like she's getting the hang of it."

"Sounds like you're going to have to buy another punching bag." Jameson stood a little straighter as a louder smack came. "Was that a kick?"

Abe swallowed down the last of his shake before rinsing his cup. "That woman has a lot she needs to get out."

The louder smacks came faster and more often, each one drawing Jameson's attention to the stairs. "You got ice packs?"

"I'm almost fifty." Abe grabbed the water from the fridge. "What do you think?"

176

Jameson leaned to peek down the stairs as the hits continued to come faster and faster. He lifted his brows before turning Abe's way. "I think if you want to keep up with her, you should probably drink another one of those shakes."

CHAPTER 14

"I'M FINE."

Abe glared at her as he shifted the ice pack across her shin, holding it in place. "If you say that one more time I'm going to lose my shit."

"You didn't tell me I could hurt myself." Elise wiggled her swollen fingers. They hurt less than they did a few minutes ago, which meant the Advil was probably kicking in.

"You needed me to tell you that if you wailed on an object hard enough you could effectively beat the shit out of yourself?"

She smiled at him from her spot on the sofa. "I was pretty effective, huh?"

Her body was a little sore and achy, but that wasn't a big deal.

What was a big deal, was how fantastic she felt. "You should have seen how far I could make the bag swing."

Abe looked her over. "I can probably imagine."

He looked unhappy as hell.

Almost as unhappy as he looked the night before when she accidentally made herself bleed.

"I didn't mean to hurt myself." She didn't want him to think he'd offered up another means to an end she'd been trying to stop for years. "I really didn't realize it was happening." Elise took in another of the deep breaths she'd been able to pull in since coming up from the basement. "It just felt so good to hit that thing."

She'd thought about turning on the music, but once she started punching the bag there was nothing else that entered her brain.

Which was kind of strange.

She thought maybe she'd mentally put a few faces on the bag. Imagine dishing out some of the comeuppance the universe seemed to forget was waiting to be served.

But it didn't happen. Instead she just hit and kicked and shoved, each one feeding the next until she had to sit down.

Then lay down, staring up at the ceiling, too tired to be upset about anything.

Not the almost kidnapping.

Not the almost murder.

Not any of the things that came before them.

For the first time in as long as she could remember, everything was peaceful.

Quiet.

"I'm going to order you some shin guards and a set of gloves." Abe reached for one of her bruised hands, gently running his fingers across the knuckles. "Until then, try to keep it under control."

Elise nodded immediately. "I will. I promise." She didn't want to risk Abe not letting her back down there.

Especially now that she knew how good it felt to force out a little of what lived inside her.

He reached out to trace one hand down her face. "I'm glad it made you feel better."

She smiled. "Me too."

"Rico said he'll be here in ten minutes." Tyson was currently on camera duty, keeping an eye on the monitors on the table while Jamison and Wade made continuous laps around the property. Brock was back at headquarters, checking in with Shawn, Pierce, and Eva.

"Are you hungry?" Abe pulled the blanket back over her body before sliding out from under her feet.

"A little." She wasn't used to sitting around as much as she had the past couple of days, so her stomach wasn't growling like it usually would be by this time in the day.

She'd spent over an hour in Abe's home gym this morning, not even realizing how long she'd been down there until she came out, sweaty, sticky, and slightly more relaxed.

By the time she was out of the shower, Tyson came in with a computer Heidi sent over. The laptop was pretty stripped down, and the internet was strictly limited to reduce the chances that someone might be able to track her activity, but she could get to her spreadsheets and lists, along with the list of contacts she kept, because it turned out she was the only one who knew the name of the fence company they used.

180

That gave her more than enough to occupy her afternoon. Unfortunately, by the time she stood up from working at the table, her body was starting to feel the effects of her battle with the bag.

And it turned out the bag might have come out ahead.

"What did you order for dinner?" She'd been existing on crackers and cheese and Danishes since coming back from Cincinnati, so the food was almost worth all the hassle.

Almost.

Abe gave her a slow smile. "That's a surprise."

"I'm starting to think you like surprises."

"If I didn't then I'd be in the wrong line of work." Abe opened the fridge and pulled out the pitcher of water he always kept filled and chilled. "You want something besides water to drink?"

Elise shook her head. "I only really drink water now."

"Now?" He poured her a glassful and brought it to the coffee table she'd eaten her last three dinners at.

"I used to only drink Diet Coke." She picked up the glass and took a sip. "Heidi gave me shit about it. Said I was going to preserve my body from the inside out."

Heidi was the first woman she'd ever really connected with. Hell, she might have been the first *person* she'd connected with.

Nothing she said phased Heidi. Heidi didn't judge anything she did. She was completely accepting.

Completely nonjudgmental.

181

"So she made you stop drinking it." Abe poured himself a glass of water before coming to sit next to her on the sofa, working his way back under her feet and shins.

"Yeah. Pretty much." Elise leaned to set her glass onto the table. "She just started bringing me glasses of ice water all the time and leaving them on my desk." It was the beginning of their friendship.

No one had ever really taken care of her before, and Heidi's actions made her feel something she'd never experienced.

Accepted.

Heidi was the first person to really understand and accept who she was.

"That sounds like Heidi." Abe stroked along her feet. "She'll make you do what's best for you whether you like it or not."

Elise laughed. "Everything she does, she does whether people like it or not." Watching how Heidi handled an unaccepting world made her feel empowered to do the same. "She genuinely doesn't care what other people think about her."

"That's an amazing place to be."

Probably. She'd never been there before.

Because while Heidi didn't worry what other people thought of her and lived her life in a way that was authentically her own without shame or guilt, Elise struggled to do the same.

Shame and guilt were part of her everyday life.

She thought about them nearly every hour of every day.

And no matter what she did they never left.

"Looks like I've got about five different things in this bag." Rico came up the stairs, saving her from getting any deeper into a conversation she really didn't want to continue. Abe already knew so many things that she tried to hide away, thinking of offering up any more of her shortcomings was terrifying.

"Elise gets her pick." Abe relaxed back on the couch, stretching one arm across the cushions while the other hand rested on her shin. "Everyone else can pick after that."

"I wouldn't have expected anything else." Rico came straight to her side, carrying the shopping bags full of food. "I know how much she likes picking what she eats."

It was a luxury she hadn't always had.

Growing up in a single-parent household meant the meals were as basic as it got. Hotdogs. Baked beans from a can.

Sometimes frozen pizza if she was lucky.

For her father, feeding her was one more hassle he'd been left to deal with after her mother's death.

One more task he'd been burdened with. One more responsibility he had to handle on his own.

And he resented it just as much as all the rest.

Elise peeked into the bag when Rico set it onto the floor beside her. The smell of garlic and tomato swirled around her as she pulled out the first container.

"This smells like it might be Italian food." She forced her attention to the food in front of her. "I didn't know there was an Italian place in Fairbanks."

"It just opened." Abe watched as she sifted through the containers, peeking inside each one before moving to the next. "Anything look good?"

"Everything looks good." So far she'd seen lasagna, spaghetti and meatballs, fettuccine Alfredo, and what appeared to be gnocchi soup with spinach. "I'm not really sure how to pick."

"Can you pick two?"

She could probably narrow it down to two. Elise pushed the soup and the spaghetti and meatballs to one side, before reloading the lasagna and fettuccine into the bag. Then she picked the bag up and handed it over to Rico. "Hopefully I didn't pick what you were wanting."

"I've got a whole extra bag of food." He shot her a wink as he walked to the refrigerator.

Elise looked to where Abe sat beside her. "You ordered one of everything?"

"I want you to have what you want." His eyes held hers. "You've had a rough couple of days, and I was hoping that some good food might make you feel a little better."

"It'll probably make me feel better than wailing on the punching bag did." She smiled a little. "But only because this won't really fight back."

It hadn't occurred to her that punching the bag could result in a little bit of physical trauma.

But now she knew.

Abe was going to order her shin guards and gloves so next time maybe she wouldn't end up so battered.

It was still worth it though.

"Most people don't end up like this the first time they take on a punching bag." Abe lifted the lid off of the soup and dropped in a plastic spoon. "Leave it to you to be an overachiever." He passed the soup her way before digging out a bag of freshly-baked bread. The bag also contained a few foil-wrapped pats of butter. He fished one free and went to work spreading the softened butter across a slice of still-warm bread. "You don't do anything halfway, do you?"

Elise moved the soup around, carefully scooping up the different ingredients to create a perfect bite. "I try to do my best."

When your entire existence has been so problematic for someone who was supposed to accept you and love you no matter what, you ended up trying to prove your worth to everyone.

It was an impossible task because not everyone would think you had value, and unfortunately to a young girl that felt like one more failing.

"All I can say is your best and everyone else's best are two completely different things." Abe handed her the bread.

She took it, managing a little smile in spite of the painful turn the conversation had taken. "Thanks."

Abe's eyes fell to the soup she hadn't yet tasted. "How is it?"

"I feel like you already know."

"Maybe. But I want to know what you think."

Elise lifted the bite she'd been working on and slid it into her mouth, chewing through the fluffy gnocchi.

The combination of creamy broth, tender spinach, and bits of sweet carrot was divine. "Oh my gosh. This is so good."

"I know." Abe passed across the spaghetti and meatballs, along with a fork. "Now try this one."

Elise eyed him as she swirled the fork in the pasta. "I didn't think that you liked food."

"Of course I like food."

"Let me rephrase that." She managed to fork off a little chunk of meatball and added it to the bite. "I didn't think you cared about food."

"I don't care about food." His gaze stayed fixed on her. "I care about you."

The loaded fork hung in front of her mouth as she stared back at him.

"Does that really surprise you?"

"A little." Reality would tell her all the signs were there.

Everything Abe did indicated how he felt.

But she wasn't great about accepting reality. Not when it was happy.

"I thought maybe I was more of just a pain in your ass." That was easier to reckon with. Easier to palate.

Because that's what she'd always been. The hassle. An obstacle.

"I didn't say you weren't also a pain in my ass." Abe smiled. "But I don't necessarily want to live a life with someone who's not at least a little bit of a pain in my ass."

There were so many things she could read into that statement.

Terrifying things.

All she wanted was for a man to fuck her.

186

Was that too much to ask?

Apparently.

"Sounds like you're a glutton for punishment then." Elise shoved in the bite of pasta and meat, needing something else to occupy her mind.

"I would argue the same about you." Abe watched as she chewed through the bite. "Because I'm sure I'm a bigger pain in your ass than you are in mine. And you're still here."

She laughed a little around the food in her mouth. "Where am I going to go?"

"Don't act like you wouldn't be trying to figure a way out of here if you were tired of my shit."

Elise passed the spaghetti and meatballs his way. "If you want me to leave you should probably stop feeding me."

"So all I have to do to get you to stay is keep feeding you?" He took the pasta and immediately collected a bite of his own.

"Isn't that what they say about feral animals? Once you feed them they never leave?"

Abe snorted out a little laugh. "You should have told me that before I ended up with two of them."

Elise reached down to scratch behind the ear of the kitten who spent most of the day as close to her as possible. "He's not feral."

"At least you recognize that you are."

He wasn't as far off as he thought he was.

Abe stroked one finger down the kitten's side. "Have you decided what you're going to name him?"

"I don't think I'm very good at naming things."

"That could be a problem if you're planning on having kids." There was something different in the way Abe was looking at her.

Something… Off.

"Well," Elise took a bite of the soup she'd chosen for her dinner, "I shouldn't have any problems then."

Abe seemed to relax a little bit. "You could probably stand to lose one problem." He took another bite of the pasta he'd ended up with by default. "Or two."

"Well I tried to lose you." Elise worked to flatten out the smile creeping across her lips. "A couple times."

Abe's head dropped back as he laughed. "Good thing I'm persistent."

"I would call it annoying, but whatever makes you feel better."

They ate the rest of their dinner while watching one of the horrible shows Abe enjoyed.

And honestly, they were growing on her a little bit.

Seeing that other people's lives were just as big of a shit show as her own made her feel slightly better.

At least she'd never been to prison, so that was a plus.

And she'd never dated anyone who was in prison, plus two.

"I still can't believe you watch these shows." Based on everything she knew about Abe, it was the one thing so far that didn't make sense.

His eyes didn't move from the television screen. "When I was a kid I used to watch soap operas with my grandma."

It was almost impossible to imagine Abe as anything other than the very grown man that he was. "I don't believe you."

He turned her way. "It's true. *The Young and the Restless. Days of Our Lives.* She watched them all. Could give you a play-by-play on everything that had ever happened."

"No, I believe that you used to watch soap operas." Elise shook her head. "I just don't believe that you were ever a kid."

Abe's expression changed, moving to something that looked uncomfortably familiar. "I wasn't one for long."

CHAPTER 15

ELISE'S EYES DROPPED and she shifted on the sofa.

She was definitely uncomfortable by the potential this conversation had, and he'd seen how Elise handled discomfort.

Not well.

But hopefully she would deal a little bit better with his discomfort than with her own.

"My parents were both drug users." Abe continued stroking down the leg draped across his lap, being careful not to put too much pressure on the irritated limb. "They lost custody of me when I was three years old."

He didn't talk much about what happened to him when he was a child. He'd worked hard to make it matter as little as possible.

Bad things happened to everyone. You could use them as an excuse or you could use them as a reason.

He chose to use them as a reason. A reason to do things differently. A reason to be better. A reason to prove he could beat the odds.

"Luckily, my grandmother was able to step in and be my guardian."

He didn't remember much of his time with his parents, and most of what he did was probably influenced by stories he'd heard.

"Oh." Elise wasn't looking at him. Her eyes were fixed on the blanket covering her lap.

"I lived with her until I was ten." Those years he did remember. "She had a little apartment on the first floor of an old house. It was just me and her."

Elise was silent.

"Unfortunately, she wasn't in good health and when I was ten she passed away." He reached out to take one of Elise's his hands in his. "By that time my parents had split up and my mother had been clean for six months."

Elise finally looked up at him. Probably because she thought the story was about to have a happy ending.

It was not. Not yet

"But she didn't stay clean long." He'd spent his teenage years moving from place to place and couch to couch, crashing wherever his mother could manage to convince someone to let them stay. "I signed up for ROTC as soon as I could and went into the military the day after graduation."

He knew it was his only chance. The only way he could be more than either of his parents.

The only way he could be all his grandmother knew he could be.

"My mother overdosed while I was in basic training."

Elise went a little pale. "She died?"

191

"She died."

It was one of the many things he suspected connected them. There was a hollowness that happened when you lost your mother at a young age.

An emptiness you could sense when you saw it in someone else.

Elise had that emptiness.

But she also carried something else. Something he didn't.

Guilt.

Abe held her hand while she sat silently, letting her absorb all he'd offered, hoping it might bring her understanding.

Maybe make her feel a little less alone.

"What about your dad?" Her tone was oddly emotionless.

"I don't know. He disappeared and I never saw or heard from him again."

Elise huffed out a bitter chuckle. "Aren't you lucky."

"I guess that depends on how you look at things."

"The way I look at things you're lucky." Her voice held a bitterness he wasn't used to hearing.

"You're probably right." He was able to come into manhood with no real example of what a man should be, good or bad.

He'd never learned behaviors that had to be unlearned. He'd never seen bad actions and taken them on as his own.

But that probably wasn't what Elise meant.

"We got something." Tyson stood from his chair at the table, one finger going straight to his ear to activate the mic on his piece. "There's a car at the gate."

Abe had Elise off the couch before Tyson was across the room.

This time she seemed more prepared for the process.

One arm snagged the blanket and the other scooped up her cat, carrying both as she raced alongside him up the stairs toward the safe room on the third floor. When he opened the door Elise immediately ran in and turned to face him. "Don't get hurt."

"Didn't plan on it." Abe pulled her in for a quick kiss before closing the door and running back downstairs. This time he didn't have to tell her to lock the door. The heavy switch of the lock happened before he even hit the first step.

Tyson had a long rifle in one hand as he raced down the steps to the first floor, with Abe moving close behind him.

Dutch was already talking in their ears as the team went into action, ready to defend their property and the woman it contained. "Heidi's running the plates, but I expect it to come back as a rental."

"A rental? Not stolen?" Abe followed Tyson down the steps and out the door into the chilly evening air.

"I'm not sure we're dealing with anyone who has a permanent status in Alaska."

"That would be fucking fantastic." That would mean no established home-base. A limited stash of weapons and ammo. And an all-around less organized threat.

That would explain the hodgepodge of attacks.

"I'm not sure it's as fantastic as you think." Dutch didn't sound as thrilled by the possibility as Abe was. "What they lack in preparedness, they might make up for in idiocy."

"It isn't real smart for them to just roll up like this, is it?" Tyson was a good ten yards in front of him at this point, moving quickly through the shadows toward the gate.

"About as smart as it was for them to try to take Elise from in front of headquarters." Jamison was slightly out of breath. "I'm moving up the east side. Should be there in under twenty seconds."

Twenty seconds didn't sound like much, but a lot could happen in that amount of time.

And a lot could go wrong.

"I don't like this." Brock was stationed in front of Abe's townhome. "Something doesn't feel right here."

Abe froze.

Brock was right. This seemed too easy. Too simple.

Too stupid.

"I'm coming your way." Abe turned and moved back toward his home and back toward the woman he hoped to share it with.

"What the fuck is wrong with the line?" Jamison's confusion bordered on anger. "What in the hell is that sound?"

194

"I don't hear anything." Tyson's response was immediate.

Abe strained, trying to hear what Jamison might be talking about.

A faint buzzing did carry through the line. "I hear it."

"There's nothing on my end." Dutch paused. "Who can hear it?"

"Not me." Tyson's voice was quiet, which meant he was probably close to the gate.

"I hear something." Brock was standing outside the garage as Abe reached his side. They stared at each other for a second, listening to the odd buzzing sound.

Both their eyes slowly lifted to the sky above.

Abe shoved Brock into the open garage bay. "It's a fucking drone." He followed Brock in. "Take cover."

The buzzing came closer as Abe rushed to the back of the space to slap his hand against the button, sending the garage door closing. It was halfway down when the beeping started.

Abe knocked open the door to the townhome, managing to make it almost to the base of the stairs when the explosion happened.

Brock hit his back and they both went down together. The tread of a stair caught Abe right across the center of his chest. The impact stole his breath and made him see stars.

"I need a status update." Panic edged in around Dutch's words. "What's going on there?"

"Car's gone." The sound of Tyson's gear shifting as he ran carried through the line. "The explosion seemed to happen at the townhomes."

"Was anyone caught?"

Brock groaned as he moved to one side and slid down the stairs. "It got me and Abe." He glanced Abe's way. "But we're okay."

"Speak for yourself." The words were breathy as he tried to maneuver his way to his back. He squinted into the dusty darkness. "And I think there's a good chance both the Rovers are destroyed."

"We've got more Rovers." Dutch's typing sounded like hammers against cement. "I'm pulling up the security feed right now."

Abe grunted as he pushed to his feet. "I'm going to check on Elise."

He wrapped one arm around his middle and raked the other hand through his hair, knocking as much drywall dust loose as he could.

It would figure. The first house he buys gets blown the fuck up.

The latch flipped on the safe room right away and the door swung open. Elise's eyes were wide and her face was white.

"I'm okay." He held one hand up. "Everything is fine."

She sucked in a shaky breath, her gaze moving over him. "You look greyer than I remember." Elise came toward him, reaching out to smooth her fingers through his hair. "They blew the garage up, huh?"

"Yup." He wrapped one arm around her shoulders as they worked their way back down the stairs. "Hope you weren't partial to that Rover."

Elise peeked his way from the corner of her eyes. "Not as partial as I am to you."

****

"ARE ANY OF the other units damaged?" Elise stood at the kitchen island, mixing together dry cat food and a little tuna.

Brock went to sit at the table. "It doesn't look like it." He raked one hand through his hair. "As far as I can tell everything is still structurally sound."

"Tomorrow we will board up the garage and make sure the place is as secure as it can be." Abe poured hot water over a teabag in a mug. "But if these bastards are going to start sending in exploding drones, then there's not much we're going to be able to do."

"That's not true." Elise perked up a little bit. She set the bowl of cat food on the floor. "I talked to Heidi and she thinks that Vincent has access to some sort of anti-aircraft something."

"Anti-aircraft and anti-drone are two totally different things." Abe bounced the teabag in the mug. "Especially when we're talking about a civilian drone, not a military drone."

He didn't even know they had civilian drones that could explode, but where there was a will there was a way.

"I am pretty sure she told Vincent it was a little drone." Elise pet the kitten as it came over to dig into its dinner. "And I mean, Vincent owes us."

197

"I'm not sure he'd see it the same way." Brock winced a little as he shifted in his seat.

"I think Vincent might see it however Heidi tells him to see it." She lifted one shoulder. "I think he genuinely likes her."

"He should like her. She's got a skill set he can exploit." Brock lifted his brows. "And don't tell Shawn you think Vincent likes Heidi. He'll kill him and then we'll be screwed."

"If Shawn goes around killing everybody who likes Heidi then that's all he'll ever do." Elise stood and added some water to her kitten's bowl. "Because everybody likes Heidi."

"I would argue everyone likes all the women who work at Alaskan Security." Brock must have picked up on the edge of hurt in Elise's words. "You're all pretty fantastic."

"Right." Elise sounded unconvinced.

"Someone just pulled up to the gate." Jamison leaned toward the screen, his eyes narrowing. "Looks like it might be—"

Abe stepped in behind him. "GHOST."

Elise smiled across the kitchen at him. "I told you."

"Be careful," Abe grabbed a long rifle as he got ready to go meet Vincent at the gate, "we might start using you as an informant."

Elise's smile slipped. "At least then I'd be able to do something."

"You're doing more than you know." Abe shot her a wink. "I'll be back in just a minute."

He moved towards the front of the townhome, heading for the front door he'd never used. Up until

198

now he'd always come and gone through the garage entrance. It was more secure, offering two points of entry to slow anyone who might try to follow him in.

But the garage was out of commission for the foreseeable future.

He stepped out onto the small porch, doing a quick scan of the property. That was one good thing about the front door. It offered a nice view of the front of the property and the area around it. Unfortunately, a full visual sweep was impossible due to the adjoining townhomes.

He edged toward the stairs, leaning to peek around the corner to make sure the coast was clear. The headlights from the SUV waiting at the gate illuminated most of the road leading to the townhomes, making it easy to clearly see the space.

Once he was sure no one was lying in wait and there were no drones hovering overhead, Abe made his way down the stairs and to the private road running in front of the townhomes. By the time he reached the gate, Tyson and Wade were already there. The head of GHOST was standing just inside the gate, chatting with the other men.

"Fancy meeting you here." He reached out to shake Vincent's hand. "Glad to see you."

"Sounds like it." Vincent's eyes moved up the lane toward Abe's townhome. "Mind if I take a look?"

"There's not much to look at." Abe and Brock had already gone through the garage, hoping to find some sort of scrap to give them an idea of what they were dealing with, but came up empty. "Whatever it was came completely apart."

"Interesting." Vincent walked next to Abe as they went to the townhouse. Three black Jeeps, their windows tinted so dark they were almost the same color as the paint, followed behind them. "So it just came down from the sky?"

"Not like a bomb." Abe pulled the flashlight free from his hip and switched it on, shining it into the darkened space. "It hovered."

"Was it silent?" Vincent crouched down to squint at the piles of drywall and debris scattered across the cement floor.

"No." Abe tried to follow Vincent with the beam of light as he moved through the garage. "It was pretty loud."

"Interesting."

Suddenly the garage was flooded with light. Abe squinted at the change, using one arm to block as much of it as he could. "That's one hell of a light you got there."

"Makes it easier to find what I'm looking for." Vincent moved methodically through the space, maneuvering around the destroyed bodies of the two Rovers parked there, his boots crunching across glass and metal.

"What exactly are you looking for?" They'd been through this mess. There was nothing identifiable to be found.

Vincent suddenly stilled, slowly crouching toward the floor. He sifted through a pile of shrapnel.

"This." He lifted a tiny bit of plastic into the air.

200

"Is that a microSD card?" The thing was tiny as hell. It would be nearly impossible to find it even if he'd known to look for it.

But Vincent found it quickly. And while Vincent was a man of many talents, finding microSD cards in piles of shit wasn't something a person would naturally be able to do.

It would take practice.

"The good news is, no one was close when this happened." He dropped the card into a plastic bag one of his men held out. "The bad news is they can program these things to fly from anywhere."

"So you're saying they just set it and it goes?" Abe looked to the sky. Up until this minute he thought they'd managed to get close enough to fly a drone into their space.

Which was unsettling, considering how much security they had.

But it was nowhere near as unsettling as thinking they didn't have to be close to do so much damage.

"It's not quite that simple." Vincent went back to digging through the piles. "Usually they also have a camera, because there is still some manual flying that has to be done." He moved around another pile of debris. "They can do it remotely using the Internet."

Abe looked at Tyson as the gravity of the situation hit him. "How far away can they be?"

"As far as they want." Vincent picked out another bit of something and dropped it into a plastic bag, before passing it off to one of his men.

"This one could have been piloted by somebody in Florida."

"Or Ohio." Abe didn't realize he'd said it until Vincent's head snapped his way.

"Ohio?" The head of GHOST stood, dusting his hands off as he walked Abe's way. "You believe this has some connection to what happened in Ohio?"

Trusting Vincent wasn't really an option. The man's allegiance was to GHOST and to GHOST alone.

But at this point he might know enough to warrant a little bit of an alliance. "Elise is inside. Someone tried to kidnap her yesterday morning."

Vincent's expression was flat, unreadable. He stared at Abe for a few long minutes before finally blowing out a breath. "I can't say that surprises me."

Abe gritted his teeth. "It would've been nice to know that could have been a possibility."

He knew Vincent only looked out for GHOST's best interests, but for Christ's sake, he could have given them a heads-up that something like this might happen.

"If I thought they would try to take one of the girls I would have told you." Vincent almost sounded upset. "I assumed retaliation would be focused differently."

"Retaliation for what?" He was frustrated. He was tired. He was sore. He was fucking scared.

Scared that Elise was in more danger than he realized.

"Because of a stupid computer?" If he'd known the computer was going to be this big of an issue he would've kept the fucking thing and sent it to Heidi instead of sending it to Vincent.

"This isn't about a computer, son." Vincent looked up at the dark sky. "This is about the future of weapons." His eyes leveled on Abe's. "In the civilian sector."

CHAPTER 16

SOMETHING WAS WRONG.

Very wrong.

Elise sat on the couch, watching as the men came and went, jaws set tight, eyes completely focused but unfocused at the same time.

The only happy one in the townhouse was the kitten, who sat on her lap, purring away.

Lucky guy had no clue what was going on around him.

It felt like forever before Abe finally came in, looking just the same as everyone else.

Until he saw her.

"How are you doing, Babe?" His expression softened a little as he came to crouch down in front of her.

"What's wrong?" There was no sense waiting for him to tell her, not that he would tell her the truth anyway.

Abe took a deep breath and let it back out. "We need to go back to headquarters."

"What?" She looked around the space that felt like a safe haven in spite of everything that happened there. "Why can't we just stay here?" Elise pointed to the stairs leading to the third floor. "There's a safe room. I'll be fine."

"The safe room won't protect you from an explosive." Abe rested his hands on her thighs. "It's just not a good idea to stay here right now. Not for any of us."

"You're going back to headquarters too?" When he said we, she assumed he might take her there, but wouldn't be staying.

And maybe that was what upset her most about it. Maybe it wasn't the townhome that felt safe.

"Everyone is." Abe glanced up as Brock came in.

"Vincent's ready to go whenever we are."

"Vincent?" Elise sat a little taller.

It was never a good sign when the head of GHOST showed up.

Vincent was like a harbinger of bad news

"Vincent and his team are going to help make sure we get to headquarters." Abe's thumb stroked over the spot he'd bandaged last night. "Otherwise I wouldn't be as open to the idea."

Whatever was happening was bad enough that Vincent was going to escort them to headquarters. "Won't they just follow us there?"

"Yes." The lines around Abe's eyes seemed more prominent. "But we can't continue to protect both locations."

"I thought you said you had to protect this place anyway." He told her more than a few times. "I thought you always knew you would have to guard this place."

"Under normal circumstances we would," Abe shook his head, "but right now we're not dealing with normal circumstances."

"Because of the explosives." It was the only thing that made any sense. It was the only thing that had really changed.

"That's right." Abe's head tipped forward, his forehead coming to rest against the center of her chest. "I have to do whatever it takes to keep you safe, Elise."

He sounded so…

Scared.

"I'll be okay." She reached up to stroke down his hair. "I'm feral, remember?"

He huffed out a silent laugh. "I remember." Abe sucked in a deep breath and straightened, pulling her up as he stood. "We need to go pack."

The next few minutes were a rushed blur of trying to grab everything she possibly could, while Vincent waited outside. By the time she and Abe made it downstairs, everyone else was loaded up and waiting.

Vincent tipped his head at her.

"Hi." She wasn't particularly interested in having any more of a conversation with a man who seemed to be more of a bad omen than a guardian angel.

Abe's eyes scanned the area around them as he shoved her into the back passenger's side of a black Jeep. "We've got to move fast, Babe. We can't spend too much time out here in the open."

206

"We can't, or I can't?"

"We." Vincent answered the question as he closed the door on her.

Elise held her kitten as she glanced toward the man already sitting in the seat beside her. He was giant.

And wearing sunglasses at night.

She leaned to peek toward the driver. He was just as huge as the guy beside her.

And also wearing sunglasses at night.

Apparently they took their eighties' music very seriously.

The front passenger door opened and Abe slid into place. There was a Jeep in front of them and a Jeep behind them as they slowly headed toward the gate. Elise took one more look at the townhomes she'd helped build. It might be the last time she saw them.

Not just because they might get blown up.

But also because she might not make it out of the next ten minutes.

Her stomach clenched as they left the relative safety of the property, the vehicles staying close as they pulled out onto the main road.

"What's your cat's name?" The man beside her's voice was surprisingly soft.

Elise gave him a little smile. "He doesn't have one yet."

The man reached over to scratch the kitten behind one ear. "He's a cute little thing."

"You like cats?" Elise tried to focus on him instead of what was going on outside of the Jeep.

"I love cats." The man's lips softened into an almost curved line as the kitten purred and leaned into his touch.

"Do you have any?" Her eyes moved to the window beside him, catching sight of a line of offices.

"I travel a lot."

"I bet." She watched as the kitten left her lap and slowly walked toward the man's giant thigh. "If you had a cat what would you name it?"

He scooped the tabby up, his huge hands swallowing the kitten's tiny body. "Dallas."

"You came up with that really fast." Maybe she was the only one who had issues naming things. It just felt so permanent. So important.

The man lifted one shoulder in a little shrug. "Naming animals is easy."

"I'm going to disagree with you on that one." She'd been thinking on it for over twenty-four hours and hadn't come up with a single possibility.

"Sure it is." He almost smiled as the kitten's nose tapped against his. "You take something that's important to you and turn it into a name."

He was trying to be helpful, and in some sense maybe he was.

That didn't make what he said any easier to hear.

"Thanks." She tried to smile. "I'll keep that in mind."

"Five minutes out." The driver's voice was significantly less kind than her fellow passenger's. Maybe that was because he was in charge of safely getting them to their destination.

Or maybe her backseat companion was just a little bit nicer.

"I'm Elise."

The man beside her almost smiled. "Jareth."

"Nice to meet you, Jareth."

Jareth passed back the kitten. "You have to tell me what you end up naming him."

Yeah sure. She'd just call up GHOST headquarters and ask for Jareth. "I'll do that."

Elise tucked the tabby against her chest, holding him close as she closed her eyes and tried to relax. Everything would be fine. They were almost there. They were with Vincent.

And nobody fucked with Vi—

Suddenly Jareth's wide body hit hers, his thick arms banding around her as he twisted her down in the seat.

The Jeep lurched forward, sending her rolling toward the back of the seat as Jareth held her pinned in place.

That was when she noticed the pinging.

Like hail when it hit a windshield.

Or, more likely, like bullets hitting bulletproof glass.

"We've got someone on our right." The driver's voice was just as calm as it was before. Like he was discussing traffic patterns instead of deadly weapons. "Looks like," he paused, "is that a fucking Volkswagen Bug?"

She hadn't been in Alaska particularly long, but she'd been here long enough to realize that most people in this part of the world did not drive Volkswagen Bugs.

They drove SUVs and unmarked, windowless vans.

"Copy." The Jeep took a sharp left turn. Sharp enough that she would've rolled off the seat if her new friend Jareth wasn't holding her in place.

"We're intact." The driver continued to respond to an unheard voice. "But we took at least ten hits."

Ten.

Ten freaking bullets were shot at the Jeep she was riding in?

Another ping, but this one hit behind her, toward the back of the Jeep.

They were being chased.

"Hold on."

The whole world seemed to spin in place. Tires screeched against asphalt.

The pinging continued.

Only now it was hitting the front of the Jeep.

Where Abe was.

Elise twisted her head, managing to work it free enough that she caught sight of him.

Abe was looking straight ahead as he shifted in his seat, angling the long gun in his hands toward his window.

"No." Whatever he was thinking was a bad idea. "No!" She said it louder as his window started to lower, removing the only layer of protection he had.

Jareth's hand clamped over her mouth. "Distracting him is not something you want to do right now."

Elise squeezed her eyes shut, trying to block out what was happening.

What could happen next.

Then everything got very loud.

Guns. Yelling.

And then the sound of twisting metal. Breaking glass.

The Jeep jerked to a stop.

"Don't move." Jareth held her tight. Tight enough she couldn't move even if she wanted to.

More yelling. Some of the voices she recognized. Rico. Brock. Jamison.

But there was one voice missing. One very distinct voice.

She wanted to open her eyes. Look to see if he was there. Look to see if he was okay.

But what if he wasn't?

Elise's door opened, sending her feet shooting straight out. She hadn't noticed how hard she was bracing against it.

Someone grunted. "Hell."

Elise spread the fingers of one hand over Jareth's face, shoving him up and off her with as much force as she could muster as she launched toward the man standing beside her.

The man she'd just been terrified to lose.

And then accidentally kicked in the nuts.

"You're okay." Elise fell against him, both arms wrapping around his neck as she buried her face in his chest.

"Not sure okay is the word I would use right now." Abe's already gravelly voice was even raspier than normal.

"You're not dead."

"I'm not dead." Abe leaned into her, one arm coming to pull her closer. "Are you okay?"

"If you're okay, I'm okay." She breathed against him, trying to calm the racing of her heart. "What just happened?"

Abe turned his head to look over one shoulder. "I have no fucking clue."

Elise leaned, risking a peek around Abe's body. Like the driver stated, there was a Volkswagen Bug sitting just beside them.

"The damn thing is pink." Vincent came walking up. "Who in the hell uses a pink Volkswagen for an op?"

"Someone who knows we aren't going to pay as much attention to a pink Volkswagen." The driver of the Jeep she was riding in frowned at the two-door vehicle. "They were right. I didn't realize it until they were right on top of us." He tipped his head toward Elise's open door. "First bullet damn near got through the glass."

Elise rolled her eyes toward the window that had been inches from her head. It was peppered with circular defects.

Someone tried to shoot her in the head.

Someone tried to shoot her in the head multiple times.

"I think I might throw up." It was all the warning she could get out.

It turned out the gnocchi soup she enjoyed for dinner was a much more pleasant experience on the way down than it was on the way up.

She tried to cover her mouth. Tried to keep from adding insult to injury.

But there was no stopping it. The amazing dinner Abe supplied her with now covered the front of his black tactical pants and the top of his black boots.

In the span of two minutes, she'd kicked him in the nuts and then barfed on him.

"We need to get her out of here." Abe didn't seem bothered at all by her recent offenses against him.

He turned to Vincent as he pulled her out of the Jeep, scooping her up to carry her the way he had not so long ago.

"I've got an armored van that will be here in under thirty seconds." Vincent tipped his head toward where Jareth stood. "You two get her to Alaskan Security headquarters."

****

"ARE YOU OKAY?" Heidi raced toward her, moving a little slower than she normally would since she was currently pregnant with twin girls. "What the fuck just happened?"

"She just got shot at." Lennie shoved Heidi out of the way and grabbed onto Elise. "We just fucking saw it happen."

Elise looked at the women surrounding her. "You saw it happen?"

"Of course we saw it happen." Heidi pushed Lennie off Elise, then grabbed her in a long bear-hug. "Did you think I would just let them drive around with you?"

"I was with Vincent." She said it like it should matter, but based on what she just witnessed, Vincent clearly wasn't as impenetrable of a person as he wanted everyone to believe.

213

"And don't think I'm not going to kick his ass for letting you get shot at." Heidi shoved her out at arm's length and scanned down her body. "You didn't get hurt at all did you?"

"I mean," hurt was relative, "I accidentally kicked Abe in the nuts. And then I threw up on him. So I'm suffering in some sense of the word."

Heidi snorted. "He probably fell in love with you because of it, right then and there."

"I'm sure." Elise looked around, trying to find any sign of the salt-and-pepper head she was struggling not to get too attached to.

"He's fine." Heidi wrapped one arm around her shoulders and led her toward the rooming side of the building. "Shawn wanted to talk to him to find out exactly what happened."

"I'll be interested to hear that myself." Everything happened so freaking fast. One minute she was having a perfectly fine conversation with Jareth, and the next...

Someone was trying to kill her.

Again.

"You're not the only one." Lennie stood at her other side as they walked through the passageway connecting the main building to the rooming house.

Heidi snorted again. "I'm sure Vincent is also interested as hell to find out what happened."

"I can't imagine people go around shooting up GHOST's vehicles all the time." It didn't seem like the smartest idea for anyone to try to take on GHOST, let alone GHOST and Alaskan Security.

Which is exactly what had just happened.

"I'm glad you're back here." Heidi rested her head against Elise's as they continued to walk. "I was nervous having you so far away."

Elise didn't have the heart to tell her it was probably good that she'd been so far away.

And that now that she was here, the danger would probably be focused here too.

"How messed up did my house get?" Lennie pulled open the door to the rooming building, holding it as Elise and Heidi walked inside.

"I don't think yours was touched by the explosion at all." Lennie and Rico bought the end unit, and Abe's unit was right at the center of the building. From what she could tell, only Abe's townhouse, and maybe the one at each side, had been damaged. "So you should be fine."

"Not like it really matters now." Lennie led the way as they walked toward the rooms where Elise stayed since coming to Alaska. "No one's going to get to live there until all of this is over."

Instead of going toward the room Elise used for herself, Lennie took the stairs to the second floor.

"Where are we going?"

Lennie shot her a grin. "You my dear, have leveled up."

Elise glanced at Heidi. "What is she talking about?"

"She's just excited." Heidi huffed a little as they took the last three stairs. "She's been pulling for you and Abe since you guys went to Cincinnati."

"I wouldn't get too excited." Elise waited while Heidi took a second to catch her breath. "Abe and I were just stuck in the same place. Now we're not."

Heidi's blonde brows climbed up her forehead. "You're not?"

"No." It was pretty obvious. "We're not staying at his place anymore."

"I guess that's true." Heidi used a badge to swipe the keypad beside the door to one of the suites on the second floor. She passed the badge to Elise. "Here. This is yours for now."

"I'm staying in a suite?" Pierce must feel bad about her getting shot at.

"You're staying in a suite." Heidi pulled open the door and went inside. "I'll make sure you get a new computer and whatever else you need."

"Thank you." She gave her best friend as much of a smile as she could manage.

She'd been almost blown up. Shot at. And she could still smell the faint odor of vomit, which meant Abe's shoes probably weren't the only ones she managed to assault.

And unfortunately, none of those things could distract her from what was upsetting her the most.

"I'm probably going to take a shower and go to bed." Then pull the covers over her head and hide from as much reality as she could.

"That sounds accurate." Heidi gave her another tight hug. "Come get me if you need anything."

"Same goes for me." Lennie opened the door and lifted her brows at Heidi.

"Fine." Heidi huffed out a breath. "But she's going to have to put up with me tomorrow."

Elise's smile was a little more natural this time. "I'm looking forward to it."

216

She really was. Getting back to some sense of normalcy, even if it was the normal she tried to leave not so long ago, would be a welcome break from the insanity that had been the past couple of days.

And all of it was Abe's fault.

She should be angry at him for upending her life the way he had. Stealing the fresh start she'd worked so hard to execute perfectly.

But here she was.

Upset that he wasn't with her.

Like an idiot.

When the door clicked shut behind Heidi and Lennie she let out a long sigh. "Looks like it's just you and me." Elise set the kitten down on the ground before turning to head for the bathroom. The suitcase she'd haphazardly packed before leaving Abe's townhome sat beside the bedroom door.

At least she would have fresh clothes to change into before she curled up under the covers with the man in her life.

The kitten bounced around the bathroom while she showered off, scrubbing her hair and body within an inch of their life as she stood under the scalding hot water.

When she was done she didn't feel any better, but at least she didn't smell like vomit.

Her first win for the day.

Elise grabbed one of the towels and wrapped it around her wet hair, before using another towel to dry off her body. She tucked the second towel around her chest before stepping out into the main portion of the suite and grabbing her suitcase, rolling it toward the bedroom.

She hefted it up onto the bed, grunting a little. It seemed heavier than she remembered it being.

The towel on her head started tipping to one side, slowly sliding until it fell to the ground.

Oh well.

Elise wrangled the zipper and flipped open the top of the suitcase. The bag of cat food Rico brought home sat on top. She hadn't put it in there, which meant one of the other men on the team must have shoved it in at the last minute.

The rest of the bag was exactly as she had packed it, chaotic as it was. It took her a couple minutes to find everything she needed, but once it was all in hand she dropped the towel.

Something dark and shadowy shifted just outside the open bedroom door, sucking in her breath and sending her spinning toward it.

"That's one hell of a welcome home."

CHAPTER 17

ELISE MADE NO move to cover herself up.

He kept his eyes on hers anyway. "Feel better?"

While his gaze stayed in a respectable spot, hers raked down the front of his body. "You changed clothes."

"There was no reason to keep my gear on."

"Because it was covered in puke."

"It happens." He hadn't intended to discuss that portion of the night with her. Definitely not when it was taking everything in him to keep his eyes where they belonged.

"I don't think it happens with other people as often as it happens with me." She held up two fingers. "I've thrown up on you twice now."

"You didn't throw up on me the first time." He almost smiled at the memory. "The bushes however, you fully dusted." Abe took another step into the room they would be sharing tonight. "And you didn't answer me. Do you feel better?"

Elise lifted a shoulder, still looking completely unbothered by the fact that she was standing fully naked in front of him.

Abe continued toward her, slowly circling around her back, hoping to reduce the temptation to let his gaze wander. "I don't like seeing you upset, Elise." He leaned closer, close enough his lips almost touched her ear. "It makes me want to rectify the situation."

Elise's head tipped to one side and she peeked at him under her lashes. "I think there's limits on even what you can accomplish."

He slowly inhaled against her skin, breathing in the softly sweet scent of her body. "You haven't experienced all I can accomplish."

Her spine seemed to stretch, making her the tiniest bit taller. "What are you suggesting?"

"Anything you want." He smiled at the sharp intake of her breath. "Within reason."

That sent her spinning to face him. "Within reason." Her eyes narrowed. "Whose reason? Yours or mine?"

"Mine."

Her gaze turned to a glare. "Why yours? Because you have experience? Because I'm so innocent I can't possibly handle the full capacity of *all you can accomplish*?" Sarcasm dripped from the last few words as she repeated his own statement.

"You're angry."

"Of course I'm angry." She huffed out a bitter breath. "I'm twenty-seven years old and I can't name a cat because there's nothing that's important to me."

220

That was not where he expected this conversation to go. Most people either ended up terrified after being almost killed, or angry.

It hadn't surprised him when Elise was the latter.

"I have spent my whole life never getting attached to anything." She laughed. "It worked. Now my cat is never going to have a name because there's nothing that I care about."

"That's not true." He saw how she was with her friends. Saw how she was with the men who worked around her. Saw how important her job was to her. "You care about a lot of things."

She lifted a brow, clearly not believing him. "Like what?"

"Your friends. Your job."

"That's not what I'm talking about." Her frustration was clear. "I was willing to walk away from all of that. You were there. You saw it." She shook her head. "That's not caring."

"I would argue that's more evidence supporting my statement." He gently rested his hands over the lines running down her upper arms, not to block them out, but to show that bit of her a gentle touch.

A loving touch.

"Emotions are hard for you, Elise." He let one thumb stroke across the slightly raised scars. "Good or bad."

"I don't think there are good or bad emotions. They all feel the same."

"That's not your emotions, Babe. That's the fear you've tied to them."

She stared up at him, her jaw set.

"That's why you're trying to find a way out of feeling them right now." He slid his hands up over her bare shoulders to rest at the sides of her neck. "That's why you can't admit that there are things that matter to you. Because if something matters to you then you will feel the fear that might come from losing it."

She blinked a few times. "I can't handle it."

The broken sound of her voice tore into him. He immediately wrapped his arms around her, pulling her close, cradling her head as he pressed it into his chest. "I think you're wrong. I think you don't realize how much you can handle."

"I know exactly what I can handle and so do you. You've seen what happens when I can't." She tried to shove away from him.

"That's not what those lines are, Elise." He held her tighter, refusing to let her run away. "You did handle it then. Every single one of them represents a time you handled the pain. Not in a good way. Not in a way that is safe. Not in a way that's healthy. But you still found a way to handle it." He smoothed one hand down her hair as he rested his lips against her head. "Because you're strong."

A sob jumped from her body, curling it against his as it leapt free. "Stop it."

"You know that's not going to happen." He circled one hand down her back. "I'm not stopping, and neither are you. We're going to learn how to handle this."

"I don't need you to fix me."

"I don't want to fix you, but I will sure as hell hold the world back so you can fix yourself." That was all

222

that was stopping her. The weight of a world that was so heavy she couldn't move under it.

It was stifling her. Smothering her. Blinding her.

Keeping her from being able to see the truth.

Elise sniffed against his chest. Her eyes slowly lifted to his face. "What if I'm not fixable?"

Abe reached out to smooth one hand down the side of her damp face, his thumb swiping at a wayward tear as it slid free. "I don't think you're nearly as broken as you think you are, Babe."

Broken and damaged were two different things.

"I think you'll be surprised what happens if you let yourself see what's really around you." He caught a bit of damp hair and worked it away from her face.

"Paying attention to what was around me was never a great idea." Her lips curved in a sad smile as the fingers of one hand traced the lines on her thigh. "That was how I ended up with all these."

Unpacking everything that led to Elise being where she was wasn't anything he wanted to begin tonight. Right now he just wanted to get her comfortable. Let her sleep.

"Let's get you in your pajamas."

"I don't want to put on my pajamas." Her palms flattened against his chest. "I want to stay just like this." She inched a little closer as her hands slid towards the waistband of his pants.

"What are you doing, Elise?"

"I don't know." The purposeful way her fingers started to gather up the fabric of his shirt said otherwise.

"You've had a long day. You need to go to sleep."

"I thought you said I needed to start paying attention to what was around me?" She managed to tug his t-shirt free in one pull. "I'm just taking your advice." Her hands immediately went to his skin, moving over his stomach and up the center of his chest. "I didn't expect you to have so much chest hair." Her eyes lifted to his face, lower lip tucking between her teeth.

Abe caught her hands, lifting each one to his mouth to brush a kiss across the inside of her wrist.

Elise moved in closer, the long line of her naked body pressing tight to his.

"You need to put your pajamas on and go to bed."

She looped both arms around his neck. "Why don't you take your clothes off and come to bed."

He'd seen aggressive Elise. The woman who propositioned a man in clear and concise terms.

He'd also seen her passive. So overtaken by pleasure that all she could do was lay back and take what he gave her.

This was something different from either of those.

And infinitely more problematic.

"I don't think it's a good idea for me to take my clothes off."

"Why is that?" One side of her mouth lifted in a smirk. "Are you embarrassed by your body?"

It was a challenge. She was trying to taunt him into doing what she wanted.

And it wasn't going to work.

"Put on your pajamas and go to bed." He'd been stern with her before and it earned him the desired outcome.

"I don't think I will." Her hands skimmed down the sides of his neck and over his chest. "I think I'll just sleep like this."

****

ABE'S NOSTRILS FLARED, but he still didn't look at her.

Not anything besides her face anyway.

He'd been in the room with her completely naked for over five minutes and hadn't taken a single peek.

It was either infuriatingly insulting or infuriatingly sweet.

Either way she was getting irritated.

"I'm not going to tell you again, Elise." It sounded like he thought he was warning her.

"Good. Because I'm tired of listening to you talk." The tightness that had fisted in her chest was starting to ease, relaxing as a warmth took its place. "It's getting boring."

"Did you just call me boring?"

"Well considering you still have every bit of clothing you came in with on, you're definitely not what I would consider exciting right now." This was the point where things usually started to fall off the rails for her. She'd been in the bedroom with a man before. Naked.

Usually with the lights off.

But Abe already knew what she hid, so who cared if the lights were on?

And since they were on, she would really like to take full advantage of the situation. Get a better look at the body she'd had a peek of last night in the dark.

But here he stood. Clothed.

"I'm not taking my clothes off, Elise." Abe still had that slightly stern edge to his voice, and honestly she kinda liked it that way.

There was something about a man being bossy.

Especially when she had no intention of giving in to him.

"That's fine. You don't have to take them off." Her hands went to the waistband of the new tactical pants he wore. She had the top button flipped open and the zipper down before he realized what was happening. By the time he grabbed her wrist, her hand was already in the front of his pants, fingers wrapped around the straining line of his dick. "You're not wearing any underwear."

"Didn't have a spare pair on me." His jaw ticked just a little as she shifted her grip, but he didn't pull her hand away.

"That's a happy accident." Usually right now she would be laying on the bed holding her breath, uncertain what was about to happen.

A little scared. A lot intimidated. Definitely hesitant.

But that's not how she felt right now.

And in every other instance, she was always uncertain about whether or not the man with her wanted her. And when it came right down to it, they didn't.

But this man did. There wasn't a doubt in her mind.

226

And being wanted made her feel different. It made her feel bolder.

"I'm not sure how happy it is."

"It is for me." Elise pulled the front of his pants out, freeing up a little more space.

She hadn't touched a single inch of his body. Not because she didn't want to.

But wanting and executing were two different things. One only required desire.

The other required bravery.

And up to this point in her life she wasn't particularly brave. Not when it came to things like this.

Elise let her eyes drop between their bodies as she worked the thickness of his cock free.

A breath of air pulled into her lungs.

Abe's was the first penis she'd ever seen in the full light in real life. Anything else she witnessed was either in the dark, or in porn.

Neither really did this justice.

It was definitely more than she was expecting.

Much more.

A flutter of intimidation threatened to lock her down. Steal the confidence she'd only just discovered.

But that was what landed her where she was. Fear.

Abe was right. It dictated her life. Controlled her reality.

The fear of sadness. The fear of loss. The fear of guilt. The fear of embarrassment. The fear of judgment.

Even the fear of happiness. Because happiness was the first step to all the other fears.

And it was time to stop letting fear and everything it fed rule her life.

Elise dropped to her knees, facing her fear head on.

Literally.

She didn't wait to breathe. She didn't wait to blink. She didn't wait to think. Time had never been on her side, and now was no exception.

Time fixed nothing. Helped nothing. Changed nothing.

She wrapped her lips around him, closing her eyes as she took in as much as she could handle.

"Christ." Abe's hand went to her head, his fingers lacing into her hair.

His reaction emboldened her even more. She wrapped her fingers around the base of his cock as she pulled away, rolling her tongue across the head before sinking over him again.

The fingers in her hair fisted tight, holding her steady as he pulled away, stealing himself from her.

Elise scoffed.

Abe hauled her to her feet, pinning her body to his as he took her down to the bed.

"That wasn't very nice." She tried to reach for him again, but Abe grabbed her hand.

"You're not very nice." His weight pressed into her, the meeting of their bodies preventing her from reaching for him again.

"I thought I was being very nice. I thought men liked when women were on their knees."

Abe growled into her ear low and deep. "I will have you on your knees for me, Elise. But not tonight."

"But you—"

"If you're about to argue that you should be allowed to do to me what I do to you, then you can save your breath." His eyes were dark as they stared down into hers. "Our rules are not the same."

She scoffed again. "That's not fair."

"I'll remind you of that when my head's between your thighs."

Her legs pressed together at the thought, bringing a smirk to his face.

She shot him a dirty look. "Shut up. I should be able to do to you exactly what you get to do to me."

"Oh you'll get to do it, Babe." His fingers traced along her neck. "I promise one day you will be on your knees with my cock in your throat."

Her stomach flipped the thought.

"But today is not that day."

She wanted to work up the gumption to be angry about it.

Because she *was* angry about it.

But right now his fingers were sliding down her body. Moving over her collarbone. Tracing along the swell of her breast.

And that seemed to be all her brain wanted to focus on. It was like he could hijack it with nothing more than a barely-there touch.

He was a sexual terrorist in the best possible way.

His lips moved along her neck as his palm worked her breast, fingers closing on the nipple.

She'd been stupid all these years chasing men her own age.

It never occurred to her that an older man might be the way to go.

Or maybe Abe was just the way to go.

"What do you want from me, Elise?"

It was a loaded question. One she would've hesitated to answer a week ago.

A day ago.

"Everything." What she wanted from him had no limits. No boundaries. No end.

It was touch. It was closeness. It was sex.

It was peace.

The kind of quiet she'd never experienced. Something that might only be found in the comfort of being understood and accepted without judgment.

She arched into him, trying to get closer. Closer to the same man she planned to run from not so long ago, thinking it would fix everything.

Thinking she could start over again.

It wouldn't have worked. Not because she couldn't find a new place to live. Find a new job. Build a new life.

The issue was that, for the first time, she would've left something behind.

Something that might be irreplaceable.

"You can't ask for something you're not willing to offer."

Elise squeezed her eyes shut tight, closing off the fear. Locking it out. "I know."

The ache was there. The one she tried to cut away. Dig out the only way she knew how.

But for the first time she didn't want the ache to leave.

Because the ache was tied to Abe.

If it left, then that meant he left.

Abe's head tilted up, his nose nearly touching hers as he stared down into her eyes.

It was impossible to breathe around the deepening fist tightening in her stomach.

He brushed along her cheek with the backs of his fingers, dark gaze unwavering as it held hers.

She waited for him to say something, and for a second she thought he might.

Instead his forehead dropped to hers, resting gently as his hands came to cradle her face.

His touch was warm and gentle. The way he held her was more intimate than anything she'd ever experienced. The closeness anchored her. Calmed her.

Pulled her in. Fixed her in this moment instead of all the others that usually ruled her life.

For the first time she was ready to take a step forward. One that took her into the belly of the beast she'd been running from.

Elise lifted her chin, tipping her head to bring her lips to meet his.

CHAPTER 18

HE CAME INTO this with so many good intentions.

So many things he wanted to do. Ways he wanted to handle what happened between them.

Nearly every single one of them had fallen through.

And it was all because of her. Not because of the defiance and strength she showed the world. Not because she was willing to fight him every step of the way.

No. Every single time Elise took him down it was quiet. A soft moment where she showed him what no one else was allowed to see.

What she hid from the world. From herself.

A moment like this.

Her kiss was barely a brush of her lips against his, but it carried an impact strong enough to lay waste to all his plans.

Destroying them.

Destroying him.

He needed space. Room to think. To reset.

But leaving her was impossible. Putting distance between them, unfathomable.

Her hands went to his hair, fingers gentle as they moved along his scabbed scalp, tracing the line there the same way he'd traced hers.

She held him tighter, her legs tangling with his as her naked body moved under him, the barrier of his clothes keeping him from feeling the softness of her skin.

Abe yanked at his shirt, wrestling it up and off, the need to feel her making his execution clumsy.

But the glide of skin against skin made it worth the struggle.

Elise sucked in a breath as her tits rubbed against the hair of his chest, her nipples pulling tight almost immediately, dragging his attention their way.

There was so much of her he hadn't yet appreciated. Discovered. Devoured.

Owned.

He latched onto one nipple, sucking it into his mouth on a deep pull that rolled her hips and arched her back. Every move she made dragged him deeper into a pool he wouldn't be able to escape from, and he let it happen.

He would let himself drown if that's what it took to be close to her.

The heat of her hand closed around his straining dick, wrapping tight as she fisted his length. He groaned into her skin, need making him a little rougher.

A little more wild.

More demanding.

He thrust into her palm, the head of his cock bumping her belly as he fucked her hand. "Tighter."

Elise immediately did as he asked, her perfect grip forcing him to grit his teeth as his balls pulled up tight, threatening to spill their contents all over the smooth skin of her stomach.

One more thing that would have to wait for another day.

A day where he was stronger. Close enough to the surface to catch his breath.

"Enough." He pulled free from her hand the same way he'd pulled free from her mouth.

Elise scoffed exactly how she had before. "I wasn't done."

"You were absolutely done." He shoved at the front of his pants as the zipper started to dig into his skin. "If you're going to be demanding then I might need to rethink this."

"You knew what I was when you walked in this bedroom, Babe." She smirked up at him, looking more than a little problematic. "You could've walked right back out."

"You were naked." He shook his head. "That's not something I have any interest in walking away from."

"Then you should take full advantage of it." One brow barely lifted. "Just in case the opportunity doesn't present itself again."

"The opportunity will definitely present itself again." He caught one of her legs, pulling it out to the side and letting his hips settle between her thighs. "Probably in the next few hours."

Her eyes widened.

234

"Don't pretend you didn't know what you were getting into. You knew just as well as I did." He nosed along her neck, breathing in the scent of her skin. "And you have a lot of time to make up for."

And at least three months of it belonged to him.

He rocked his hips, sliding the ridge of his cock along the center of her pussy, teasing them both.

She was already wet enough that the glide slick and satiny.

But it still wasn't enough. Not for tonight.

Abe grabbed her other thigh, spreading it wide like the first as he slid down her body and laid his mouth against her pussy, burying his face in the hot and the wet.

Taking it as his own.

Her clit was already hard and swollen, making it easy to pull between his lips with a steady pulse as he pinned her in place, bringing her right to the edge before stopping.

Elise let out a loud grunt of irritation as she fought his hold, trying to get her legs back together.

"Relax." He licked across her clit to redirect her attention.

"I don't want to relax. I want to get off."

"Good. I want you to get off too." He sucked her clit again, bringing her almost to climax before stopping.

"I swear to God, I'll kill you. Right here, right now."

"If you kill me now then you'll never get fucked." He pushed up to his knees and shoved down the pants hanging at his hips. "Not by me anyway." He kicked the pants to the edge of the bed. "And I think you definitely want to get fucked by me." Abe

235

slowly lowered back between her thighs, his eyes holding hers.

Elise glared at him, her nostrils flared. She watched as he once again put his mouth on her. Once again lapped at her clit. And once again almost let her come.

She flung one arm across her eyes. "I hate you so much."

"You've said that already." He snagged a condom from the pocket of his pants and rolled it down the length of his dick. "You didn't mean it then, and you don't mean it now."

"I definitely mean it now." She whimpered as his mouth met her flesh one more time. He made slow passes across her clit with his tongue as he eased two fingers inside her. Her thighs shook a little and her cunt clamped against his fingers.

He stopped one final time.

"You're an asshole."

Abe ran his lips up her stomach, continuing to finger fuck her as he paused at one puckered nipple, teasing it with his lips and teeth. Every bit of her had to be ready for this. Every part of her strung tight with need.

Because there was no way he would allow this to be anything except what she deserved.

A promise of what was to come.

What they could be.

He stroked his thumb across her clit as his mouth found hers. He rubbed it until she was writhing, desperate for release.

Abe eased his hand free, sliding his fingers from her body before slowly dragging the head of his dick along her slit.

Elise inhaled at the change, her eyes opening as he notched against her and slowly pressed closer.

He rocked in the tiniest bit before pulling back. Then he did it again, this time going just a little farther before easing back out.

He wanted to give her time to adjust. To relax.

Inch by inch he worked his way in until he was fully seated, the length of his dick held tight by the heat of her pussy.

Abe dropped his head beside hers, taking a deep breath, steeling himself against the threat of an early completion. One that would leave them both feeling less than satisfied.

"Um." Elise's voice was quiet. "I'm no expert on this, but I think you're supposed to move."

"I think you're supposed to be quiet and give me a minute." He struggled to unclench his teeth as he spoke.

Elise wiggled a little bit under him, the shifting of her body making the moment even more difficult.

"You're about to find fucking very anticlimactic, Babe." He gripped her hip with one hand, trying to hold her still. "I just need a second."

"Do you need a second, or do you need a minute? Because you asked for both, and I'm trying to schedule out the rest of my evening."

He huffed out a little laugh. "You're a pain in the ass."

"And you're an asshole, but you don't hear me complaining."

"What was that you were doing a couple minutes ago?" Abe reached between their bodies, finding her clit with his thumb.

Elise gasped, her thighs immediately tightening at his hips as her cunt clenched around him.

He pulled in one last deep breath before fisting his free hand in the pillow behind Elise's head and easing his body out of hers. He continued to rub her clit as he pressed back in in a slow glide. Her expression barely tightened as he filled her again.

"You okay?"

"It's just—" she sucked in a breath as he pulled out and pushed in, "a lot."

"Careful." Another slow and steady thrust. "You're stroking my ego."

"Well you wouldn't let me stroke your dick."

This was what brought him here. This was why he knew she was the one for him. She talked to him. Bantered with him. Gave him as much shit as he gave her.

"One day I'll let you jerk me off. You'll see it's not as exciting as you think it is."

Her lower lip tucked between her teeth for a second before releasing. "It sounds pretty exciting to me."

His next stroke was a little faster. A little deeper.

"What else sounds exciting to you?" She needed to know she could tell him anything. Ask him for anything.

He would give it to her.

No questions. No judgment.

"Lots of things." Her eyes were closed now, lips parted.

"Like what?"

"Shut up. You're ruining my experience."

"I am your experience, Babe." He worked the thumb against her clit faster. "Without me, there would be no experience."

Her hand clamped over his mouth. "That's better." Elise rubbed her lips together, head tipping back just a little as her body started to move with his, finding the rhythm he set. "Much better."

Her fingertips dug into his skin a little as she rocked faster, meeting each glide of his body into hers.

"That's—" she made a little noise. "That's—"

Her nails dug into his cheek as her whole body went tight, legs, face, pussy.

She came undone, shuddering, cursing, laughing.

Elise's arms dropped to the mattress above her head. She smiled as she caught her breath, looking calm and relaxed and free.

Abe worked his body free of hers.

"Wait." Her smile slipped and her eyes widened. "You didn't—"

He stretched out beside her pulling the covers up over her naked body. "This wasn't about me, Elise."

She turned to him. "But—"

"No buts." He smoothed back her hair. "Go to sleep."

"But you didn't—"

"I don't need to."

Her lips tipped into a frown. "Did I do something wrong?"

"Considering you almost ended up with me coming in your mouth, on your stomach, and in your hand, yeah. You did some things wrong." He pressed a kiss to her lips. "But I won't hold that against you."

He pushed up off the mattress and headed to the bathroom, snapping off the condom and tossing it into the trash before going back into the bedroom.

Elise was still frowning at him. "I'm not happy."

"You should get used to it. I'm probably gonna make you not happy a lot."

She crossed her arms over the blanket covering her chest. "Fine. Maybe next time I'll make you not happy."

"I'll look forward to it." He slid under the covers beside her and moved in close, wrapping one arm around her body and pulling it against his. "Now stop being a pain in the ass and go to sleep."

****

"WHAT IN THE hell happened to your face?"

Abe reached up to run the fingers of one hand over the tiny moon-shaped scratches dug into his cheek. "No clue."

Pierce lifted a brow. The owner of Alaskan Security clearly didn't believe his explanation. Luckily Pierce was smart enough not to take it any further.

Probably realized he didn't actually want to know.

"Did you find anything out about the people in the Volkswagen?" He got up early this morning, leaving a warm welcoming bed, to come meet with

Pierce and Vincent to go over the events of the day before.

"Besides the fact that they're dead?" The head of GHOST shook his head. "Not much yet."

Pierce sat behind his desk, looking as polished as he normally did in his expensive suit.

But the lines around his eyes made it clear he was concerned. "Neither of the men in the vehicle carried identification of any sort. We are currently running photographs of them through a database. Hopefully we'll get a hit there."

Abe turned his attention to Vincent. "What did you find on the computer I sent?"

"That's classified information."

"Fine." Abe relaxed back in his seat. "I'll ask Heidi."

"Ms. Rucker does not have that information." Vincent said it like he really believed it.

Which was kind of funny.

"Not sure if you're aware of this, but Elise, the woman involved in yesterday's altercation, is Ms. Rucker's best friend. I can promise you if there is a shred of information that will help us identify the men trying to kill her, Heidi will find it."

Vincent's weight barely shifted from one side to the other. "Ms. Rucker had the opportunity to have access to everything GHOST knows and does. She declined."

"She declined to work for you." Abe shook his head. "Her access to all of GHOST's information is completely unrelated to that."

Vincent stared at him for a few long seconds. Finally his eyes turned toward Pierce. "We were able

241

to find some information that led us to some accounts located outside of the US. These accounts were associated with men who are known to be developing weaponry and selling it for civilian use."

"No shit." He was getting real fucking tired of Vincent's bullshit. "What else did you find?"

"What else did we need to find?" Vincent's head snapped Abe's way. "If these men believe there's a possibility the federal government will find out what they're doing, they will do anything to stop it. They could make billions of dollars selling their technology to anyone willing and able to pay for it."

"How many civilians can pay for something like that?" Abe shook his head. "I don't believe that's all there is to this."

"Civilian is a loose term, son." Vincent looked between Abe and Pierce. "You think there aren't places just like this one all over the world who are willing to pay any amount of money to access what you witnessed last night?" He tipped his head. "Because I can guarantee you there are. And right now, they're in a race to see who can get there first."

Pierce's eyes moved from Vincent to Abe and then back again. "What about terrorist organizations?"

"Terrorist is also a loose term. What do you call a man willing to spend millions on a bomb he can place and detonate from anywhere in the world? Do you call him a civilian, or do you call him a terrorist?"

"So these people." Pierce's eyes hardened. "These terrorists. They believe we have the computer that can identify them."

"Define we."

"Alaskan Security. They believe Alaskan Security currently has possession of that computer."

Vincent slowly shook his head. "No." His gaze slid Abe's way. "They believe you and your lady have the computer."

CHAPTER 19

"DID YOU NAME him yet?" Heidi dangled a feathery toy in front of the kitten's face.

"Maybe." Elise slid her feet into the high heels she set out to wear this morning. "I was thinking maybe Danish?"

"Oh my gosh I love that." Heidi smiled wide as the little kitten grabbed a hold of the end of the toy, smacking at it with his paws as he chased it across the floor. "And you love Danish. It's perfect."

"Is it?" Jareth told her to pick something important to her, and it seemed silly to pick something like a Danish.

But when she thought about Danishes, she thought about Alaskan Security. All the mornings she spent there. All the people who took a few minutes to check in while they ate a Danish of their own.

"It is. He looks like a Danish." Heidi glanced her way, looking her up and down. Her brows came together. "Did you change your hair? You look different."

"Hair's still the same." Elise grabbed her bag from the counter. "Nothing is different. I'm still the same boring me."

Heidi started laughing, tipping over a little as she did. "Boring my ass." She wiggled her brows. "Did you bone Abe yet?"

"Maybe." She'd always tried to talk a good talk. Make it seem like she had done more than she really had.

But now the talk seemed less important.

"Dammit. I told you everything about Shawn."

Elise scoffed. "You absolutely did not. Don't pretend like you did."

"Well I told you about every guy before him." Heidi worked her way up from the floor, which was no easy feat, considering her belly was getting bigger every day.

Elise reached out a hand, gripping tight and helping hoist Heidi up off the floor. "And they all sucked."

"They did suck." Heidi looked her up and down. "So can I take that to mean Abraham does not suck?"

"Abraham does not suck." Elise pulled open the door. "Come on, I'm hungry for a Danish."

"Me too." Heidi hooked one arm through Elise's as they walked toward the main kitchen in the rooming house. "I'm so glad you're back here. I missed you."

"I missed you too." Elise stood at the counter as Heidi worked her way through the assortment of food spread across it. "I'm sorry I was going to leave."

"Don't be sorry. I think about leaving here all the time." Heidi dropped a cheese Danish onto her plate. "Usually when Vincent pisses me off. Or when Pierce pisses me off. Or when Shawn pisses me off." She pursed her lips. "So it's usually every day. Sometimes twice a day."

"Yeah, but you don't actually try to leave and end up getting kidnapped."

"Don't let them hear you say you were kidnapped. Because kidnapping only counts if—"

"I know. It only counts if you actually make it into the car." Elise grabbed the plate. "He did knock me out though. That counts for something, right?"

"I'll have to ask Shawn." Heidi grabbed the water she carried everywhere with her. "I can't keep it all straight. They have so many stupid rules."

"I'm going to make a chart. Blow it up into a poster size. Print it out, have it laminated, and hang it in all the break rooms." Elise opened the fridge and grabbed a bottle of water, tucking it under her arm as she followed Heidi to the walkway connecting the rooming building and the main offices.

"You should make a little one too. One we can all carry around with us and whip it out whenever we need it." Heidi opened the door to the main building. "We could call it a bullshit brochure." She snorted out a laugh, but her smile was short-lived.

Vincent stepped out of Pierce's office and stood in the hall in front of them.

Heidi scowled at him. "Morning."

Vincent tipped his head their way. "Ms. Rucker, Ms. Foley."

246

"Don't give me that fancy bullshit." Heidi stared him down. "You almost got my best friend killed yesterday." Her brows lifted. "And the day before that." Her eyes narrowed. "I hope you gave Pierce the information he needed to handle this, otherwise I'll have to find a way to make your life a living hell."

"What makes you believe my life isn't already a living hell, Ms. Rucker?"

That stopped Heidi in her tracks.

Elise stared at Vincent. The man was as stoic as it came. Practically emotionless.

It was impossible to imagine him miserable.

It was also impossible to imagine him happy.

Or sad.

Or any other sort of way normal humans were.

Pierce stepped out of his office, with Abe right behind him. "GHOST and Alaskan Security are working together to solve the problem that belongs to both of us."

"Well it's nice to see you're finally taking responsibility for something." Heidi had recovered from her temporary shock. "Because you're the one with the stupid fucking computer everyone is all wound up about."

"The computer was sent to me, Ms. Rucker. I did not seek it out myself."

"Well I can promise you we won't be making that mistake again." Heidi took a drink of her water before continuing. "Next time we'll be keeping it and you can try to get into our system to find the information we collect, because it took me almost three months to get into yours."

Vincent's eyes barely widened, making it clear he had no idea Heidi managed to get into the data recovered from the computer.

It was a tiny reaction, but one Heidi did not miss. "What? Did you think I would just sit around waiting for you to share what you knew with the rest of the class?"

Vincent and Heidi were caught in a stare down. At this point it was anyone's guess who would win.

"In my office. Now." Pierce spun on his heel and marched straight into his office.

Heidi didn't even bother asking who he was talking to. She smirked at Vincent as she walked past, following Pierce.

Elise took a bite of her Danish as she watched Vincent. "I think he was talking to you too."

Vincent didn't respond as he turned and followed Heidi into Pierce's office, closing the door behind him.

"I tried to warn him." Abe came to her side wrapping one arm around her waist and pulling her close. "How's your Danish?"

"Perfect." She leaned into his lips as he pressed them to her temple. "How was your protein shake?"

"Not as good as a Danish." He grinned. "But a necessary evil."

"Definitely evil." As much as she hated to, she had to step away from the warmth of his embrace and go into her office. She was already behind, and the only way to catch up was to buckle down and do what needed to be done.

Which unfortunately, did not include standing around with Abe.

Sadly.

"What's on your docket for the day?" Abe followed her into the office directly across the hall from Pierce's.

"Well," she stared at the desk she'd tidied up before she tried to leave, "I guess I need to get back to work."

"I'm sure everyone around here will be thrilled." He dropped down into the chair across from her desk, stretching his legs out in front of him. "What are you doing for lunch?"

"Are you going to get all obsessed with me now?" Elise smothered a smile as she turned away from him.

"Babe, I've been obsessed with you. You just didn't know it yet."

This time she couldn't stop her smile. "I usually just grab something simple and snack for lunch."

"Perfect." Abe stood up. "I'll be back to pick you up at the end of the day then."

"Pick me up? Where are you taking me?"

"Home." He tipped his head. "As close to home as we can get right now." Abe came close, his hands coming to rest on her hips. "Our dinner options are pretty limited for a while. But I promise I'll make it up to you soon."

"You better. A girl can't live on Danish and Danish alone." She paused, mulling over her next words. "I'm thinking about naming the kitten Danish. What do you think?"

"I think it's fantastically inaccurate." He smiled as he leaned in to press a kiss to her lips. "No one will realize he's a savage."

"He's not savage, he's feral."

Abe shot her a wink as he backed towards the door. "Just like his mama."

Then he was gone, leaving her to do what she said she had to do.

"Ugh." Elise dropped down to her chair and let her head fall back against the rest.

"What's the matter? Abraham wouldn't give you any office dick?" Heidi came straight in and sat down in the seat Abe had just vacated. "Usually threatening to go take care of things myself nips that right in the bud."

"That's a good idea. I'll hang on to that." Elise flipped open the lid of her laptop. "But I was not actually trying to get him to give me any office dick."

The idea of office dick never occurred to her.

But now that it had…

"Don't get distracted right now. I know it's hard, but Abe's dick will still be there when you're done working." Heidi snorted. "Hard."

"Did you come in here to make sexual innuendo jokes, or are you going to tell me what was on that computer?" It was the reason she and Heidi were friends. Neither of them took anything too personally. Neither of them got offended when the other one said what they meant.

And they both tended to be considered aggressive.

Which she used to think was a bad thing, but now…

"Technically I don't know what was on the computer." Heidi turned to peek over one shoulder at the open door, before leaning closer. "Yet." She lowered her voice. "But I will. I've got a program running that should be able to decode the encryptions Vincent used."

"He encrypted it?" Elise shook her head. "What an asshole."

"I'm not sure he does it to be an asshole." Heidi took another drink. "Specifically." She huffed out a breath. "I think he does it thinking the more we know the more danger we would be in."

"More danger? We could be in *more* danger? In case Vincent missed it, they've tried to kidnap me once and kill me at least three times." Luckily they hadn't succeeded in any of it, mostly because of Abe.

"What I don't get is why they would think we're the ones who have the computer. Anyone who knows anything would have to realize we're working with someone bigger than us." Heidi huffed out a breath. "I mean we can make bodies disappear for Christ's sake. That shit doesn't happen by magic."

"Why do you think they're coming after us then?"

Heidi dropped her head back and groaned. "Unfortunately, there's only one reason I can come up with." She straightened, eyes leveling on Elise. "I think Vincent told them we had it."

****

"I KNOW IT'S not fine dining, but I was hoping it would work in a pinch."

Elise lifted her eyes to where Abe sat across from her. "It looks just as good as anything I could get in a restaurant."

"That doesn't explain why you haven't put a single bite in your mouth." He lifted a brow. "Are you scared?"

"No." She scooped up a bite of noodles with the take-out style chopsticks Abe dropped in the bowl, shoving them into her mouth as proof she wasn't scared of his cooking.

Which seemed pretty on par with her cooking, so that was nice.

Abe's expression sharpened. "What happened today?"

"Nothing." She didn't bother trying to hide the mouthful of food as she spoke. At this point Abe had seen the worst she had to offer, which made talking with her mouth full seem like it wasn't a big deal.

"That's fine if you don't want to talk about it." He collected some of his own ramen and took a bite.

"It's not that I don't want to talk about it." She poked at the fried egg he'd added on top of their cardboard bowl ramen.

"But there is something."

She moved around a few of the green onions he'd sliced and sprinkled over the egg. "Maybe."

"I don't expect you to want to talk to me about everything right away, Elise."

She looked up to find his eyes on her. "It's not that I don't want to talk to you about it."

"You don't have to explain it. You're allowed to keep things to yourself." His eyes moved over her face. "As long as you're okay and safe, that's all I care about."

That was where this got a little sticky.

252

If Heidi was right, and Vincent was the reason these people set their sights on Alaskan Security, then she might not be safe.

None of them would be.

Abe included.

"Heidi thinks Vincent told these people that we have the computer."

It wasn't fear for herself that pulled the words from her mouth. It wasn't even fear for her friend that prompted the confession.

It was fear for Abe.

And for the first time in her life, she had zero desire to run from it.

Abe was very still, elbows resting on his knees, hands clasped in front of him as he looked across the coffee table at her. "Has she told anyone else she thinks this?"

"I don't know." Knowing Heidi, it was difficult to tell what she might have done with the information. She could be keeping it to herself so she could use it to her benefit.

She could have told all of Intel.

She might have called Vincent and ripped him a new asshole because of it.

There was just no telling. Heidi was unpredictable before, but now that she was pregnant?

Her best friend was completely—

Feral.

Abe picked up his chopsticks and went back to digging at his soup. "Vincent mentioned that he believed these people were focusing on you and me because they believed we had the computer."

Elise's throat tightened on an involuntary swallow. "So maybe Vincent didn't tell them Alaskan Security had the computer. Maybe he told them *we* have it."

Abe barely nodded. "Maybe."

"Well wouldn't that just suck a bag of dicks."

Abe snorted. "Did Heidi expand your vocabulary, or did you expand hers?"

"Depends." Elise managed a little bit of a smile. "She learned *suck a bag of dicks* from me."

"I'm impressed."

"Just because I hadn't had sex didn't mean I was innocent." She ate a little bit of the perfectly-cooked egg.

"Babe, you're the least innocent person I've ever met."

She scoffed, but the comment felt oddly flattering.

"Don't act like you didn't already know." He tipped up his bowl to drink a little of the broth.

Elise went back to digging through her soup, the conversation bringing on a sense of melancholy.

Staying in Alaska was going to be complicated. Not because she didn't like it here. Not because she didn't enjoy the people around her. Not because she didn't love her job.

The problem was that those things made it difficult for her to continue on the way she had been going.

Being around people who made her feel accepted made it more difficult not to accept herself.

254

But the process of learning to accept herself was going to be unbelievably painful.

One part in particular.

"My mom died when I was little." She didn't look up from her soup. "She killed herself."

She waited for the inevitable *I'm sorry*. When it didn't come her eyes moved to the man across from her. Abe sat silently, watching her with a patient gaze.

"My father said she was overwhelmed. That I cried too much at night. That I made too many messes. That she couldn't handle being my mother."

The patience in Abe's eyes evaporated in an instant, the soft understanding immediately replaced by an anger so sharp it would make her take a step back if she didn't know him so well. "Where is your father now?"

"I don't know. He got remarried after I graduated high school. Went to live with his new wife and her kids."

"What about you?"

"It was actually better. I didn't have to face him every day anymore. Didn't have to deal with the way he looked at me." Her father really believed the things he told her.

He really believed she was the reason her mother killed herself. It was there in everything he said. Everything he did.

Abe's nostrils flared as he leaned back against the couch, raking one hand through his hair. "He's lucky I can't leave right now, because if I could—"

"If you could then I would still want you to stay here." Dealing with her childhood was always an insurmountable task.

A mountain she could never consider trying to climb.

But in this moment she realized she didn't have to climb the mountain.

The mountain was already behind her.

"You know it's not your fault, right?"

Elise thought on it for a minute. She was older now than her mother was when she died.

While the life she lived was very different from the one her mother had, she could still examine it through an adult's eyes. "I know that."

Abe studied her for a minute. "Good."

"Tomorrow I might not know it though." She held his eyes. He needed to know it was a possibility. That she would still have moments where everything was too much. Where she doubted herself.

"That's okay. We'll cross that bridge when we come to it."

"It's not a bridge. It's a mountain."

The line of his mouth softened. "Fine. We'll cross that mountain when we come to it."

Elise tipped her head in a little nod. "Okay." She went back to her soup, taking a couple more bites as she kicked off her shoes. "Since you made dinner tonight does that mean I have to make dinner tomorrow?"

"Absolutely it does. And you better bring it." Abe smiled at her across the coffee table as he switched on the television and moved through the screens to find his favorite trashy show. "And my instant ramen is going to be hard to beat."

CHAPTER 20

"WHEN DID SHE tell you this?" Pierce leaned back in his chair and took a sip of the scotch he'd been nursing since Abe walked into his office.

The owner of Alaskan Security looked more than a little tired.

Hell, they were all more than a little tired at this point.

They'd managed to go for years, flying under the radar, handling what needed to be handled, all without running into the sort of problems they'd had in the past year.

"A couple hours ago."

"Does she know you're here telling me?"

"Yes." They'd discussed it at length.

Decided together this was their only option.

"Ms. Rucker told me this morning that she was able to obtain the data, but explained it was completely indecipherable."

"Technically that was true this morning." Apparently Heidi wanted Vincent to think that while she had managed to get to the information, she was unable to decode it. "But I think that changed this afternoon. From what Elise said Heidi was able to identify what appeared to be a list of names."

Pierce went very still. "Names?"

Abe nodded. "She believes it's a list of the people involved in the money laundering website." He paused, hating to voice the next bit. "Which was possibly being done to hide the funds changing hands during the buying and selling of weapons like what we witnessed last night."

As awful and violating as the website Kyle and Rob supplied videos for was, it was the simplest part of this situation.

"They were moving millions through that site." Pierce poured more scotch into his glass, polishing off the last bit in the bottle in one swallow.

"Yup." And Alaskan Security was responsible for taking it down, shuttering their payment system in an instant.

"Christ." Pierce's glass hit the table hard enough that Abe almost expected it to shatter. Luckily the tumbler held it together.

Hopefully they could do the same.

"Has Heidi found the locations of the names on the list?" Pierce was working through this the same way he and Elise had.

Abe shook his head. "Not yet, but my guess is she'll probably stay up all night until she figures it out."

Elise was Heidi's best friend. Knowing Elise was wrapped up in this would make Heidi ten times more dangerous than she usually was.

And that woman was dangerous as hell.

259

"Where are they now?" Pierce didn't look exceptionally excited about the prospect of confronting Heidi and the rest of her cohorts.

Neither was Abe, which is why he came to Pierce for backup. "Right now there's at least five of them in my room."

Pierce paused. "Which five?"

This was going to make Pierce even less happy. "Heidi, Elise, Lennie, Eva, and Mona."

Pierce raked one hand through his hair, knocking his slicked-back style loose. "Fuckin' hell."

"I thought you might say that." Abe stretched his legs out in front of him. "Almost half of them are sober, if that makes it any better."

"I'm confident their level of sobriety is irrelevant." Pierce was the whole reason the women were in Alaska in the first place. He was smart enough to realize that the female perspective was something they were lacking, and that obtaining it was what could set them apart from their competition.

And maybe that's why things had changed. Maybe their competition realized what a threat they were now.

"All right." Pierce stood from his chair, tucking the button at the front of his suit into place. "Let's go get this over with."

The halls were silent as they walked back to the rooming building and up to the second floor, which made the noise that came out when he opened the door all the more jarring.

It didn't take a full headcount to see that the number of women in his room had grown since he left. Members of Intel were everywhere. Lounging on the couch. Stretched across the floor. Perched on the stools at the small bar adjoining the kitchen.

And every one of them appeared to be having one hell of a great time.

Which made him feel a little guilty that he was about to piss on their parade.

Mona was the first to notice them. Her cool blue gaze rested on Pierce, raking up and down his body in a slow sweep. One pale blonde brow slowly lifted.

Pierce cleared his throat.

The women continued on as they were, eating, drinking, and chatting, oblivious to the two men standing there.

Pierce took another step, moving deeper into the suite. He cleared his throat again.

This time Elise looked up. She leaned into Heidi's ear and whispered something.

Heidi's head slowly turned their way. "It took you freaking long enough."

Both Pierce's brows jumped up.

Heidi hoisted her way out of the chair she was sitting in. She went to the bar and snagged a file from the top, holding it out as she walked their way. "You can decide what you do with this."

Pierce took the file and flipped it open, his eyes quickly scanning the top page. "You already know the identities of the men listed in the computer."

Heidi snorted. "Of course I know. Is that something you think I would drag my ass on?"

Pierce flipped the file closed, holding it in one hand as it dropped down to his side. "Is Vincent aware that you have this knowledge?"

"Now you're starting to offend me." Heidi crossed her arms over her chest, resting them on the swell of her growing belly. "No. Vincent doesn't know that I have this knowledge." She rolled her eyes up and to one side. "He should though. If he paid attention to anything but the stick up his ass."

"I'll be sure to make that suggestion."

"I already have." Heidi smirked. "He doesn't seem open to self-improvement."

Pierce's eyes moved across the suite. "Is there anything I can get you ladies before I go?"

Pierce was a smart man. Smart enough to know a large part of his company's value was contained in this small space.

"Just go find those dicks before they try to kill my friend again." Heidi's expression turned very serious. "Because if they hurt her, I will do way worse than kill them."

"That will be unnecessary." Pierce's gaze dragged across to where his wife sat. "The situation will be handled."

"I sure as fuck hope so." Heidi pointed a finger from each hand at her pregnant belly. "Because I sure as heck don't want to deal with these two in a teeny tiny suite. I really want to be in my house by the time they fall out."

"Of course you do. I completely understand. I will do everything in my power to ensure you have a safe home to bring your daughters to."

Heidi's eyes softened. "I know you will." She grinned at the owner of Alaskan Security. "Because you don't want two crying babies here any more than I do."

Pierce smiled back at her. "That is accurate." He turned to Abe. "Collect Rogue. We will meet in ten minutes."

Abe tipped his head in a nod. "We will be there." He looked into the suite one final time, catching Elise's eyes.

She gave him a soft smile and a little wave.

"Hopefully Heidi has everything we need to find these bastards." He pulled his eyes from where Elise sat. "Because Heidi will have to get in line to fuck them up." Abe walked out into the hall, pulling his phone from his pocket.

"As will you." Pierce passed him, heading straight for the stairway to the main floor. "Ten minutes."

"Yup." Abe had already dialed Shawn's number.

He picked up on the first ring. "Do you need me to come get her?" He sounded almost hopeful, a sentiment Abe now understood.

"Definitely not. She might be saving everyone's ass. I'd let her do whatever in the hell she wanted to do." Abe walked fast, knocking on Wade's door before moving to the next suite to knock on Brock's door. "She found a list of names from the computer."

"You're shitting me."

"Nope. Pierce has them in a file. We're meeting him in ten minutes to go over everything."

Brock pulled open his door, beer in hand. Wade stood right behind him.

Abe waved them his direction as he continued to talk to Shawn. "I don't know how she did it, but hopefully she's right. I'm ready to get this bullshit over with."

"You and everyone else."

"I've got Brock and Wade. I'll get Tyson and Jamison. You get the rest of the team." Abe didn't wait for Shawn to answer before disconnecting the line.

Right now wasn't the time to worry about proper phone call etiquette.

"We're meeting Pierce in ten minutes." Abe checked his watch. "Eight minutes."

"Did you say Heidi found the names of the motherfuckers on the computer?" Brock hopped along behind him, working one foot into a shoe as he tried not to spill his beer.

"She said she did. Pierce has what she found." Abe rushed down the stairs, going to the first floor where the single rooms were located. He banged on Tyson's and Jamison's doors just like he had Brock's and Wade's.

"That would be fucking fantastic." Brock tossed his empty bottle in the recycle bin as they passed the kitchen in the rooming house.

Abe called down the hall as Tyson and Jamison opened their doors. "We've got a meeting."

By the time they reached the primary conference room, Pierce was already there, along with Shawn, Rico, and Nate. Shawn sat next to Pierce, looking through the file with him.

"Anything interesting?" He hoped to God there was something worthwhile in that thing, but he had his doubts. Heidi was amazing. Her abilities unmatched.

That's why Vincent tried to seduce her away from them.

But everyone had their limits. And if these guys were trying to do what it seemed like they were—

Finding them would be next to impossible.

Shawn raised his brows and tipped his head to one side. "There's a lot interesting in here."

"Is it what Vincent claimed it was? Is this about weapons?" Abe pulled out a chair and sat down, trying to force himself to relax.

Usually that wasn't an issue. There was nothing more he enjoyed than going out on an op. The possibility of excitement. The probability of danger.

But up until now nothing that was on the line belonged to him.

And it appeared that might change things.

"It would that seem if it is, GHOST did not find that information on the computer." Pierce looked down at another paper before passing it Shawn's way. "If they did, Ms. Rucker did not include it in her report."

"Then she didn't find it, which means it wasn't there." Shawn passed the paper in his hand Abe's way. "But that doesn't mean she's not currently looking for where GHOST did find that information."

"She's currently hanging out with the rest of Intel in my room." Abe focused on the lines of text in front of him, looking for anything familiar. Any names that jumped out at him.

"That doesn't mean she's not looking. She's usually got at least three programs running at all times." Shawn sent another piece of paper Abe's way. "My money says she'll be here in under fifteen minutes."

"Good. She can explain these reports to us." So far he'd counted ten names on the papers. Some of them were clearly American, but many of them were not. "These guys are all over the place."

"I would count that in our favor." Pierce passed the final paper around. "My hope is that none of the large players will be in this area at all."

Another thing that would work in their favor. "If they were, things would have certainly been more organized."

"I am making the same assumption." Pierce steepled his fingers, touching his pointers to his mouth as he stared across the room.

Abe sent the stack of information down the line, passing it off to Wade and Brock as Dutch and Reed came into the room. Dutch sat down at Pierce's other side. "What did she find?"

"More than I expected." Pierce dropped his hands and tipped his head toward Shawn. "I don't want to wait for her. Call her and have her come here now."

"I'm happy to do that, but you should know she's probably not going to come alone."

"Even better." Pierce rubbed both hands over his face. "I'm interested to see what Intel thinks of this."

Shawn swiped across his phone and pressed it against his ear.

His eyes roamed the room as he waited for Heidi to pick up.

The sound of her laughing on the other end of the line was loud enough for the room to hear. "Sounds like you're having a good time." Shawn was quiet for a second as Heidi spoke, her words loud but too muddled to identify. He glanced toward Pierce. "We need you in the conference room. We have a few questions."

Shawn set the phone down on the desk in front of him.

Pierce leaned forward. "Is she coming?"

Shawn dug the tips of his fingers into his eyes. "She's coming."

"How much are we telling them?" Jamison was probably the only one in the room who didn't already know the answer to that question. It was the only way they could continue from here.

Intel would have to be on the same page as everyone else. Always.

"Everything." Pierce's eyes moved from man to man. "From this point forward, Intel knows everything."

"What about Elise?" As much as Abe knew he should be concerned about Intel's knowledge of the situation, he was more worried about Elise. She was making so many strides so quickly, and at some point she would have a setback.

Hopefully knowing what was happening would keep that under control until all of this was over.

Because he would kill anyone who set Elise back.

Pierce leaned forward, folding his hands on the table in front of him. "I don't think it will matter. She will know everything whether we tell her or not."

Abe heard the women before he saw them. Their voices carried down the hall, pulling every man in the room to his feet.

Mona came through the door first, her lips lifted in a small smile as she crossed the room.

Heidi and Eva followed her, then Lennie and Elise, followed by the rest of the women who worked at Alaskan Security.

A tribe of untouchables, ready to take down any threat in their path.

"Please," Pierce motioned to the vacated chairs around the table, "sit."

"No thanks." Heidi stood, her arms crossed. "My sciatica is acting up." Her eyes went to the folder. "I'm assuming you looked at that?"

"Of course." Pierce shifted a little on his feet as every woman continued to stand, lined shoulder to shoulder. "I am interested to hear what you think."

"What I think?"

"Not just you." Pierce looked down the line of women. "All of you."

Heidi looked toward Eva. "You want to go first?"

Brock took a step toward her, but Eva's eyes snapped to where he stood, narrowing as they pinned him in place.

These women didn't need backup. Not when they had each other.

Abe lowered into his seat, taking his place in the current situation.

The rest of his team followed suit, allowing the women to hold the floor they owned.

"I think we're sitting at both ends of the spectrum." Eva pointed to the file in front of Pierce. "The guys listed in there are at the top. They are the ones with the money and the power."

Mona picked up where Eva left off. "The men we're dealing with here are close to the bottom. Not quite as far down as Rob and Kyle and Chandler were, but pretty close."

"And they're panicking." Lennie smiled Rico's way before flattening her lips out and finishing her thought. "We are suspicious that the men in that folder don't even know they've been exposed."

"So you believe what we're dealing with right now is damage control." Pierce looked toward Abe as the gravity of the situation settled over the room. "They're hoping to get the computer back before we find this list of names."

Heidi tipped her head from one side to the other. "Sort of. Technically the list of names probably wasn't on the computer."

"That's our guess as to why it took Vincent so long to find them." Harlow's eyes leveled on Abe. "He had to connect some pretty slim dots. Dots that only he would have access to."

Sending the computer to Vincent had been one of the most difficult calls he'd ever had to make. Partly because he believed in Intel's abilities so much more than he believed in GHOST's.

But at the end of the day, he'd decided they were too close to be able to effectively do what needed to be done. Not a single one of them was impartial. Not in the way they needed to be. Not Intel, and sure as hell not Rogue.

"Do you think Vincent knows anything else?" Pierce focused his question on Heidi. She seemed to be the one who understood the head of GHOST the best. Maybe because, had the cards been dealt a different way, she might be the next in line to take his position.

"Vincent always seems to show up when he's out of ideas." Heidi smirked a little. "So my guess is that he's out of ideas and out of intelligence."

"Fantastic." Pierce's shoulders relaxed as everyone in the room stood a little taller.

Once again they were in the position of being needed by Vincent, and that was a useful place to be.

"What do we have?" Pierce scanned the line of women. "Anything of value?"

Harlow checked her watch. "We should have something soon." She smiled at Heidi. "We've got a few things working."

Harlow on her own was one of the biggest assets at Alaskan Security, as was Heidi.

But put them together?

Honestly, Vincent had to know he couldn't compete.

And that was before you factored in the rest of Intel. The women were a force Vincent simply couldn't touch.

But Vincent wasn't a stupid man. He had to know all this.

"Shit." Abe dropped his head back to stare at the ceiling.

"What's wrong?" The alarm in Pierce's tone was obvious.

"Nothing. Technically." Abe turned to Heidi. "I think Vincent will start giving you information if you stop having so much fun finding it."

Heidi stared back at him.

"You're not really getting one over on him. He knows you're going to find it. He waits until you do, knowing we'll be able to take it farther than he can."

"I'm not sure that's the case." Pierce's skepticism made sense. It was still wrong. "Vincent has access to more than we could dream of."

"That's true, but he's missing something way more important than information." Abe's eyes settled on Elise. "Emotion."

The room went quiet, eyes moving around the space. Husbands looking at their wives. Men looking at the mothers of their children. Friends looking at friends.

"I don't think that's entirely true." Mona focused on Heidi. "Respect is an emotion."

Heidi's face shifted with a slow, sly smile. "That means Vincent is one of us."

"Don't tell him that. He'll get all butthurt about it." Harlow rolled her eyes. "He likes to think he's the fucking tin man."

Pierce steepled his fingers again, tapping the tips together the way he did when he considered something big. His eyes finally lifted, moving around the room. "If Vincent is one of us, then we are on his team as much as he is on ours." His gaze went straight to Heidi. "That means no more games."

She huffed out a loud sigh, head dropping back. "Fine."

CHAPTER 21

"LOOKS LIKE YOU had an interesting evening." Abe scanned the suite, his eyes moving over the cracker crumbs and paper plates strewn across nearly every surface.

She'd been working to clean up the mess for the better part of a half-hour, while waiting for Abe to return from wherever he was. "I'm guessing your evening was just as interesting as mine."

He tipped his head to one side. "Interesting is relative." He snagged a couple of empty wine bottles from the coffee table. "Mine had less booze and less food."

"Good. Just the way you like it." Elise held out the bin for recycling.

"I'm letting myself appreciate food more than I used to." He tossed the bottles in before turning to gather more. "I'm trying to find balance in my life."

"I'm not sure balance is something that really exists." Elise went to the sink and ran a dish rag under the hot tap. "I think everyone believes it does, but in reality nothing is ever balanced."

She'd spent her life believing she was the only one unbalanced. The only one struggling to find some sort of peaceful resolution for all the problems and difficulties she faced.

But now Elise was pretty sure everyone felt exactly the same way she did.

Lost.

Maybe they didn't take things to the same extreme she had, trying to find that balance and that peace, but they still struggled. Still fought in ways she probably couldn't understand. The same way they couldn't understand her ways.

Abe's brows slowly lifted. "Interesting assessment."

"Thanks. I'm trying something new." Exploring her own emotions was a dangerous thing, something she wasn't currently sure she was capable of really doing.

But analyzing other people's feelings?

That she was comfortable with. And hopefully it would be a gateway. A safety zone of sorts as she inched closer to where she wanted to be.

"I would say balance is easier to attain the fewer things you have to juggle." Abe picked up the empty trays from the bar and stacked them in the sink. "Up until recently, I thought I led a pretty balanced life." He went to work rinsing the remnants of cheese and cracker, and vegetables and dip, from the trays. "But my life was pretty simple. I think the less simple your life is, the more difficult it is to find balance."

"Why did you choose simple?" Asking Abe questions about his life was as tricky as asking herself questions about her own. The potential pitfalls were too many to count.

What if Abe wanted something very different than she did?

What if he imagined the picket fence with kids running around the yard calling him daddy?

If he did, then ultimately it was better to find that out now. When losing him might still be something small enough she could deal with it.

"Because I'm selfish." He lifted one shoulder. "I liked my life the way it was. I didn't want to sacrifice any of it."

Elise struggled to swallow. "Oh."

His answer clarified nothing, and only created more questions, all of which seemed unaskable.

Their possible answers, unhearable.

"I never wanted the same things most people want from life, Elise." Abe opened the small dishwasher and loaded in the trays. "I wanted to experience the world. I wanted freedom. I wanted to live a life that belonged only to me." He shook his head. "That's not what most people want, and I knew that."

"What do most people want?"

He turned to face her, leaning against the counter as he dried off his hands. "What you see happening all around us. Marriage. Children. The All-American dream."

"That doesn't sound like a dream to everyone." For some people it was a nightmare.

A scenario that filled them with dread instead of happiness and longing.

274

"I don't want to have children, Elise." Abe held her gaze, his expression as serious as the situation warranted. "Not now, not ever."

He said it easily. Without fear of judgment.

The way only a man could.

Because the same statement coming from a woman was chastised. Un-believed. Unendingly questioned.

You're too young to make that decision.

You'll change your mind.

Every woman wants a child.

She'd heard them all. "Is that why you think you're selfish?"

How can you be so selfish?

That was her least favorite response when someone found out she didn't want to have a child. Because her reasons were anything but selfish.

Abe's brows came together. "You know selfish isn't a bad word, don't you?"

"Of course it's a bad word." Her whole life she'd been called selfish by everyone around her. Her father. People who claimed to be her friends. Coworkers.

Men.

"Being selfish isn't a bad thing." Abe slowly came her way, tossing the towel onto the counter as he walked. "Not if what you're doing doesn't hurt anyone else."

Elise laughed. "That's not how people act." God forbid you do something because it's what you want. What you need.

They lived in a society that created people, women especially, who felt guilty for taking time for themselves.

Living life for themselves.

Women were supposed to put everyone else first. Everyone else's feelings. Everyone else's desires.

Everyone else's needs.

Then suffer in silence when their own weren't met.

"People take it personally when you don't put them first." She'd seen it time and time again.

"Not the right people." Abe stopped right in front of her, one of his hands catching her arm, the tips of his fingers tracing down her skin as they moved toward her hand. "The right people want you to be happy. They want you to take care of yourself. They want you to live the life you want."

"I must not know very many of the right people then." She spent her life suffering in silence. Knowing that her pain was hers alone. That no one else cared because they were only worried about themselves.

"Don't you?" Abe sounded skeptical. "Because I think there's a whole team of people who want you to be happy."

Elise's eyes drifted to the door leading to the hallway of the rooming building. "They don't know I'm unhappy."

"What do you think would happen if they did?" Abe's voice was soft. Gentle.

Being unhappy was a secret she'd guarded fiercely her whole life. One Elise went to great lengths to keep hidden.

"I think they would judge me." And she wouldn't blame them if they did.

She judged herself.

"You're not giving them enough credit." Abe's blue eyes held hers. "You are expecting them to disappoint you."

"Everyone always does." It wasn't a personal attack. Everyone included herself.

She'd probably disappointed herself more than anyone else had.

"The wrong people will always disappoint you, and up until now you've known a lot of the wrong people, Babe."

"How do you tell the wrong people from the right people?"

Abe's lips lifted in a slow smile. "The right people will always show up for you. Even when you don't want them there. Even when you've tried to run away from them."

"So you're saying the right people are a pain in the ass?"

His smile widened. "Absolutely."

"This wouldn't have anything to do with me calling you a pain in the ass, would it?" His smile was almost contagious. Somehow Abe could take the heaviest conversation and keep her from feeling its weight. Keep her from sliding toward dangerous waters.

"I mean," he lifted her hand and brushed his lips across the inside of her wrist, "you're the one who said it."

Elise let out a sigh, one that sounded much heavier than she felt. "Now I can't tell you when you're being a pain in the ass, because you will just think I'm saying you're a nice person."

"You like how I did that?" Abe's lips continued up the inside of her arm as he laced it around his neck.

"You're a sneaky man." It was true in every sense of the word.

He could creep up on men and take them out with a single shot.

He could move past walls built over a lifetime, finding his way into protected spaces without any warning.

Without any sound.

"All those years of training have finally paid off."

It was easy to slip into a conversation that was so much more relaxed than it should be. "I'm pretty sure that's not how anyone intended for them to be used."

"You'd be surprised what the intended use is." Abe's fingers slid along the side of her face, his palm cradling her cheek. "It's all about picking your battles, Babe."

"Is that what I am? A battle?" She couldn't work up the tiniest bit of offence at the possibility.

Because if she was a battle, then he'd decided she was worth fighting for.

"For sure." Abe's lips whispered across hers. "Best one I've ever been in."

She smiled against his mouth. "It's probably not over."

"I'm counting on that." Abe nipped at her lower lip. "I'm hoping it will go on forever."

"You want me to fight you forever?"

278

"You're a warrior, Babe. You can't help it."

The ease of the moment slipped away, dragging all her focus to his eyes. To the honesty there.

The understanding.

Abe didn't think she was difficult when she argued.

He didn't think she was a bitch when she disagreed.

He didn't think she was a pain in the ass when she fought.

He thought she was a warrior.

It was one little change. A tiny shift in how someone else viewed her.

And it made her question how she viewed herself.

"I never thought of it that way."

His thumb stroked over her cheek. "I know."

Her mind stumbled along this new possibility, fighting for what she didn't think existed.

Balance.

Maybe Abe was right about more than she realized.

Maybe balance was possible.

Maybe it just didn't look the way she thought it did.

Maybe balance was more about understanding. Acceptance.

Two things she'd never tried to turn inward.

"You're really smart."

His lips lifted at the corners. "It comes with age."

"You are kind of old." Elise reached up to slide her fingers across the grey scattered through his hair.

"You're welcome."

"It is kind of working out in my favor, isn't it?" She moved a little close. "And to be honest, the grey hair really does it for me."

"That's good since it's probably only going to get greyer with you in my life."

Elise managed a scoff just as he hefted her up, one hand banding across her back as the other lifted one of her legs, wrapping it around his waist as he carried her though the suite. "If that's how it works then my hair will be grey next week."

"Good. We'll match then." He tossed her onto the bed. "They say couples start to look alike anyway."

"There's worse people I could look like." She caught her lower lip between her teeth as Abe peeled off his shirt. "The chest hair might be an issue though."

"You like it." He crawled over her.

"I do." Elise immediately spread her fingers across his chest, digging into the slightly rough texture of the hair in question. "But I don't think it would look as good on me."

He nosed up the side of her neck. "Anything would look good on you, Babe."

There was no stopping the laugh that came all the way from deep in her belly. "I'll remember that when I have chin hairs."

Abe's lips dragged over her jaw then his teeth scraped her chin in a teasing bite. "I'll tweeze them out for you." He tipped his head, giving her a grin. "Or braid them. Lady's choice."

"There's something wrong with you."

His hand caught her shirt, dragging it up her body. "Are you complaining?"

"I should." She raised her arms over her head, making it easy for him to work the t-shirt free. "But you do buy me dinner a lot."

"I knew that was the key." His lips worked down her neck and across her collarbone. "I knew I could win you over with food."

"I told you, you were sneaky." Her breath caught as his hands raked down the straps of her bra, dragging them lower until the cups flipped forward, baring both her breasts in a single second.

Abe's mouth immediately caught one nipple, the wet heat engulfing her sensitive flesh, sending her eyes closed and her head back.

His hand worked under her body to snap the fastener free, the band of her bra going loose before being pulled off and tossed away as Abe moved to her other breast, rolling it under his tongue and between his teeth until she was fighting for friction, trying to ease the ache building between her legs.

She wanted to feel full again. Stretched in the way she had the night before when his body rocked into hers. "Please fuck me."

Abe's head lifted. "I thought we moved past that."

"I said please." She twisted, searching for some sort of pressure. Something that might fill the void. "That should count for something." She wiggled one hand between their bodies to find the waistband of the tactical pants he always wore. "And I waited until we were already in the bed to ask."

"And you consider all that a step in the right direction?" Abe lifted his body up just enough that she could work the button and zipper of his fly open.

"Of course." Elise slid her hand into the opening. "What would you consider it?"

"Still pretty impatient." He grabbed at his pants with one hand, shoving them down.

She smirked a little. "Says the man who's going to tear his pants trying to get them off." She watched as more of his body came into view. "It's like you're in a hurry to be naked with me."

Abe's eyes lifted to hers as he kicked the pants away. "I'm in a hurry to get inside that sweet mouth of yours."

Her whole body went hot and her thighs and stomach clenched. She stared at the length of his cock as he crawled up the bed, the thought of it sliding between her lips sending her tongue out to skim across them in preparation.

"Christ." Abe's voice was a deep growl as he stopped right in front of her, one hand coming to the back of her head as his dick teased across her mouth. "You are fucking dangerous, Babe, you know that?"

She tried to lean forward, but his fingers fisted in her hair, keeping her pinned in place.

"You take what I give you, no more." The words were raspy and a little rough. "Understand?"

She didn't. Not completely, but admitting that would stop whatever this was, and that wasn't anything she was willing to allow to happen.

She'd expected Abe to treat her like some sort of innocent who had no clue how things worked in the bedroom.

But she had a clue. She had lots of clues.

Just because she hadn't had the sex didn't mean she wasn't decently versed in it.

Thank God for Pornhub.

"Yes." Elise licked her lips again, but other than that she held very still, trying to find any patience she might possess.

"Open for me."

If it was possible to come from words alone, that might have done it.

There was something in the sound of his voice. The deepness of it. The graveled demand as he stared into her eyes, hand tangled in her hair.

She stared up at him, letting her lips part, heart racing with an anticipation she'd never experienced.

An excitement she didn't think would ever be hers.

The flared head of his cock pushed past her lips and across her tongue, filling her mouth the same way it filled her pussy. She'd barely gotten a taste of his skin before he was pulling back.

She tried to follow him, but the hand in her hair held tight, keeping her from getting any more than he allowed.

All she could do was wait as he slowly eased back in, fucking her mouth with careful thrusts as his free hand dipped into the pajama pants she still wore. As his dick slid into her mouth his fingers found her clit, stroking it with the same steady pace, until

283

she was whimpering around him with the need to come.

His cock pulled from her mouth and his fingers abandoned her pussy, abruptly stealing both the sensations feeding her desire. "What the fuck?"

"I know. You hate me." He yanked at her pants, ripping them off her body. "You'll get over it."

"Like hell I will. I'll—" The perfect pressure she'd been wanting cut off the rest of her words, stealing them as Abe's body pushed into hers. Stretching.

Filling.

Taking.

This time it wasn't slow and careful. This time it was smooth and steady. A single stroke that impaled her body with his.

It stole her breath and her thoughts. Refocused all of it on the throbbing it caused.

He eased out, but immediately pushed back in, moving faster than he had before, pressing deeper as his fingers worked across her clit.

There was no pain. Not even a trace of the discomfort she'd felt before.

"Still hate me?"

"Maybe. You should probably try harder." Elise gasped as his mouth immediately closed around her nipple, sucking in tandem with the thrust of his hips.

The stroke of his fingers.

Her hands grabbed onto the sheets. The pillows. His skin. His hair.

Holding on as he proved there wasn't even the tiniest bit of hate for him anywhere inside her.

What she had for him was so much more.

284

His mouth pulled from her breast, popping loose as his strokes became stronger. Longer.

Faster.

She sucked in a breath as her legs started to tense.

"Good girl." The praise was a ragged whisper. "Come for me."

She didn't mean to do it.

Didn't mean to give him exactly what he wanted when he wanted it.

Next time she would try harder to be difficult.

But this time there was no stopping it. No controlling the waves as they took her down.

Swallowed her up.

"That's my girl." He rocked into her, each shove of his body bouncing hers as her pussy clenched tight, each spasm dragging her orgasm higher.

He suddenly felt deeper. Bigger. Harder.

Then he buried himself fully, hips shoved tight to her as he groaned out her name where his face was pressed into her hair.

His breathing was ragged and rough, heating the skin of her neck and ear.

It was a little concerning. "Are you okay?"

"I hope you're not thinking you just gave me a heart attack."

She pressed her lips together, trying not to smile. "Maybe you should go back to your protein shakes and egg whites just in case."

Abe lifted his head, his eyes lined with amusement.

And something else.

"Careful, Babe." His body slowly eased from hers. "I might spank your ass next time for that."

CHAPTER 22

"I SHOULDN'T BE here." Elise looked around the room filled with everyone currently stationed at headquarters.

"Of course you should be here. Pierce said everyone." Abe pulled out a chair and tipped his head toward it, motioning for Elise to sit down.

Elise did one final scan of the large conference room, before slowly lowering into the seat. Abe sat down beside her, resting one arm across the back of her chair as he leaned close. "You are just as important as everyone else here."

"Right. Because without Danishes how would anyone here survive." Elise held her work binder close to her chest as she continued to watch everyone around her.

Currently it was Rogue, Stealth, and a few members of Shadow staying on the property, and Pierce had called them all to this morning's meeting, along with Intel.

By the time everyone was seated, the room was packed with the men and women ready to take on their most recent threat.

Pierce sat at the front of the room with the team leads. He looked like he'd hardly slept. His hair was loose and there were dark circles under his eyes.

Heidi sat with Mona, Eva, and the rest of Intel. She waved her hands around in Elise's direction.

Abe leaned into Elise's ear. "I believe your presence has been requested." As much as he wanted to keep her with him, Elise might benefit more from being close to her friends right now.

The right people.

Heidi beckoned Elise with one waving hand, her eyes widening.

"If you don't go over there they will all come over here, and then this will take even longer."

"Fine." She tried to sound a little put out, but the soft smile on her face made it obvious how much she appreciated them wanting her.

How much it meant that she was clearly one of them.

Elise made her way across the room, shimmying between the chairs of men as she headed towards where Intel sat. Mona scooted down a chair, leaving a spot for Elise directly between her and Heidi. As soon as Elise sat down, Heidi grabbed her in a squeeze and didn't let go as Pierce started the meeting.

"Once again we find ourselves in the position of having to defend Alaskan Security." He wiped both hands down his face. "From something that was not directly our fault." He dropped his hands and sat straight. "Unfortunately I can only assume this will be our new normal."

"You think we're always going to have to do this?" Mona's head tipped to one side.

Pierce sighed. "I'm aware others have a different opinion from me, but I believe it is best if we approach this as if it will be the way we conduct business from here on out."

One of Mona's pale blonde brows lifted.

"I think it is important that we recognize there is the possibility that our new business model will continuously keep us in the line of fire." All Pierce's focus was on his wife.

Mona crossed her arms.

"Up until recently, much of Alaskan Security's business was defending people like the men attacking us now. It afforded us a certain level of safety within that circle." Pierce's gaze moved to where Rogue sat. "For all intents and purposes, we were one of them. We provided them with a service no one else would."

It was how Rogue began. Offering private security to the worst of the worst. Drug dealers. Criminals. Anyone and everyone that traditional security companies refused.

It was a lucrative business. One that helped put Alaskan Security in the financial position it was in. Unfortunately, it was also a tough business for anyone with even the smallest amount of morals.

"Do you think that has put a target on our back?" Wade had been the first of the group to voice his concerns about continuing to conduct business with people on the wrong side of the law.

"I think it's a distinct possibility." Pierce turned to Intel. "When this current situation is resolved, I would like complete investigations done on all Rogue's past clients."

"Don't we currently have a past client in a safe house?" Harlow tapped the end of her pen against her chin. "That daughter who drove Wade crazy?" Harlow looked from one side to the other. "We're probably lucky no one's come looking for her yet."

"Christ." Pierce rubbed his eyes. "One thing at a time, Ms. Mowry."

"I don't think we're a one thing at a time sort of company anymore, Pierce." Harlow shook her head. "I think we're a *ten balls in the air* sort of company now."

Heidi snorted beside her. "Balls."

"I will look into Courtney. I'll work up a full report on her family and everyone who could possibly be a danger to her." Eva was scribbling across a pad of paper as she wrote. "Are we sure no one has come looking for her?"

"If they did, they didn't make it very far." The lead for stealth spoke up from his spot at the table. "We've been with her around the clock, and so far we haven't heard a peep from anyone."

"So this girl's just been locked up in a cabin in Alaska for months, and no one has looked for her?" Eva sounded skeptical.

She had every right to be. Rogue had been called in to protect the daughter of a well-known drug dealer twice before. It was strange that no one had made an attempt to get close to her since she'd come to Alaska.

Pierce squeezed the bridge of his nose. "I considered it a blessing."

"I mean, it could be." Eva cringed. "Or—"

Pierce cut her off. "This morning we are not dealing with the *or*. This morning we are dealing with our current problem."

Heidi lifted a finger. "One of our current problems."

Pierce stared across the table at Intel.

Harlow grinned back at him. "Remember when you wanted to hire a whole team of women because you thought it would be a great idea?" Her smile widened. "How's that working out for you?"

"I have no complaints." Pierce leaned back in his chair, scanning the women of Intel. "What do we know about the men attempting to regain ownership of the laptop?"

"You always say men. Like men are the only ones capable of doing something like this." Heidi flipped open the folder on her lap.

"In my experience, men *are* the only ones capable of doing something like this."

"I guess I'll take that as a compliment." Heidi huffed out a breath. "Anyhoo, it does seem like it's men doing it this time."

Harlow stood, carrying her laptop toward the podium at the front of the room. She plugged it into the projector, turning as the screen at the front of the room flashed to life. "So far our best lead is actually that pink Volkswagen." She clicked through a few screens to display a photo of the car in question. "While it was successful at avoiding suspicion, it's an easily identifiable vehicle."

"And also not something that can be rented. Especially not in Alaska." Mona's arms were still crossed over her chest. "Vincent impounded the vehicle, but we were able to get enough information from the photos Abe was smart enough to take at the incident." She shot him a smile. "The color is not standard for that vehicle, which greatly limits the number listed by the DMV."

"The Volkswagen belongs to a woman named Lauren Collins." Harlow opened another window on her laptop, and the face of a pretty, young woman populated the screen. "Unfortunately, Lauren has not reported her vehicle stolen."

Heidi grinned at Pierce. "Plot twist."

"So you believe this woman is involved?" Pierce's eyes moved to where Rogue sat.

Abe glanced across the room. The discomfort of the men around him was palpable.

Of course they all knew women were just as capable of doing evil as men, but that didn't make it any easier to stomach the possible outcome when that was the situation.

"Possibly?" Harlow pulled up a report. Lauren's name was at the top of it. "She's never done anything wrong though. Not even a traffic ticket. It's hard for me to imagine someone going from zero to one hundred like this."

"It's possible she just fell in with the wrong man." Lennie's expression was tight. "It can happen to anyone."

"At any rate," Harlow pulled up the picture of the pink Volkswagen and Lauren Collins, putting them side-by-side on her screen, "this woman appears to be involved in this somehow."

"Which leads us to," Mona stood next, taking her laptop to the podium, and plugging it in, "this guy."

The women scowled at the photo of the man on the screen.

"This is either Michael Mosley or Sebastian Simms." Mona pulled up a few more photos of the same man. "I'm not convinced either of those is his real name, but so far it's all I've been able to find."

"Lauren had a couple of pictures with him on her Instagram profile. We did a reverse image search and came up with this guy." Harlow turned to look at the screen as it flipped to a list of addresses. "What we found most interesting was his possible addresses." She pointed toward the third address down. "This one," her pointing finger moved up to the most recent one associated with Michael Mosley, "and this one."

"That top one is Lauren Collins' address." Mona stepped in at Harlow's side. "The other one was the home of Rob Greer." She turned to face the room. "The man whose laptop they are looking for."

Pierce perked up a little. "So you believe Michael Mosley is the connection?"

"Of course he's the connection." Heidi shook her head. "He spent a little time making nice with a girl up here so he could come in and fuck up her life."

"But he wasn't one of the men who tried to shoot me." Elise stared at the image on the screen. "Those men are dead."

"Right." Mona pointed at Elise. "Close your eyes."

Elise immediately did as Mona suggested.

Mona went to her computer and pulled up a separate screen, this one a split image of two dead men. "We're currently scanning the web for any sign of these men. Unfortunately we haven't had much luck finding either of them. Possibly due to the fact that the picture we have is of them dead, and the pictures on the web are all of them alive."

"Neither man had any sort of identification on him at the time of the incident." Heidi sighed. "So Vincent doesn't know who they are either."

Brock snorted. "Sure he doesn't."

"If he did I would be able to find it." Heidi shook her head. "And there's nothing."

"Then it appears our best chance at stopping this is to go pay a visit to Lauren." Pierce looked as displeased by this development as Abe was. He turned to Shawn. "When can your team be ready?"

"We can be ready now." Shawn tapped one finger against the desk as he thought it through. "But I'm not sure walking up to her front door in the daylight is our best plan of attack."

"Agreed." Pierce tipped his head in a nod. "We wait until dark. Then we move."

"Wait a minute." Heidi held one hand out. "Why *can't* we go up to her house in the daylight? This woman is probably caught in the middle of this and has no idea what she's gotten herself into."

"Unfortunately for her, I am not willing to put her safety above yours." Pierce's expression was unyielding. "We will do what is best for Alaskan

Security and what is going to keep the people here safe."

"Are you shitting me right now?" Eva shook her head. "This woman could end up caught in the crossfire all because she made a bad decision and met a guy over the Internet?" She snorted. "Literally every woman in the world could be in her position."

"Be that as it may, I will not put the safety of one above the safety of many." Pierce glanced at the men at his side. Each one of them nodded in agreement.

"But she's innocent." This time it was Elise who spoke up in defense of a woman none of them had met.

"You don't know that." Pierce wasn't going to back down on this. "She could be just as guilty as everyone else involved."

"Or she could be another one of their victims." Elise appeared to be as unwilling to back down as Pierce was. "Don't treat her like she is guilty when you don't know the truth."

"This isn't about her guilt or innocence Ms. Foley." Pierce's tone was gentle. "This is about the safety of the people who work with us."

"You can keep her safe too." Elise sat tall, her gaze unwavering.

"We will do everything in our power to keep her safe." Abe spoke up, hoping it would help calm Elise's fears. For some reason she was taking this very personally, and that meant he would too. "If she is innocent, I promise she will be safe."

Elise's eyes moved over his face. After a few long seconds she gave him a small nod.

"It's settled then." Pierce turned to Shawn. "Rogue goes out tonight."

The women of Intel must have been appropriately satisfied, because they all stood together and left the room without another word of argument.

Elise glanced back his way as the crowd of women caught her in their midst, dragging her along. She gave him a little smile and wave just before disappearing into the hall.

"You know you can't keep that promise." Brock's tone was quiet. "There might not be shit you can do about what happens to this girl."

"We have to." Abe met his friend's gaze. "This could have happened to any one of them."

"And we couldn't have done shit about it if they got caught in the middle either." Brock raked one hand through his hair. "I don't like it any more than you do, but Elise needs to know that girl could get caught in the middle."

"All we can do is our best." Pierce stood. "But I will always put my people's safety first." Pierce's eyes met Abe's. "And I would hope we are all on the same page there."

"I don't know that we are." Abe held his ground, ready to stand up for the woman all of Intel was ready to stand up for. "If that girl is innocently caught in the middle of this then I will get her out of there."

"You will do what is best for your team." Pierce said it like it was the end of the discussion.

But he didn't only have an entire team of women willing to stand up to him.

"I will do what is right." Abe met Pierce's stare. "And protecting an innocent victim is always what's right."

Tyson stepped in at Abe's left shoulder. "I'm with him."

Reed stood at his right. "So am I."

Pierce's eyes shifted between them. "If you are unwilling to meet the expectations of the op then I will be forced to replace you."

"You're seriously going to cut us out because we want to protect this poor woman?"

"At what cost?" Pierce raked one hand through his hair. "You don't seem to recognize the position I am caught in right now. These people are trying to kill my men." Pierce's eyes narrowed at Abe. "But not just my men. You of all people should understand the gravity of our situation."

"And you of all people should understand how easily a person could get caught up in something like this." It happened to Eva and Mona. Both women went into business with a man tied up in this whole mess. Both women ended up dragged into the line of fire because of it and were lucky to make it out alive.

"I do understand. That's what you don't seem to be seeing." Pierce's tone took on a desperate edge. "I understand better than anyone what can happen." He pointed to Stealth. "I built an entire company because of it. A company that I will protect at all costs."

They were all caught. Wedged into a place none of them wanted to be.

"Of course we will do our best to ensure this woman's safety." Pierce shook his head. "But her safety will always be secondary."

CHAPTER 23

"UGH." HEIDI DROPPED her head back.

"What are they saying?" Elise stepped closer, the fingers of her right hand tracing along her upper thigh.

"Abe's still holding his ground." Heidi's eyes rolled Elise's way. "But I'm feeling like he's fighting a losing battle with Pierce."

"This is so hard for him." Mona sat on the edge of Heidi's desk, her arms wrapped around her middle. "He has to feel like he's picking between his men or his sister."

The room fell quiet. Everyone at Alaskan Security now knew what happened to Pierce's sister. That she lost her life because she chose to get close to the wrong man.

"There has to be some way to get Lauren out of the middle of this." Elise slowly lowered to the floor, propping her back against the side of Heidi's desk. "Or at least some way to figure out if she's involved or not. Because if she's involved..."

"If she's involved, then there's nothing anyone can do to save her." Harlow sat in front of her computer, fingers working across the keyboard. "But we've dug into her. Found out everything there is to know. If she is involved, then she's hella good at hiding it."

"Can we just call her? Tell her to get the fuck out of there?" Elise checked her watch. They had plenty of time to get Lauren to safety as long as they acted now.

"That would be fine as long as no one else is listening. If someone hears us call to warn her then they'll know we're onto them, and that she's our link." Harlow's eyes lifted above her screen. "And we probably won't have to worry about her getting caught in the middle anymore."

A chill settled into Elise's stomach. "You think they would just kill her for that?"

"These men are willing to do anything to get that computer back. If the names that we have are discovered then those guys are as good as dead and they know that." Heidi pulled her earbuds free and dropped them onto the desk. "There has to be some sort of a way to get her out of that house without making anyone suspicious."

"Are there any cameras close to where she lives that we could watch?" Eva nibbled on the corner of a cracker before taking a sip of ginger ale.

"The closest camera I found is from a convenience store across the street." One of the screens on the wall behind Harlow flashed to life. A second later a foggy scene populated it. "But it's blurry as hell."

Heidi snorted. "Maybe we could go clean it."

"If we're going to take it that far then we might as well just watch her ourselves." Harlow turned to face the screen. "But I'm not sure that watching is going to do us any good."

"No. We need to get her out of there." Mona started to pace. "If we can figure out how to take her out of the equation then Pierce doesn't have to make that call."

The worry on Mona's face was evident. As strong and confident and unbreakable as Pierce appeared, he was still just a man. A man who would probably never forgive himself if something did happen to Lauren.

"What if we're thinking about this the wrong way?" They'd been trying to get Lauren out of the house so she wouldn't be there when Rogue moved in. "What if we get this Michael, or whatever his name is, out of the house? Rogue could just take care of him and then Lauren could go on her merry little way, free from whatever stupidity this man brought into her life."

"It's not that easy. She's still caught in this. If we found her then so will everybody else." Harlow leaned back in her seat and kicked her feet up on her desk the way she did when she was thinking. "But getting the asshole out of the house might be a great idea."

"But what in the hell do we use to get him out of the house? I can't imagine he's dumb enough to not realize he's in a whole world of trouble." Eva blew out a little breath as her skin paled. "It would take something significant to get him to leave the safety of wherever he is."

"Good point. We don't even know that he's in that house." Harlow tapped her pen against her chin. "I think step one is finding out if he's in the house. If he is, then step two is figuring out how to get him out and away from Lauren."

"How do we find out if he's in the house?" Elise squinted up at the camera feed. "Because that thing is going to be no help."

"Pierce did say he didn't want me fucking around with Vincent anymore, right?" Heidi's eyes were wide and her expression was innocent as she picked up her cell phone. "And he did say that we work with Vincent as much as he works with us, right?"

Everyone looked to Mona. Right now she was the final decision on this. She was the one who knew Pierce. She was the one who had to make this decision.

Mona barely tipped her head. "Do it."

Heidi tapped her screen.

Vincent picked up immediately. "I changed my number, Rucker."

"And I didn't let it hurt my feelings." Heidi rubbed her lips together, glancing at Mona for one final nod of approval. As soon as it came she continued her conversation. "I need you to do some surveillance for me."

"You need me to do some surveillance for you? That's not how this works."

"Don't act like you're the one with all the power here, Vincent." Heidi smiled, the expression clear in

302

her words. "You need me as much as I need you. That means on occasion we have to exchange services."

"Does this mean you have a service to exchange?"

"Of course. I always have something to exchange. That's why you kidnapped me and tried to make me come work for you."

Vincent snorted what might be considered a laugh by someone like him. "I could argue you still essentially work for me."

"If I work for you, then you also work for me, which brings me back to my initial question. I need you to do some surveillance for me."

"That's not a question, Rucker. That's a demand."

"Potato *potato*." Heidi grabbed the top paper from the file in front of her. "This is something you're going to want to do anyway, so don't act like I'm making you sacrifice some huge amount of your time for an irrelevant task."

"I'm listening."

"I know. You're a pain in the ass, not stupid." Heidi was probably the only human on the face of the earth who could get away with calling the head of a pseudo-government entity a pain in the ass. "I think we found someone involved in this little situation we're both dealing with. I was hoping you could get some eyes on an address to see if this guy is actually there."

"How did you figure this out?" Whether Vincent was curious, or jealous, or suspicious, was impossible to say. He sounded an equal amount of all three.

"What do you mean, how did I figure this out? I figured it out the same way I figure everything else out. I got a whole room full of women working together here. There's nothing we can't do." Heidi paused. "Which brings me to my next request."

"Two requests in one day. You must think I'm feeling generous."

Heidi laughed. "I'm sure generous is a word no one has ever used to describe you."

"You would be incorrect."

"I'm not banking on your supposed generosity, Vincent. My money is on your willingness to do your job." Heidi scooted her laptop in front of her. "I want you to go get a set of eyes on the house of the woman who owned the Volkswagen."

"The Volkswagen was reported stolen this morning."

"Cool. I don't care." Heidi's eyes suddenly lifted to meet Harlow's. "Are you already watching that house?"

Vincent was silent as Heidi and Harlow continued to stare at each other.

Harlow's eyes narrowed as she spun to face the screen behind her. "Fucking Vaseline."

"Are you shitting me right now, Vincent?" Heidi glared down at her phone. "You know I was trying to be nice to you. I was going to call and give you all the information I had, but here you are not only withholding information, but also doing your fucking best to sabotage any chance we have to deal with the situation that's going to come back to bite our asses and not yours."

"Rogue was planning to go in there tonight, and here you are sitting and watching, knowing everything that's happening." Elise pushed up to her feet, shoving her face right against the speaker of the phone. "For what? Just because you don't want to get your little fingers dirty? You act like you're some sort of God sitting back and watching all the little people of the world try to handle their messes from above while you know all the answers."

Mona snatched the phone away. "Vincent, I swear to God if you don't stop with this bullshit we will cut you off." Her pale blue eyes were sharp. "No more of our help. No more using us to your advantage. No more letting us take the fall. You'll be on your fucking own."

It was time to test Pierce's theory. To see if Alaskan Security and GHOST really had a mutually beneficial relationship.

"Fine. What do you want from me?"

"Who's at the house?" Mona held the phone as she continued to pace around the room.

"One man. One woman. Last night they had a domestic dispute."

Mona spun to face the women in the room. "Were the police involved?"

All this worry might have been for nothing. Lauren might already be safe. Moved to another location by local law enforcement.

"Negative."

Mona's skin paled. "Then how do you know this happened?"

"At nineteen hundred hours the female came out of the front door screaming. The male chased her down and dragged her back inside by her hair."

"And you just watched that happen?" Harlow's feet dropped to the floor and she stood up. "What the fuck is wrong with you?"

"People in my position have choices to make, Ms. Mowry. Choices you should thank God will never be yours."

Elise fought the urge to dig at her leg as the familiar ache settled into her gut.

But this time the ache had nothing to do with her, not really.

This time the ache was for a woman she'd never met before. A woman she might never have the opportunity to meet.

A woman who might not see the end of this day.

"We have to help her." She knew what it was like to feel lost and broken, and chances were good that was how Lauren was feeling right now. "We have to do something."

Vincent snorted. "And what is it that you would do? Walk in there and take her from the place?"

It sounded simple.

And sometimes simple plans were the best. "Why couldn't we?"

"Because that's exactly the kind of bullshit that will get her killed."

"But it sounds like you're saying she's probably going to end up getting killed anyway, so isn't it worth the risk?" They needed to save this woman. Help her.

Show her that there were good people in the world.

"Let Pierce deal with this."

"You would like that wouldn't you?" Mona snapped at Vincent. "You want to reap all the rewards of working with us and let us take all the heat."

"You think Alaskan Security doesn't get any rewards? Where do you think all the men you kill go? Do you think they just disappear?"

"If the only perk you're offering us is having you as a cleaner, then I think you know we could find similar services elsewhere." Mona was definitely turning out to be just as good of a negotiator as her husband. "You can either be on our team or you can go be on a team by yourself, but we are tired of you trying to toe the line."

"You're willing to risk all this for one woman?"

"That's what you don't understand, Vincent." Mona met Eva's eyes. "This isn't just about one woman. This is about all women."

"We're going to do this with or without you, Vincent." Heidi took a drink of her water, making him wait to hear the rest of her statement. "Which means you're either with us or you're against us."

"You're a pain in the ass, you know that?"

Elise smiled. "We do know that."

"Fine. I'll be in touch."

The line went dead.

"I can't tell if he was pissed or impressed." Mona handed the phone to Heidi.

"It's usually both." Heidi was working on her computer. "I have an idea."

"You always do." Harlow walked around to stand behind Heidi. "What are you thinking?"

"So, this dude." Heidi waved one hand around as she continued to work. "Michael whatever his name is, he definitely sucks, which means he probably doesn't care what happens to Lauren as long as he gets what he wants."

"I would say that's a safe assumption." Harlow watched Heidi's computer screen.

"And this dude wants that computer, right?"

Elise moved in closer. "Right. The computer that Abe sent to Vincent."

"Correct." Heidi's fingers worked across the keyboard. "What if we gave him his computer back?"

"Like a trade?" Mona sounded skeptical.

"Not a trade he would know about." Heidi finished typing and turned to face them. "What if we use the computer to lure him away from the house, and then we went in and took our half of the trade?"

"You just want to kidnap her?" Elise's fingers went back to her thigh. She'd been kidnapped.

Almost.

And almost was too close for comfort.

"You think she'll just willingly go with a bunch of scary-looking men?" Heidi shook her head. "Vincent's going to have to kidnap her."

"Vincent might have to kidnap her." Elise looked Mona's way. "But we wouldn't."

Heidi spun in her chair to face Elise. "You want to go get Lauren?"

She'd spent years suffering. Punishing herself for mistakes and bad decisions. Letting someone else suffer for a similar reason didn't sit right. "Yeah. I want to go get Lauren."

****

"WHO DO YOU think is going to be in the most trouble for this?"

"That depends." Harlow adjusted the earpiece tucked inside her ear. "Does it go well?"

Elise yanked at the bulletproof vest Vincent made her wear under her shirt, trying to get it to feel comfortable. "It's going to go well."

"In that case all of us."

Elise stared across the van at Harlow. "Who would be in trouble if it doesn't go well?"

Harlow was looking at her laptop. "Also all of us." She grinned, her eyes lifting to meet Elise's. "But if it goes well we'll have one more person on our side."

Smuggling her and Harlow out of headquarters turned out to be way easier than Elise expected it to be. Vincent pulled up, they walked out, climbed into the back of his van, and off they went.

"Do you think they'll figure out we're gone?" Elise pulled her coat on over her shirt, adding another layer to disguise the fact that she was wearing a vest that probably cost more than the car she used to drive.

"Only if Abe or Dutch come looking for you or me." Harlow pursed her lips. "So we've probably got about fifteen minutes."

"If you do this right we won't even need fifteen minutes." Vincent was in the front passenger's seat, his expression stoic as he looked out the windows.

"My team is currently at the drop-off location. The minute he leaves the house we move in. You get your ass in there, grab the girl, and get the fuck back out."

"Right." She could do this. It would be simple.

The van pulled to a stop a few blocks from the house they were going to.

A phone started to ring. Vincent tapped the screen set in the center of the dashboard. He didn't have the chance to say anything before the person on the other end of the line started yelling.

"Where in the fuck are they?"

Elise blinked at Harlow as Pierce continued screaming at Vincent.

"I'm sick and fucking tired of you acting like you can do whatever you want."

Vincent didn't seem to react at all, just sat in his seat, letting Pierce go.

"Bring them back right now."

"I will bring them back in fifteen minutes."

"If you don't bring them back now, I will come get them."

Vincent scanned the area in front of them. "That's fine too. You know where we are." He reached out to end the call, cutting Pierce off. "You ready?"

She was not ready. Not even a little bit.

Pierce's reaction made her question the sanity of the decisions she'd made over the past hour.

"Do you want me to go get her?" Harlow whispered the question. "I'll do it."

Elise shook her head. "I can do it."

They'd narrowed it down to her, after taking into account pregnancy and temperament, deciding she was the one most likely to be able to get Lauren to leave the house.

"He just left." The driver didn't make a move to pull away.

"We'll give it five minutes."

Elise rocked a little in her seat, fighting the emotions clawing at her insides.

Emotions she used to avoid at all costs.

Five minutes flew past, and before she was able to fully catch her breath they were moving, each second taking them closer and closer to the little house where Lauren lived with a man who was bringing her nothing but pain.

It was a situation Elise was familiar with.

One no one saved her from.

"You've got thirty seconds, Elise. Be ready."

"Rogue is already loaded up." Harlow paused, listening to Heidi's voice in her ear. "They'll be here in four minutes."

The van jerked to a stop, and the man riding in the back with Harlow and Elise yanked the door open, stepping to one side as she climbed out after him. He held his post as she rushed up the sidewalk, her high heels clicking along the cement. As soon as she reached the door she knocked, knowing there was no time to waste.

At any moment the man living with Lauren could come back and find her here.

And then it wouldn't just be Lauren on the line.

The door opened and a woman with chocolate brown hair and wide eyes stared out at her. One of those eyes was circled with an ugly mottle of green and brown bruising. Her left cheek was dotted with tiny scabs, as if she'd been dragged across a rough surface.

Elise tried to smile, but it was impossible. "You need to come with me. It's the only way you'll be safe."

The woman's eyes widened even more as they held Elise's.

Like she was trying to tell her something.

But before Elise could ask any questions, a heavy hand locked onto her arm.

And yanked her into the house.

CHAPTER 24

"WHAT IN THE hell were they thinking?" Dutch's voice was in Abe's ear.

"Pierce said he wanted me to work with Vincent." Heidi was still holding her ground on the whole thing. "And if it was one of us, you guys would've done the same damn thing."

"But it wasn't one of you. You don't know shit about this girl." Dutch was clearly hanging on by a thread. When he found out Harlow had gone out with Elise and Vincent he completely lost his shit. Threatened to join Rogue as they left.

It took more than a little convincing to talk him into going back inside where he was more valuable.

Abe was the last man into the van, knowing it put him in the position to be the first man out. He had one hand on the door handle, ready to move the second they arrived.

"Two minutes." Rico sped down the side roads to avoid any danger of slow traffic as he moved them toward the small house just outside of Fairbanks.

The same house where Elise was currently trying to convince a woman to leave with a complete stranger.

If anyone could do that it would be her.

"You look awfully fucking calm." Tyson sat right across from him.

"Not a good time to be upset." Not that he would be upset. Not the way most people would expect.

Because he understood why Elise did this. He understood why they all did this.

He watched each of the women join Alaskan Security. Saw the different things that brought them here, and all the reasons they stayed.

And every one of those reasons meant they had skin in this game.

This situation would hit very close to home for every member of Intel.

And Elise was no exception.

Whether it was one they were dating, one they were in business with, or one who was their father, they all knew what it was like to suffer because of a man. These women each understood how Lauren could be in the position she was in, and they all had very important reasons for doing what they'd done.

That didn't mean he liked it. That didn't mean he agreed with the way they'd gone about it. But he still understood.

And intended to do anything he needed to back them up.

"One minute."

Every man in the van sat a little straighter at Rico's time call.

314

"We've got a problem." Dutch's words were clipped and short.

"What's the problem?" Abe's fingers twitched on the handle, itching to throw the door open the second he could.

"Elise is inside the house."

Of course she was inside the house. That was her entire reason for going there. "She's gotta get the girl out."

"No. She didn't go in the house on her own."

"Thirty seconds."

Abe stared across the van at Tyson as Dutch's words sank in. "Who's in the house?"

"Vincent's not sure. He said our guy left, but he hasn't arrived at the pickup spot yet."

"We'll get her." Tyson's words were strong and sure. "She'll be out of there in no time."

The van jerked to a stop. Abe immediately threw the back door open and was out. Tyson and Reed were close at his side, with the rest of the team following.

"I'll go to the back. Tyson tipped his head toward the thick line of hedges running along the side of the property. "You two go around the front. We'll hit them at each end at the same time."

Abe tipped his head as he and Reed separated from Tyson and the rest of the group.

"I'll grab Elise. You grab Lauren. Then we get the fuck out of there." Abe kept his voice down as they crept along the side of the small house.

Heavy blankets covered the windows, making it less likely they would be seen as they moved in.

"Do you see any cameras?" Reed craned his neck, looking up at the roofline as they crawled past the first window.

Abe stopped, pausing at the backside of the thick evergreen bush providing cover. He leaned to peek between the bush and the house. Tucked right against the eaves, into the foliage of another evergreen bush, was a single camera. It was nearly impossible to see but would give whoever was inside a perfect view of the front door they were approaching. "Shit."

"There goes the element of surprise." Reed tipped his head away, directing his next words to the men on the other end of the line in their ear. "Check for cameras. We've got one on the front."

"I don't see any back here, but that doesn't mean there aren't any." Tyson's voice was hushed. "We're in position. Ready whenever you are."

Abe held back a second longer, knowing the minute he stepped toward the front door he would be giving them away. "We keep both girls safe, understood?"

He made a promise to Elise and he intended to keep it. She would never have put herself in this amount of danger if it wasn't something desperately important to her.

And that made it desperately important to him.

"Understood." Tyson's agreement came immediately.

Luckily he and Tyson were on the same page.

"We'll move on the count of three." Abe shifted around, working into a position that would make it easier to move quickly to the door. "One. Two—"

A single shot made the rest of the countdown irrelevant.

"We've got gunfire." Abe jumped from his spot behind the brush and immediately put his shoulder into the door.

Time slowed down just like it always did. For most people situations like this seemed to fly past, lost in a blur of adrenaline and chaos.

But that's not how it worked for him. Not anymore.

Abe took two steps back and went at the door again, putting his shoulder into it as hard as he could, rocking it on its hinges.

"Step back." Reed was right behind him. The second Abe was out of the way, Reed put his boot in the middle of the door, managing to knock it the rest of the way loose.

Abe immediately went in, gun in front of him as he stepped into the darkness of the small house.

A second shot came as soon as he crossed the threshold, followed by a high-pitched scream.

He moved quickly through the front living room, cutting across the worn carpet as he made his way in the direction the rest of the team should be. Reed stayed right behind him, moving in tandem with Abe as they closed in on their target.

They reached the doorway to what appeared to be a kitchen, each man tucking close to one side of the opening.

"Don't make me shoot this thing again." The command was sharp.

"If you shoot that again we're all going to be deaf." Elise's response was immediate.

She was okay. Still breathing. Still fighting.

"Good. Then I won't have to listen to your fucking mouth anymore." The man in the kitchen with her didn't seem to appreciate Elise's backbone as much as Abe did.

"This isn't going to work out well for you." Elise's voice was strong and sure.

"It seems like this isn't going to work out well for *you*." The man responding to her sounded almost amused. Amused and loud. "Because I'm the one who's going to be walking out of here alive."

"If you think that then you're a fucking idiot."

Abe almost smiled at the tone of her voice. Elise sounded completely unbothered by where she was and what was happening around her.

It likely wasn't true, but the fact that she was holding it together made him proud as hell of her. Made it clear that she and Intel had made the right call when they chose her to be the one to come here.

"Well it looks like I'm the one getting ready to go out the door, and you're the one who has a gun pointed at her." The man's voice got even louder as he came closer.

Abe met Reed's eyes across the opening. Reed barely tipped his head in an acknowledging nod.

This guy had no clue they were there. Probably ended up temporarily making himself deaf shooting his gun in such a small space.

All they had to do was wait, and he would come to them.

Abe closed his eyes, taking a slow deep breath before opening them again.

318

It was the same thing he'd done the morning Elise was almost kidnapped, and it was just as difficult to do now as it was then.

Patience was something he'd learned. A skill he'd cultivated and grown. One that rarely ever failed him.

And it wouldn't fail him now, as long as he could maintain it.

"Did you think I was this stupid?" The man's shadow crept across the floor.

"Do you want me to answer that honestly?"

Reed's eyes widened as he stared Abe's direction, like he couldn't believe the words coming out of Elise's mouth.

When this was all over they might need to have a discussion about the best ways to handle these kinds of situations, but right now the fact that she was holding her own made him nothing but proud.

"I'm not fucking stupid."

"I guess we have differing opinions then." Elise paused. "Because the way I look at it, anyone who has two of the most dangerous forces in Alaska camped outside their house, is a fucking idiot."

The man choked out a laugh. "I looked into your company. Alaskan Security is nothing more than a bunch of rich people babysitters."

That explained a lot. Now it made more sense why this guy and his small-time buddies thought it would be a good idea to come up here to retrieve the computer personally.

"Right. That's why we've killed three of your friends."

The man's shadow stopped moving. "What?"

FRIENDLY FIRE

Shit.

"You didn't know?" Elise snorted. "Where did you think they went? On a vacation? Maybe to live on a farm in the country?"

Yeah. He was definitely going to have a talk with her about how to act in situations like this. The dos and donts of antagonizing and already antagonized psychopath.

Especially one that had a gun.

"Are you fucking kidding me right now?" The shadow that had been coming their way started to move deeper into the kitchen. "If your fucking company killed my brother—"

Experience told him he couldn't wait any longer. There were certain things there was simply no coming back from, and when family was involved there was no telling what could happen.

Abe took a single step into the doorway, gun immediately lifting to where he knew the man was standing based on the positioning of his shadow and the sound of his voice. In the single second it took for his finger to pull the trigger, the man's eyes came his way.

Elise grabbed the woman close at her side and dragged her towards the dirty floor.

But when Abe's gun discharged, it wasn't only one shot that rang out.

It was two.

CHAPTER 25

CHAOS IMMEDIATELY FILLED the kitchen.

It started before her body even hit the floor. The gunfire. The screaming. The yelling.

It was inescapable.

Elise held Lauren tight, keeping the other woman on the floor as men raced into the room around them, clogging her view of what was happening.

And what had already happened.

She craned her neck, trying her best to look around, hoping to find proof that the man who'd had his weapon pointed at her seconds ago was taken down. Some sort of confirmation that the danger was over.

That she and Lauren were both safe.

"He shot him." Lauren's dark eyes were wide as they snapped around the space. "He shot him." She sounded almost...

Upset.

"He was going to kill us." Elise wanted to shake the other woman. Did she not understand what was about to happen?

"He shot him." Lauren started to rock. "He shot him." She sounded like a broken record at this point.

One that almost made Elise question what she'd just done.

But she'd seen the look on Lauren's face when she showed up. The fear. The panic. The concern.

"He was going to kill you." She tried to reason with the woman, hoping to explain the gravity of the situation they were both in. "He already tried to do it once."

Lauren's face was beat up and swollen, so while he might not have tried to kill her, he definitely wanted to do damage, and right now that was close enough.

The memory must have registered, because Lauren's eyes finally came Elise's way. "What?"

"Last night. He beat the shit out of you."

Lauren shook her head in a jerky move. "Not him." She lifted a shaky finger to point at the open back door. "Him."

Elise lifted up, straining to get a better look at where Lauren indicated.

That was when she realized the man in Lauren's life wasn't the only one down.

Any fear she still had for herself was gone in an instant. Elise scrambled to her knees and crawled towards the collection of men standing around their wounded partner.

"Nope." Arms banded around her middle and pulled her up from the floor. "You don't need to go over there right now." Abe dragged her towards the front of the house, holding tight as she fought him.

"He shot Tyson." She grabbed at Abe's arms, trying as hard as she could to make him let her go. "That bastard shot Tyson."

"I know. But there's nothing you can do for him right now." Abe managed to get her through the front room and out the door. "You need to let them handle it."

Her whole body went cold. "This is all my fault."

She should have done more to keep the gun pointed in her direction. She should have kept him talking longer. Bought more time.

Abe's hands turned rough, gripping tight as they spun her to face him. His blue eyes were hard as they stared down into hers. "None of this is your fault."

"How is this not my fault? I'm the one who went in there." She was the one who came up with the idea. The one who insisted they save Lauren at any cost.

And now she knew the cost.

"We should have listened to Pierce. We should have let him do what he wanted." The world started to spin out around her, threatening to take her down. "This is all my fault."

"Give her to me." A second set of hands yanked at Elise's coat, managing to rip her away from Abe. "Look at me."

Elise could barely manage to face Harlow.

"Are you listening?" Harlow's expression was serious and stern.

Elise nodded.

"We decided on this together. And I can tell you right now that if you hadn't come up with this

323

someone else would have." Harlow didn't blink as she continued on. "And it would've been someone else who went in there, and chances are good they wouldn't have handled this as well as you did." She barely smiled. "Because you did one hell of a job."

Elise sniffed, trying to contain her running nose. Harlow couldn't know the full extent of what happened, because if she did she would be looking to place blame too. "He shot Tyson."

"In the leg." Abe was close to her side, his hand rubbing across her back. "They already got a tourniquet on, and they're loading him into the van right now."

Elise's eyes dragged across the yard to where four members of Rogue carried Tyson. Tyson's eyes met hers. They were lined with pain, but he still managed a smile and a wink.

"You did well, Ms. Foley." Vincent stepped in beside Harlow.

Harlow turned to shoot him a glare. "She did better than you did. How in the hell did you not know there were two men in this house?"

"I don't keep a psychic on staff, Ms. Mowry. There are always unforeseen variables in this business."

"Well your unforeseen variable just shot one of our men." Harlow's voice was icy and sharp. Her eyes snapped across the yard where members of GHOST were milling around. "And I can't help but notice that not a single one of your men ended up with so much as a paper cut because of this op." Her glare came back to Vincent. "An op that should have been yours from the beginning."

Vincent held her stare as the seconds ticked past. Finally his eyes lifted to the house as one of his men came out, carrying a large black duffel bag. "It would appear we are at a crossroads."

Harlow's eyes narrowed. "What in the hell is that supposed to mean?"

"It means you should tell Pierce that I will be in to see him in the morning." Vincent took the duffel bag from his man, opened it, looked inside, and passed it back. "Until then I can promise this situation is under control."

****

"HOW ARE YOU doing, Babe?" Abe's hand held hers tight as they walked toward the large conference room in the main office building.

"Honestly?" Elise took a deep breath. "I don't know."

She'd been wrangling with the previous day's events all night long, trying to come to terms with what happened.

Trying to find peace with the decisions she'd made.

Trying to allow herself to share the burden of those decisions and what they resulted in. Her friends had done their best to convince her, with most of Intel spending the majority of the evening in her suite, but she was still struggling.

Yes, they'd come up with the plan together.

Yes, they'd all voted for her to be the one to go to the house.

And yes, they were all in agreement that they'd done the right thing. Lauren was safe.

Broken, but safe.

The men who were threatening them directly, were all eliminated.

And everyone from Alaskan Security made it out alive.

But not unscathed.

"It might take you a while to figure out how you are." Abe pulled open the door to the conference room. "This life isn't an easy one. You'll second-guess yourself a lot."

"I wasn't supposed to be a part of this." She came here to be an office manager, but somewhere along the way she ended up part of this mess. "I was just supposed to order Danishes and coffee."

"And look at you now. You're one of the team." The lighthearted way Abe was handling everything made it a little easier not to fall into the pit threatening to swallow her up. "Whether you like it or not."

"I'm not sure I'm a fan." Elise lowered into one of the chairs lined around the room. "How do you sleep at night?" She'd struggled to find any rest, the possibilities and *what might haves* keeping her awake most of the night.

"Next to you." Abe wrapped one arm around her shoulders and leaned close. "And I've got to tell you, I wish I started doing it sooner."

"That would have been creepy. Especially since I didn't like you before."

"You barely like me now, Babe." He smiled as he leaned to press a kiss against her temple. "You keep making me kill guys to prove my affection."

326

"How are you so nonchalant about this?" There was no judgment. It was an honest question.

She was glad he'd killed the guy yesterday. Also glad he'd killed the guy who tried to kidnap her.

But for some reason, she was still struggling. More so with what happened yesterday.

Possibly because Tyson got hurt in the process.

"I'm not always nonchalant." The tips of Abe's fingers brushed against her shoulder. "If something happened to Lauren, I would not be feeling the same way I do now."

"What if something happened to me?"

Abe's eyes immediately hardened, his entire expression turning to stone. "Nothing would have happened to you, Elise. Not ever."

"But it could have. He had that gun pointed right at my—"

"*Not ever.*" Abe cut her off with short, sharp words.

Before she could try to continue the conversation, Pierce strode into the room, immediately followed by someone she wasn't expecting to see.

Vincent.

"I appreciate everyone meeting us here on such short notice." Pierce sat in the center chair at the long table dominating the front of the room. "There are some new developments in the way we will be conducting business from here on out, and I would like to go over them with you."

Elise glanced to where Heidi sat next to Shawn. Normally he would be at the head table with Pierce, but this morning everyone was seated in the chairs facing the table, team leads included.

Heidi widened her eyes, making it seem like she didn't know exactly what was happening.

Which would probably be a first.

"Up until now, GHOST has been a primarily silent partner, but in light of recent events it appears that will no longer be possible." Pierce's eyes moved to Vincent. "Not without Alaskan Security taking on substantial and unwarranted risk."

"What exactly does that mean?" Mona sat with her arms across her chest, eyes moving to where Vincent sat at Pierce's side.

"At this point, we aren't sure. This is new and uncharted territory, so for the foreseeable future we will simply be taking it one step at a time." Pierce directed most of the answer to his wife, his eyes only moving to the rest of the room for the last couple of words.

"Can we assume the first step is the handling of the situation that resulted in the injury of one of our men yesterday?" Harlow held the same position as Mona, arms crossed, lips turned down in a frown as she stared at Vincent.

"GHOST has taken on the responsibility of dealing with the bulk of the civilian weaponry problem. There could be time in the future where we will be called in to assist on an op involving this issue, but as of right now, any connection to Alaskan Security has been severed." Pierce sounded pleased with the outcome.

He should be. If they continued to be the target of whoever was creating and selling these weapons, there was no doubt Alaskan Security would end up blown off the face of the earth.

"How exactly was the connection to Alaskan Security severed?" Heidi sounded much more skeptical than Pierce did.

"I invite you to come to GHOST headquarters to see for yourself. We welcome your assistance and your input on this project." Vincent did not sound as pleased as Pierce did with the new situation.

"So it's a project now?" Heidi's eyes skimmed Vincent up and down. "Interesting."

"You know as well as I do, Ms. Rucker, that this will be an ongoing process. It is impossible to know how many connections have been made to Alaskan Security. It will take time to identify them all."

"And we are allowed to have eyes on that process?" Harlow sat up a little straighter in her seat.

Vincent glanced at Pierce before looking back at Harlow. "Yes."

The members of Intel exchanged glances from their spots across the room.

Mona faced her husband. "What does Vincent get out of all of this?"

For the first time Vincent looked pleased, the normally flat line of his mouth barely lifting at the corners.

"I get access to Intel."

EPILOGUE

"IT'S NOT AS pretty with the blinds on it." Elise frowned at the large window in their living room.

"But it will be much more difficult for anyone hoping to shoot through it to get their eyes on a target."

"I guess that is a perk." Elise dropped down to sit on one of the sofas. Danish immediately jumped up into her lap, spinning two times before settling down. "Do you really think we need to worry about that now?"

"Babe, we are always going to have to worry about that." Abe eased down onto the sofa beside her, draping one arm across the back as he reached out to scratch behind Danish's ear. "It's the nature of the business."

"I'm pretty sure I didn't sign up for this." Elise's head dropped to his shoulder. "I was just supposed to be ordering pens and legal pads."

It was what she fell back on whenever the reality of her life in Alaska got to be a little too much.

Downplaying her importance there. What she brought to the table.

Because Elise was so much more than an office manager.

"And you can still do that." Abe kicked his feet up on the coffee table. "You just have to also dodge bullets occasionally."

Elise laughed. She was finally relaxing a little bit after getting way more caught up in Alaskan Security's most recent mess than anyone expected.

And thank goodness she did. He couldn't imagine anyone else would've been able to keep that guy talking long enough for them to get in position. Elise had been the perfect mixture of unthreatening but also challenging enough to keep the man's focus on her while Rogue got their ducks in a row.

"I'm glad we can finally be back in the townhouse." Elise took a deep breath as she looked around the space. "The suite wasn't bad, but this is so much better."

"Agreed." They'd been stuck at headquarters for nearly a month while the fence was reinforced at the townhomes, and his window was replaced. "I missed our bed."

"I missed the shower." Elise smiled a little. "I love that freaking thing."

"You should. You're the one who picked it out."

Elise twisted to face him. "You knew I was the one who picked out all the finishings in the basic townhomes?"

"Of course I did. Why do you think I didn't change anything?" He'd been on the list to buy even before he found out Elise was making the final design decisions. Once he found out she was the one picking cabinets and tile and light fixtures, he decided to leave everything exactly how she intended for it to be.

Just in case.

"I'm not sure if that's sweet or presumptuous."

Abe lifted one of her hands to his mouth. "Probably a little of both." He brushed his lips across her knuckles. "What do you want to do today?"

"Maybe go have at the punching bag a little."

Her answer surprised him. "Of all the things in the world, that's what you want to do?"

"What else can we do?"

They'd been locked down for an additional three weeks, just to be sure Vincent really was able to erase their ties to the computer and the problems that came along with it.

And while there still may be some issues that came up, it appeared that, at least for the time being, they were relatively safe.

As safe as anyone who worked for Alaskan Security would ever be.

"We can do anything."

"We can't go to the beach."

"Technically we can," Abe tipped his head to one side, "it will just take us a while to get there."

Elise snorted out a little laugh. "I'm sure Pierce would love it if we all packed up and flew to the beach."

"He did it. If he can do it, we can do it too."

"He did it when he got married. It was his honeymoon."

"Are you saying that's the exception we need to get a trip to the beach?" He'd be willing to do way worse things if that was what it took to get Elise where she wanted to go.

Especially since he had every intention of making sure this woman was his in every sense of the word.

Elise stared at him. "What?"

She seemed genuinely confused, which made sense. They hadn't discussed much beyond the fact that she would be coming to live with him in the townhome.

Along with Danish.

And initially, he thought that would be perfect. That as long as she was at his side every night, he would have more than he ever could have wanted.

But the idea of having a ring on his finger was starting to grow on him.

"I'm saying, if you want to go to the beach but you think we need a good excuse, we could always just get married."

"I'm still confused." She barely shook her head. "You can't want to marry me. You don't even love me yet."

"I thought love was implied after I killed the second guy for touching you."

"He didn't touch me. He just pointed a gun at my head."

"Well in that case, maybe I didn't have to shoot him after all."

Elise didn't laugh.

"You don't look as thrilled with this as I expected you to be." He kind of thought she would jump on board with the plan right away.

But he should have known Elise would surprise him.

"Well, considering you never told me you love me," she lifted one finger, "you haven't actually proposed to me," Elise added a second finger, "and I don't see a ring to make me think that's in the works," a third finger went up, "it seems like you're just flying by the seat of your pants right now. And I definitely don't think marriage is anything anyone should do on a whim."

"Just because this is the first time you're hearing it, doesn't mean this is the first time I've thought about it." He leaned closer to her. "And for the record, I love the fuck out of you, you're going to marry me, and now I know what we're going to do today."

****

"YOU'RE KIDDING." HEIDI grabbed her and yanked her in through the door. "Let me see it."

"I think he's crazy." Elise kicked the front door of Shawn and Heidi's townhome closed as her best friend peered down at the ring on her finger.

"They're all crazy. But at least he's crazy with good taste in jewelry." Heidi moved the solitaire from one side to the other with her pointer finger. "That thing is gorgeous."

"I really thought he was kidding." She didn't actually think Abe was kidding. She just didn't really think he'd follow through.

Definitely not right away.

"He just wants to lock you down." Heidi grinned. "Because he's smart."

"Smart and crazy." Elise followed Heidi through the townhouse and into the living room space. She pointed to the large window. "I hate these blinds."

She'd gone through every possible shade that would fit the large windows she picked out, finally settling on the least of all the evils.

"It's better than getting shot at." Heidi plopped down on the large sectional in the living room. "And I think they look good. They match the blinds and the rest of the townhouse."

"Yeah, but the windows looked so pretty uncovered, and they let in so much light." Her disappointment didn't really have anything to do with how pretty the windows were, or the light they let in.

Her disappointment primarily focused on the fact that she'd failed.

She was the one who chose a window without really thinking of all the possible problems that could come along with it.

It was so easy to place blame on herself. Even now, when she was happy and loved, her natural tendency was to try to blame herself for anything that went wrong.

Maybe it would always be like that. Maybe it was something she would struggle with forever.

And that would have to be okay.

"I think I'm going to hang some curtains around it. Sort of dress it up a little bit. Make it stand out a little more." Heidi's eyes widened. "What do you think of those little lights on wires?"

"You want to dress the window up with curtains and twinkle lights?"

"Why not? The window is the focal point of the room."

It was supposed to be the focal point of the room, but now it was just another window with blinds.

"You know, if you don't want to keep the blinds on your window, you could plant a tree back there." Heidi tapped one finger against her chin as she stared across the room like she was envisioning it. "Eventually the branches would block the window enough that you probably wouldn't need a blind anymore."

"Maybe." It would still defeat the purpose of the window in the first place, which was to let in as much light as Alaska would ever allow.

Elise dropped down onto the couch next to Heidi and let out a long sigh.

She was dwelling on it. Stewing on something that didn't really matter. The blinds on the windows didn't bother anyone but her.

And she still couldn't find a way to give it up.

Normally, that alone would have made her disappointed in herself. Added to the guilt she was already feeling for failing.

But she didn't feel disappointed. Actually she felt a little proud.

Because even with everything that happened in the past month, that ache in her gut, the one she tried to cut out for so many years, hadn't shown up.

That didn't mean it would never come again, but at least right now she was coping in a way she never had before.

And there were so many people she had to thank for it.

Starting with the one beside her now.

Elise angled her body towards Heidi's, pulling one leg higher onto the couch as she settled in for a very long conversation. One she'd only had with one other person in the world.

But secrecy gave things more power than they deserved. And she was tired of keeping secrets.

Tired of letting them rule her life.

Elise reached out, taking Heidi's hand in hers. "I need to tell you something."

BONUS BIT ONE

"DO YOU LIKE it here?" Brock shifted the deep green gliding chair a little to the left.

"I don't know." Eva leaned against the wall and let her body slowly slide down to the floor, legs dropping open to make room for her big belly as her butt hit the ground. "Whose fucking idea was it for us to have a kid?"

"I guess that depends on how you look at things." Brock pushed the chair a little more. "What if we put it here, with that little lamp right next to it?"

"I'm sure it will be fine." She started the morning out gung-ho, ready to tackle the rest of the nursery before she got too big to do anything.

But her enthusiasm for the project wore off really quickly.

"Let's leave it here for now, but we can move it if you change your mind." Brock came her way and held out both hands. "Why don't you come try it out."

"I just got here." Eva let her head fall back against the freshly-painted wall.

They'd finally been able to move into the townhouse they bought from Pierce. She should be thrilled. Ecstatic to finally be in her own space. To have a home that she could decorate however she wanted.

But all of her get up and go had definitely got up and went, leaving her behind.

"Come on." Brock grabbed both of her hands and gently hefted her up off the ground. "I guarantee this chair will be way more comfortable than the floor." He led her to the ultra-padded glider she'd ordered when she first found out she was pregnant.

Back before the morning sickness and regret had kicked in.

Not that she regretted having a baby. She was thrilled that in just a few short weeks she would be cradling a tiny human in her arms.

Most of her regret centered around the pregnancy itself.

It was complete bullshit.

"You know your mother liked this?" Eva slid down into the chair, her ass hitting harder than it would have if she hadn't been carrying another entire person in her gut. "*Pregnancy is a beautiful thing, Eva. You're bringing new life into this world, Eva. It's a miracle, Eva.*"

She'd heard it all. Multiple times.

Brock's mom was just trying to make her feel better, she knew that.

But still.

It was the last thing she wanted to hear when her stomach was rolling and her skin was breaking out in a cold sweat.

"My mother didn't have twenty-four-hour morning sickness for nine months." Brock crouched down beside her, resting one hand across the widest part of her belly. "Otherwise I can promise you she would have stopped at one."

"Well hopefully you only want one, because I think this has cut any chances you had for more down to nothing." It didn't help that she was pregnant side-by-side with Heidi.

Even carrying twins, Heidi was having a perfectly fine time cooking up her crotch goblins. No morning sickness. No stretch marks. No misery.

Just some sort of irritating pregnant glow, that made her skin clear and pink, and her hair thick and shiny.

Meanwhile Eva was kissing the porcelain god, and the only hair on her body that seemed to be growing was on her legs.

"Maybe this just means that you're getting all the hard stuff out of the way now and once the baby gets here it will all be smooth sailing." Brock was really trying hard to put a positive spin on this.

But they both knew that was never going to happen. "You think our kid is going to be easy?"

"That does feel like I'm reaching a little high, doesn't it?" He eased his butt to the floor and leaned his head against her stomach. "Based on genetics, chances are good it will be a complete pain in the ass."

Her face started to pucker up, and her throat started to tighten. "What if it is?" The last word dragged out on a wail as she started to cry.

For the fifth time today.

"What if it doesn't sleep?" Eva didn't even bother wiping the tears as they came out. "What if I can't get it to eat?" Her nose started to run, forcing her to suck in a deep breath to keep her snot from joining the tears' downward path. "What if it hates me?"

"First of all, I'm pretty sure infants don't really have any feelings, good or bad, about their parents." Brock reached up to wipe at the wetness on her cheeks. "Second, I am positive we will be able to feed the baby something."

"What if I can't breast-feed?" The whole concept of it seemed so foreign.

Almost unnatural in spite of her doctor's claims that it was 'the most natural thing on earth'.

"Then we will feed the baby formula. Babies don't care. They just want milk."

She sniffed a little. "Are you sure?"

"Positive." Brock seemed so confident in her ability to be a good mother.

Way more confident than she was.

"And, if we end up using formula, that means I can help you. I can take the night shift so you can sleep."

He was trying so hard to make her feel better, but all he was doing was making her feel worse.

Eva started to cry again. "I'm so tired."

She hadn't gotten a full night's sleep since she crossed the six-week mark. It was like someone flipped a switch and she went from a perfectly functioning human being, to someone who couldn't even make it through breakfast without rushing to the bathroom.

"I know." Brock continued to stroke her face. "But we're on the home stretch."

"No we're not. It's going to be even harder once I have the baby."

She knew how it worked. Right now she was just dealing with nausea and incontinence.

Once the baby was out she would deal with feedings, diaper changes, sleep schedules…

And probably still incontinence.

"You don't know tha—"

Their doorbell rang, cutting off Brock's repeated attempts to soothe her.

"It's probably Mona. She wanted to come see the nursery today." Eva tried to work her way up from the glider, but the damn thing kept moving, making it impossible for her to get any sort of footing. "I hate this fucking thing already."

"I'll buy you another chair." Brock grabbed her under the arms and lifted her up and out, waiting until she was steady on her feet before hooking one arm around her as they headed for the stairs.

The doorbell rang again as Eva waddled her way through the living room, past the stacks of boxes that held the crib, the co-sleeper, the stroller, and any other array of crap one needed to take care of a baby.

There was a lot of it.

"We'll have to clean that up before the shower." She lost her mind somewhere along the way and

342

ended up asking to have the shower at their townhouse.

At the time it seemed to make the most sense. Why take things multiple places? If the shower was at their place, everything would already be where it needed to go.

But now it was one more thing to add to her already overwhelmed plate.

"I'm sure that won't be a problem." Brock led her to the door, sticking right by her side just as he had through all the long nights, and all the early mornings.

If it wasn't for him she would have had to wash her hair twice a day, but somehow he always knew when she needed him to show up and hold it back so she didn't puke on it.

"Have I told you how much I love you?"

"Not since I held your hair back this morning." He reached for the door and pulled it open.

Eva stopped short, staring at the person on her front porch.

She blinked a few times, positive she was not seeing what she thought she was seeing.

This must be a new pregnancy symptom.

Delirium.

And this one might be the most fucked-up of them all. Especially since it seemed to know what she most wanted in this world.

It wasn't until she looked down to see the rolling luggage beside their visitor that she realized she might not be seeing things.

"Is that a *me* suitcase?"

Her Gram-Gram twisted the bag, turning it so Eva came face-to-face with herself. "Hell yes it is." She gave her a wink. "Hopefully no one shoots you between the eyes." Gram-Gram stepped inside, dragging her Eva bag along behind her. "Where am I staying?"

"Your room is down here." Brock closed the door before walking toward the bedroom on the first floor. "We'll be staying on the second floor with the baby."

Gram-Gram followed him into the room, dropping her bag just inside the door before coming out and grabbing Eva in a tight hug. "How you doing, Peanut?"

Eva started to tear up again. "Pregnancy is stupid."

"Damn right it is." Gram-Gram leaned back to look at her. "Complete bullshit." She smiled, reaching out to pat her on the cheek. "But if you don't do it you'll never get to have a granddaughter." Her eyes were soft and warm and everything Eva needed to see. "And I promise that makes it all worth it."

BONUS BITS TWO

"GOOD MORNING."

Tyson worked both eyes open, fighting his way through the rest of the fog clouding his brain. "Is it morning?"

"It is for you." The smooth voice that woke him up continued on. "It's also a good one, if you had any concerns about that."

The skin of his bicep suddenly squeezed. Not in an uncomfortable way, it was just odd.

"Is that too tight?" The sweetly smooth voice was closer, bringing a warm scent that carried a hint of vanilla and flowers along with it.

"I'm good." He blinked, managing to finally get his eyes open as a soft touch moved down his arm.

"How's your stomach?" The woman at his side was staring at the computer in front of her, clicking the keys with one hand as she checked his IV with the other.

He pressed one hand against his middle. "Hungry."

"I can imagine. It's been a while since you ate." She checked her watch before looking at the screen. "At least ten hours."

"How long did the surgery take?" Tyson tried to lift his head to look down at the leg that brought him to the hospital.

"About six hours." The nurse turned to fully face him, but her eyes didn't move to his as she went to work adjusting the blankets covering his body. "Do you remember them talking to you when you came out of the operating room?"

Tyson rubbed his burning eyes. "Not really."

He remembered being in recovery. He remembered Eli being there.

Other than that, there wasn't much he remembered besides being rolled into his room.

"I'm sure your surgeon will be in to check on you soon, so you can ask him any questions you have." The nurse's eyes finally came to his. "You need anything before I go?"

Tyson stared up at her. The soft curve of her cheeks. The perfect line of her wide nose. The pale brown of her eyes.

"I know you."

He'd seen this woman before. Thought of her more than a few times since. Wondered if it would be appropriate for him to come back, see if maybe she thought of him too.

"Do you make it a habit of landing yourself in the hospital?"

He checked her badge, scanning it for her name.

Naomi Bloom.

346

He might have to make it a habit if it could gain him some time with this woman. "My friend was in the hospital. You were one of the nurses that took care of her."

Naomi's black brows lifted. "It's possible. I take care of a lot of people." She finished adjusting the blankets before turning to grab the computer cart at her side.

"She was shot too. Here at the hospital."

"Sounds like maybe you should be rethinking who you're friends with." Naomi's eyes met his before jumping away. "If y'all keep getting shot."

"Where are you from?" Tyson tried to work his way a little more upright, hoping it would help her see him as something other than a patient.

"I live in Alaska." Her lips lifted in an amused line. "Otherwise it would be a hell of a long commute."

"I mean where did you live before Alaska?" He didn't want her to leave just yet. She hadn't remembered him last time, and he didn't want to run into that problem again. "You don't sound like you're from here."

"How does someone from Alaska sound?" She spoke a little slower, taking a little more care with how she formed her words.

"Not like they're from the South." He smiled. "I heard that drawl."

Naomi eyed him, her honeyed gaze moving over him for a few long seconds. "Georgia."

He tried not to look too excited at the scrap of information she'd offered. "I've been to Georgia. It's nice."

"It's hot."

Tyson grinned. "Everywhere is hot compared to Alaska."

"Good point." It almost seemed like she was about to smile. Like she might be enjoying their conversation.

And he wanted to keep it going.

"Is that why you moved here, to get away from the heat?"

Naomi's expression immediately shuttered, closing down immediately.

"Yup." She started pushing her cart toward the door. "I'll have someone bring you something to eat. The kitchen isn't open right now, so it will be one of the cold box lunches we keep in the fridge."

Tyson sat up straight, ignoring the twinge in his leg when he moved. "Wait."

Something just happened. Things were going fine and then suddenly they weren't.

And as far as he could tell, there was no explanation for it.

Naomi stopped just inside the door but didn't look his way.

"When are you coming back?" He checked the clock on the wall. It was two in the morning. She should be right in the middle of her shift.

If he did this right he could make up for whatever he'd said to make her shut down.

Smooth it over and figure out a way to convince her to let him see her outside of here.

"You sound awfully eager to have me back in your room, Mr. Muller." A tiny bit of warmth was back in her words.

"Call me Tyson." He worked on an easy smile. "And I just remember how well you took care of my friend's wife when she was here."

He wanted to make it clear the friend he had was that and that only.

A friend.

"It's my job." Naomi turned to him, one brow lifted. "And I will be back shortly." Her full lips twitched, like she was about to smile.

Maybe Naomi Bloom was just as excited to spend time with him as he was to spend time with her.

She gave her computer cart a little shove. "To take out your catheter."

****

Printed in Great Britain
by Amazon